CONSUMED

CONSUMED

JUSTIN ALCALA

Copyright © 2019 Justin Alcala.

First published in 2014 by Zharmae Publishing Press.

This edition published in 2019 by BLKDOG Publishing.

No part of this publication may be reproduced, stored in a retrieval system, or transmitted in any form or by any means, electronic, mechanical, photocopying, recording, or otherwise, without written permission of the publisher.

All rights reserved including the right of reproduction in whole or in part in any form. The moral right of the author has been asserted.

This is a work of fiction. Names, characters, businesses, places, events, locales, and incidents are either the products of the author's imagination or used in a fictitious manner. Any resemblance to actual persons, living or dead, or actual events is purely coincidental.

www.blkdogpublishing.com

CHAPTER 1

"Hysteria in London," that's what the papers are calling it. Outbreaks of cholera and tuberculosis throughout Western Europe have every Jack and Judy beating down the doors of Parliament. Backed into a corner, the Whigs have tried to *woo* back England's taxpayers by making public spectacles of their latest "Disease Control Regulations". Tightened immigration, newly reformed hospitals, drained city cesspools; you name it, they've tried it. Unfortunately for me, that also means us bluebottles working extra hours guarding the Thames from waste dumpers. Can you imagine it? They have half of Scotland Yard just twiddling our thumbs around that damnable river while every scab in the metropolis gets away with murder. The Houses must be dull to think we can properly protect the public day in and day out after twin shifts. Reports are already starting to pour in about dog-tired constables abandoning posts, roughing up civilians and refusing to back up other policemen at the call of the whistle. I wish there was something that I could do, but to be honest, I have my own problems.

When I first received the promotion to Detective Sergeant, I thought it would make circumstances easier. Catherine's consumption had already become quite expensive and any extra shilling I could get my hands on was something to put towards her remedies. However, as her condition worsened, so did her groans and whimpers, and soon our landlord was threatening eviction. That's how I ended up where I am today. It was just another grey day at work when some brigand I'd been booking overheard me moaning to some of the boys at the station about my wife. He offered a solution. *Kubla Khan* he called it, but I was savvy enough to know what he meant. Opium, dried latex obtained from poppies was big on the streets, and word is that it could get a fellow so glocky that he couldn't tell the difference between dreams and reality. I thought for sure it could help my wife's pain and before long found myself looking for a *Mr. Chen* inside London's Limehouse district.

Now it wasn't easy, as most of the ladybirds and dippers who frequented the dens knew I was a rozzer from my days in uniform. Nevertheless, after a couple of sovereigns, I'd finally made right with a Chinaman who promised a weekly supply. Bed ridden, Catherine was reluctant to smoke the opium at first, but in time I convinced her otherwise, and the results were profound. Her pain almost immediately ceased. I can still recall sitting by her bedside nightly, watching as she melted away in euphoria, conjuring what I thought I'd never see again- *her smile*. So, for a brief hiccup in time, we'd restored our past, holding conversations devoid of any suffering or torture. It wouldn't be long before she invited me to join her, and starving to preserve our reconnection, I overlooked my duties as a police officer in order to make her happy.

After my first puff, I understood why Catherine's suffering had so easily washed away. A delicate stream of pleasure flushed under my skin, filling every part of my body with silk. Later, once the drug had taken full effect, it felt as if an imaginary musician had loosened each tightly strung nerve in my body, strumming them until they were thoroughly sedated. My toes curled, stomach retracted, and cheeks puckered. It was remarkable. Then, as I built up to the pinnacle of this electrifying high, doubt polluted my mind, and I worried that my heart could not endure the stimulant. But, just as I'd nearly panicked, a lethargic sensation showered over me, extinguishing my anxiety by singing me to sleep. The effects lasted a few hours, and when I finally awoke, spooned under me was Catherine, slumbering with her Christmas grin.

I knew it wasn't a cure, but it had a way of delaying the inevitable, if not for just another night. So went our routine. I would return home from a long day of work and join my wife for another round of tar procured from the den. Together we'd smoke and laugh until our faces turned plum, then fall into a state of mesmerism. As aberrant as it sounded, the routine was something I quite cherished, and still do to this day.

But because fate is fickle, fortune foul, and destiny depraved, one day while returning home, I found Catherine sprawled across our kitchen floor like a fox freshly butchered by hounds. Her sickly auburn blood stained her sleeping gown and filled the chamber pot as well. Apart from the occasional bloody gurgle, she lay motionless. As I rushed to her side, I could no longer ignore the veracity of what was at hand. Catherine sat at death's door. With life barely flowing in her veins, I hurried to call her physician, but much as expected, there was little he could do. Catherine had succumbed to her consumption, passing the next morning.

To further exacerbate things, not shortly after the funeral, I began feeling abnormally ill. It started as fatigue, but gradually progressed into chills, night sweats and fever. Before long, my chest began to burn and I was coughing up blood. I had contracted Catherine's illness and was now going through the early stages of what she had suffered. The agony from my ailment and grief of being a widower was more than I could bear, and to help from being driven mad, I continued to visit Mr. Cheng, buying enough tar for just one. But then one night, just as I had nearly given up, *he* came, and everything changed.

It was the start of another grueling day and I was both physically worn from my condition as well as emotionally hollow from the stress. I was reluctant to tell anyone on the force about my disease, as I feared that they'd sack me for sure. At work, I went through the motions, pretending to be someone who still cared. Superiors were correctly addressed, cases fully investigated and criminals properly processed. I received the deepest sympathies from blokes in the Yard about Catherine, but truth be told, I always knew no one *really* cared. It wasn't their fault. People naturally put themselves first. They were far too concerned with the outbreaks at their front door then to indulge in one man's sorrows.

From the barber to the butcher you'd hear nonstop gossip: *"I've heard that thousands are dead across Europe."*

"Someone told me it's worse in the States."

Even the most respected priests and politicians were blathering. It was embarrassing. Nevertheless, as life carried on that evening, I returned home from a pair of shifts to stumble upon a most peculiar sight outside my home. A prelude of what was in store for me.

My third story rental glowed like a lighthouse in the moonless eve. More surprising though, was the fact that the curtains were drawn back and a single shadowy silhouette crept near our window. *Had my kind neighbor, Ms. Abigail, possibly stopped in to check on me?* Charging up the stairs, I opened my door to a scene out of the worst of penny-dreadfuls. Lingering in my bedroom was a gangly one-armed chap, no older than seventeen. He wore a black long coat pinned off at one shoulder and was rawboned with midnight hair. His dopey face carried a pair of sunken eyes that gawked at me with admiration. I drew the revolver from under my coat, pointing it at him threateningly as I stumbled inside. The intruder studied the gun barrel for a moment before locking his eyes on the small red birthmark that protruded from between my glove and jacket.

"The witches' mark," he whimpered anxiously before sniveling like a pup begging for scraps. His clothes were simple, and as I continued to examine him, I could see that he was wearing a porter's sark beneath his coat. His irises shined an eerie hue of gold, the way candlelight flickers off of coins, and a set of mauve veins webbed around his neck. Tense with anxiety, I clicked back the revolver hammer, aimed it at his forehead, and readied to fire. He knew what came next, because finally he opened his mouth to speak. A set of jagged teeth protruding from beneath his thin lips mouthed those next eerie words.

"Don't worry Detective Brannick," he whispered. "I'm here to guide you."

Already at wit's end, I knew I needed to take action or else I might blame myself later. Not wishing to kill the boy nor risk my own safety, I tried to think of something unconventional instead. Perhaps stern negotiations were in order. Frantically, I spit out the first derogatory threat that came to mind.

"Try anything stupid young mincer and I'll blast you proper!" *It was not exactly the point I wanted to get across, but it would have to do.* The boy spewed out a subdued cackle.

"I'm sure you will Nathan," he said calmly, "but it's hardly necessary."

He straightened his back, finally allowing me to see his full stature. He was a towering young man with bushy hair that made him appear even taller. The fingers on his lone hand were long and lean, the untrimmed nails gleaming at the ends. His jacket was weathered with soot, and as I continued to glare at him, I couldn't help but notice the emanating aroma of freshly turned soil. He slipped towards our side window with a spiderlike grace, unclasping the small hook that held the glass panel shut. The curtains flapped violently as the winds breached inside.

"You'll be hearing from *him* soon," he said threateningly, "and if you're as talented as he says, you'll follow the trail."

He staggered over the sill and glanced at me briefly before leaping out with his arms spread like a crow. I raced to the windowsill, and after swimming through the drapes, pointed my revolver downward towards the alleyway. However, much to my astonishment, instead of a broken boy, I found nothing more than the abandoned cobblestone path. He had vanished.

I rushed to shut the window before investigating the rest of the flat, but found that it hadn't been wronged. While initially it was relieving, it didn't take long for the fear and suspicion of what had just unfolded to settle in. I had grown accustomed to the criminal world and its many transgressions, but never imagined it would intrude into the safety of my own home. After the shock wore off, I gathered my thoughts.

Who was he and why did he come? I had no answers. While I hoped he was just a young thief down on his luck, his words haunted me. It was the mention of *him* that lingered- making me fear that another aggressor was involved. Perhaps it was a past criminal I had put to justice or a forgotten enemy I had made long ago. Regardless, for that night, and every night thereafter, I'd make sure to fasten each lock, secure each window and sleep with my revolver nearby. This lad was a harbinger, but for whom, I did not know.

CHAPTER 2

SERGEANT HONORED FOR HIS EFFORTS IN PIMLICO POISONING

On Thursday, Scotland Yard Sergeant Nathaniel Brannick, was honored for his efforts in the Pimlico investigation. The small ceremony took place within the Metropolitan Police Headquarters in London, honoring the policeman for his part in the inquest of Adelaide Bartlett. Inspectors assigned to the case claim that it was Sergeant Nathaniel Brannick's organization during the investigation that assisted detectives in identifying foul play.

It was New Year's Eve, December 31, 1885, when Edwin Bartlett returned home after visiting the dentist. He'd gone to sleep alongside his wife, only to be found dead the next morning. Doctors found that Edwin's stomach was filled with liquid chloroform, but his wife claimed that he had been very unhappy as of late and likely took his own life. However, after looking further into the case, Sergeant Brannick discovered that not only had Adelaide been having an affair with Edwin's younger brother, but she had also been secretly hoarding a small collection of prescribed chloroform from a Dr. Alfred Leach.

Sergeant Nathan Brannick, a former royal navigator of the HMS Black Prince, moved to London after his tour of duty. He entered the academy in late September of 1881, and created quite a stir with his mentors. After working as a constable for three years, Nathaniel earned his Sergeant stripes. With his new rank, he was able to organize the men on his shift, thwarting several riots, expense thefts and black

7

market investigations. However, it would not be until Thursday that Sergeant Brannick was credited for his full worth. The thorough coordination of his policemen and astute judgment were of great assistance to what is now being dubbed as "The Pimlico Poisoning Mystery". Although the case is still being deliberated in court, it will be hard to prove Adelaide's innocence due to Sergeant Nathaniel's efforts.

It was the morning after the intruder. I'd been rifling through my criminal files in search of reports of a one-armed boy when I stumbled across an old article about me written in the London newspaper. The small piece was printed along the backside of the *Daily* next to advertisements and wanted ads, but I was told that a few of the admissions board members had read it before I submitted my request to the CID, a position most policemen at the moment were clawing to get into. Ironically, though it helped me earn the rank of detective, Adelaide Bartlett would later be acquitted. Shamefully, as I recall, I wasn't that upset, as I was more excited about shedding my stiff uniform than solving the investigation.

But then again, I was more carefree in those days. I was a handsome bruiser with arms like iron and a face so masculine it could scare off the dogs. My hair grew a thick, grizzly bear brown and my blood pumped kerosene. I had a reputation for being fearless, making me the bloke to seek out if trouble lingered. My mind was sharper too. I could get a case in the morning and close it out before dinner. In my short time as a constable, I'd put more criminals away than anyone else is my division. No doubt, I'd been in my prime, tough as nails and smart as a whip. Everything was nearly perfect. Well, everything except for...*the echo*.

Echo is a name that I made up. It's a burden that I don't really like to talk about, mostly because I fear that I've gone mad. My family had always teased me as a child, claiming that I was cursed because of the blood colored birthmark on my wrist resembling an overturned cross. Little did I know that nearly thirty years later, I'd be taking their allegations seriously. It started shortly after my father's death, and at first, I thought that it was merely a repercussion of my mental anguish. But as the weeks went by and my spirits lifted, still the echo remained. Gradually, it began to develop and before long it was all but ignorable.

It only emerges when I'm dealing closely with a violent or tragic death, like when working a murder. It's not much, mostly just a brief, but unforgettable image that comes into my head. It's a flash of what the victim had seen just before their untimely demise that triggers if I touch them. It first surfaced when I was helping doctors move Mr. Edwin Bartlett's corpse during the initial inquest for the Bartlett investigation, and it's why I knew he'd been poisoned. I'd used it several times after in order to solve some of my more paramount cases, earing me a reputation as a natural detective.

Anyhow, besides the occasional unexplainable hallucination, things were going very well. I had a successful career, a loving wife, and plans for the future. But things changed quickly after Catherine's death. I was damaged, and had a hard time looking at the world optimistically. I'd physically wasted away too. My once proud features now needed to be hidden behind clever distractions. I draped myself in trendy suits, as I'm not as healthy as I once was. I try to conceal my baggy eyes with broad muttonchops and cover my thinning hair beneath a fashionable bowler hat. People say I'm still handsome, but I sometimes feel like the last leaf on an autumn tree. I try to blame nature, but the fact of the matter is that my illness, Catherine's death, and opium have changed me for the worse.

I filed the memory-stained article back in its folder and continued to sort through my records for any signs of the one-armed intruder. I examined every cat burglar and kids-man report I came across, but each fell short of being a match. With few options left, I fed my typewriter with a fresh sheet of paper, deciding to chronicle the encounter in hopes it might contribute in the future. I vigorously tapped away at keys, recording everything about the boy that I could remember. I must have lost track of time because just as I put the final touches on my report, a heavy rapping came at my office door. The person knocking took the liberty to open it, and soon, my routine morning visitor poked his head into the room.

A pink-faced fellow with a long mustache, jolly grin and a yellowed porkpie hat bobbed his bushy brows farcically at me. It was Second Class Detective Sergeant James Davis, a man who was as serious as he was skinny. He was a tubby dimwit in his mid-forties, who should have made rank twice as many times as he did. He once tried to explain to me that he was just a carefree soul, unfocused on his career, trying to enjoy the many delicacies of life. I interpreted that as his confession of laziness. He had a wife he loathed and cheated on habitually, even though she cared for him like a child, and two sons that he avoided at all costs.

Nonetheless, what James lacked in dignity and professionalism, he made up for with city knowledge and street connections. He could reach out to any macer or thief in London for useful information, a talent that was more than helpful in our line of work. Since we were in the same division, we often found ourselves paired up by our superiors. Eventually, we grew accustomed to one another's methods, working closely together to solve a handful of major cases. And despite the fact that we were never officially notified, the two of us accepted that we were unendorsed partners.

"Morning Nathan," he said through a stupid grin as he squeezed his plump belly through the entrance. James took a seat, placing his walking stick down and unbuckling his belt so that his stomach could hang out comfortably. The chair legs underneath him squeaked in pain from his weight. I watched, repulsed, as he snorted a bogey from his throat and spit it into his coat pocket napkin. "What the deuce you doing cooped up in your office? Shouldn't you be out guarding the river with the rest of the Yard?" he asked sardonically.

"Funny."

"Seriously though, how's everything?"

"Take a look yourself." I tossed James the report and patiently waited as his eyes scrambled across it. He was bowled over.

"Is this a joke?"

"Wish it was, but unfortunately this is what I came home to last night."

"My word, half-witted beak-hunters so desperate nowadays, they'll even try to steal from a policeman." He dug in his pocket, pulling out a handful of peanuts and began cracking them over his lap, raining shells over his coat. "I'll ask a few of my blowers on the streets if they've ever heard of 'im."

"Thanks James," I said dryly.

"No seriously, I will!" James, liar-extraordinaire, earned his position largely by out bluffing the criminals he apprehended. He was a cheat, phony, and notorious bully. I sound like I'm being hard on him, but honestly I'm not. While the two of us share a mutual respect for one another, it did not come without incident. It demanded quite a bit of tolerance on both of our parts. I see him as reckless and I'm sure in his eyes, I'm an irritable, faultfinding prick.

"Blimey," he cried, "I can't even get my own peers to trust me. What has this world come to?"

"Sorry," I apologized. "It is just that I have not been sleeping properly and...well, you get the point." Davis bobbled his head, aware I had been struggling immensely with Catherine's death.

"Hey, things are tough for you right now. No love lost." I could sense awkwardness polluting the room by the mere tone in his voice. James wanted to move the conversation along. He locked his eyes back on the report, mouthing the words while peanut fragments sprayed outward. "So d 'you think he was a loony conspirator or just a bloke down on his luck?"

"I can't be certain James. You of all people should know that I follow facts. Now clean those shells off my floor." Davis hopped up from his seat, raising his hands in revolt.

"Whoa, you weren't kidding mate. Grumpy as a bearded prostitute, you are." He went and picked up a few of the scattered shells, shoving them back in his pocket before trying to sit back down, nearly falling out of his seat in the process. "So, uh, do you want put some of the boys thick around your street or no?"

"No Sergeant. I can take care of it myself," I snapped, "Don't you ask one man." Since morning, I had become starved for another fix, the pipe beckoning me like the sirens themselves. The calling had a way of temporarily stealing my ability to curb my own temper. Calming myself, I stood from my chair and straightened myself out. "Besides," I grinned playfully in an attempt to repair the mood, "that's an abuse of power." The two of us snickered and grabbed our coats, readying to start our rounds. "Let's get to the streets, I'll buy us some tea." We prepared ourselves for the brisk November winds, tightening our jackets and clasping every button. I squeezed on my bowler, checking myself in the mirror before tugging the handle of the office door. Alarmingly, poised just outside of my office was our superior, Chief Inspector Donald Swanson.

He was a sturdy looking creature with broad shoulders and a heavy brow. He always parted his hair to one side and wore an unkempt mustache that made him look like a circus walrus. He donned simple brown suits that never fit him and complimented them with wrinkled ties. He had freshly achieved his rank by preventing a Fenian terrorist attack in London, and was now Chief Inspector in our Commissioner's Office. Since then, he had enjoyed browbeating anyone ranked below him. He assisted in assigning criminal cases and managing the staff. I half respected the man for his hard work and diligence, yet half loathed him for his pitiless attitude. He tended to speak to us as if we were trying to swindle him, a humiliating quality that I found hard to ignore.

"Sir," spat out Davis, "We were *just* about to help the bobby's on the beat-"

"Shut it Davis," ordered Swanson, "and clean those shells off your coat." Embarrassed, Davis swatted at his chest as if he was he was covered in ants. *Bravo James.*

"My word Sir," Davis mumbled, "how humiliating."

Swanson motioned us to return to the confines of my work area, following us as we lumbered back to our seats. I examined our burly Chief Inspector discreetly and noticed that along with his freshly stained mustache from breakfast tea, he had a stack of disheveled reports under his arm, a single photograph strung on top. The image was of a dead woman, in her early twenties, strewn across a wooden floor. She wore an uncorseted gown and a braided choker. Her undone hair enveloped a simple face that she partially shielded with her arms. Her home in the background appeared spartan and spotless, with very little home décor.

"You may have a new case," grumbled Swanson.

"*May* sir?" I inquired. Meanwhile, Davis played coy, frozen in his chair like a frightened deer. It was his only line of defense.

"It is with the most delicate respect for your past that I ask for you to take on this case," said the Chief Inspector with false compassion. "Quite frankly, your knowledge in the matter makes you the best suited to take the reigns on this one. Unless that is, you feel you'd be more of a hindrance than an aid." He plopped down the packet of papers in front of me. I wasted no time spreading them across the table until I came across the initial police report. Davis raised his nose to the ceiling, glancing at the document as if it could stand up and bite him.

The police report read that the victim, twenty-three year old Jacqueline McCann, was an Irish immigrant from Kilrush. She had immigrated to London when she was just fifteen, escaping the violence spreading across Ireland. She lived alone in a one room flat on Curtain Road, making a living as a nursemaid. Sometime last week, Miss McCann visited her doctor with complaints of chest pains and a cough that discharged blood. After a close examination, her physician feared she had been in the late stages of consumption and quarantined her to the confines of her quarters.

It was not soon after that neighbors began to worry that Miss McCann's mental state was deteriorating, in part because of her nighttime behavior. Most discernibly, on the eve of her first day in quarantine, people living next to her reported wailing from inside her flat. It always started near dusk, terrifying children and pets. When a few concerned residents tried checking up on her however, she refused to open the door, apologizing, but assuring all was well. This episode repeated itself for seven more nights until the eighth morning when she was discovered dead in the northwest corner of her parlor. Police on the scene reported no signs of intrusion. There were no physical bruises or wounds on the corpse that led to the presumption of murder, though constables did document abnormally swollen eye sockets and small blood traces along the lips.

Nonetheless, one particular factor that police uncovered could suggest foul play. On the final night the young lady was seen alive, witnesses entering the first floor pub within Miss McCann's building reported a stranger accompanying her. From their viewpoint below her window, they described a brawn man with a short imperial mustache and pale skin pacing the apartment. He wore an *Ushanka,* or Russian fur cap, and covered himself in a black frock coat that nearly hid his tall riding boots. He appeared to be scolding Miss McCann, who onlookers stated dissolved in tears. The pub staff, which was unacquainted with the nursemaid, assumed she had been engaged in a routine spat with a suitor and dismissed the incident as trivial. Unfortunately for investigators, once word made it back that Miss McCann had been found dead on the very next morning, both patrons of the inn and neighbors alike demanded that authorities conduct a more scrupulous investigation.

Now it all became clear why Chief Inspector Swanson wanted me for the case. Though he was unaware that I'd contracted the disease, he knew that both Catherine and Miss McCann suffered from consumption. Glancing over the narrative, I could see from the corners of my eyes Swanson glowering with irascible impatience. Dropping the report back on my desk, I conjured up some medical jargon in hopes to both confuse and irritate the Chief.

"Though it is my prognosis that her red swollen extrinsic muscles, swollen irises, and bloody oral cavity indicate that this casualty stems from tuberculosis, the fact that one ill-tempered man happened to be witnessed within the victim's home near the time of her death is a relevant enough component to compel my best efforts. I'll gladly take the case." Both puzzled and annoyed, Swanson turned to Davis, who fretfully straightened out his back.

"Good," he growled, "you can take Davis with you. The both of you are exempt from water guard duty."

"Thank Moses," exclaimed Davis emphatically before realizing his doltishness. He covered his mouth with one hand and grimaced. The room went quiet enough to hear a mouse shitting. Chief Inspector Swanson glared like the devil before swallowing a lump from his throat. He clanked his wedged shoes together and stomped towards the door, clearly disgusted.

"Have a report on my desk when you're finished," he ordered before slamming my door shut behind him. Davis and I remained muted, listening as the Chief Inspector trampled along the hallway towards his office. We glanced at each other with blank faces, waiting for Swanson to be out of earshot before sniggering. *If we didn't solve this case, there would be hell to pay.*

"Fuckin' hell, my ass is sore from Saint Swanson's rogering," laughed Davis as he stood up to straighten his jacket, "but at least we're out of water guard duty."

I glanced at the mirror along the wall and inspected my appearance once more. The last thing I wanted to look like when speaking to my Chief Inspector was a used-up opium addict. Thankfully, both my sideburns and hat shaded my bloodshot eyes. I checked to make sure my revolver was properly concealed under my long coat before tightening my coat belt. After hearing the British Army had become suitably impressed with the model's reliability, I had purchased the short-barreled firearm directly from Webley and Scott. She was a beauty, I'll give her that, but luckily, I had yet to fire it in the field. Davis waited eagerly at the exit, anxiously ready to go.

"Think this Cossack did it?" he burbled while lolling on the doorway threshold.

"Bullocks," I cried, squeezing into my calfskin gloves, "It just doesn't make sense." The tanned leather stretched across my fingers, protesting with an abrading squeal. I wore the gloves not just for warmth, but also to help me avoid the echo. The odd talent only seemed to stir up when I used my bare hands, and gloves seemed to do the trick. "Most of the details are quite trivial. I mean, the midnight moaning spree, bloody lips, none of it has anything to do with murder. They are just common symptoms of consumption. I've seen it before. It's a simple combination of pain, stress and science. In fact, we are solely relying on two facts. One, that Miss McCann had a spat with some chum the night before her death, and two, that she fell into some odd post mortis position."

"Maybe you're right. But aren't Russians always up to no good?"

"Don't know," I said while straightening my coat collar as we walked out my office, "But it seems we'll have to find out won't we?" Davis smiled while wagging his walking stick.

"Might I add," I continued to lecture, "that it shouldn't matter if he's some Russian rogue, criminal mastermind or even Lucifer himself. Clear all those wishy-washy preconceptions from your head and think straight." We made our way to the main doors of the station, taking one last breath of heated air before casting ourselves into the cold. "If there's one thing I've tried to cram into that thick head of yours Davis, it's that *we* deal in facts.

CHAPTER 3

It was still early morning in London and the ash canvas from another dreary autumn dawn had all the street paraders as happy as a funeral procession. The brown smuts and black fumes from residential smokestacks, factory chimneys and boat vents polluted the skies, making the air unnaturally thick. Davis and I made our way to Curtain Road, catching a cab ride from a drunken chauffeur who unconsciously mumbled curse words between breaths. We rarely took advantage of the police carriages, as they tended to draw attention, instead using a small allowance the department gave us for transportation expenses. The bumpy ride stirred my hangover, making the headache I'd been enduring quite unbearable.

Luckily, the trek was short and we soon found ourselves before an ugly brick building towering over an infestation of beggars and rats. A trail of spit stains along the walk guided us to a dirty porch marked with fresh bicycle tracks. After knocking a few times at the front with no answer, we decided to let ourselves into the unlocked entry. We then trudged the narrow stairwell, Davis huffing like a pig until we were at the door of Miss McCann's third floor flat. I jiggled the handle, only to find that the cheap doorknob bolt securing the apartment seemed to be turned from inside.

"Now what?" wheezed Davis.

Digging in my boot, I extracted the sailor knife I'd kept hidden, introducing it to the oval keyhole. I felt around with the dagger point, pushing up the pins on Miss McCann's simple lock mechanism.

"Heavens old boy," remarked Davis, "inmates teach you that one?" Lock picking was a tricky art to master, especially with inadequate tools. I'd learned how to use a knife from a fellow sailor during my enlisted years. The seaman had perfected the technique in order to steal more bread from the supply room, and was nice enough to teach me his technique. Ignoring my partner's banter, I listened for the short clicks inside the keyhole before snapping the latch with a smile.

"No, your mother did the last time she mistakenly locked me out," I spit back, causing Davis to snort uncontrollably.

When working on the beat for as long as Davis and I had, you tended to develop an uncouth and almost cruel sense of humor with your closest colleagues. I first noticed the phenomenon when I was but a humble constable, overhearing my superiors as they relentlessly slung vulgarities at each other. I thought it pitiless and callous at first, but as time went on, learned that it acted as a means to deal with the levels of stress that badgered our line of work. Soon enough I not only started to respect it, but also adopted it, becoming quite the rapier. The hardest part was growing insensitive when co-workers delivered an occasional jab, but soon enough one learns to welcome the banter, so long as it is clever enough to catch you off guard.

Entering the apartment haphazardly, the two of us immediately reared back in alarm. For springing before us was a navy cloaked figure stumbling up from the living room sofa. Horse faced and thin, the young man stood upright, revealing his tunic badge. Squeezing on his custodian hat, he struggled to juggle his baton until finally abandoning all efforts and allowing it to roll near Davis's foot. Ignoring his folly, the constable saluted, staring up at the ceiling with dread.

"Sirs," he shouted in attention, a glossy sweat glistening from his neckline.

"Harper you dumb fuck," roared Davis. Charging like a challenged ram, James butted heads with Constable Harper, smashing their faces together violently until their noses were squashed together. "Sleeping on the job are we?" Harper began to shutter.

"Sir," he nasally pleaded through a flattened nose, "I was branded to guard this crime scene-"

"*Possible* crime scene," I corrected astutely.

"*Possible* crime scene," he retorted, "but I grew weary from my two shifts. I thought it couldn't do any harm to catch a wink in the meantime."

As Davis continued to shame Harper, I looked past them and began studying the frowning walls of the flat. Not shortly after taking in the canvas, did a few suspect details rouse my attention. In particular, a small puddle of abnormally dry and flakey blood lingered in the corner where Miss McCann's body was found. It wouldn't be enough to use the echo. Davis, spotting my locked eyes, grabbed Harper by the collar.

"Get out of my sight boy, and if I find you fucking about again, you'll get the bottom of one of my gallies just before I take your badge."

Running out the door, Harper raced down the steps, but not before tripping down a dozen on the way. Meanwhile Davis, who fashioned an amused smirk, dug out a fag from his pocket and poked it into his lips. Striking a match on a table, he lit the end, puffing at it before blowing smoke out his nostrils like a dragon.

"Damn it Davis, don't strike your match on the crime scene."

"Thought it wasn't a crime scene?"

"It will be if you don't shut your trap."

I knelt over the blood splotch, searching for immediate clues, but nothing in particular stood out. The echo couldn't help me without a body, so I'd have to use good old fashion detective work. Taking a deep breath, I cleared my thoughts and tried to become more attentive. Falling into a methodical rhythm, my mind began to flash in measured beats, inspecting nearby walls, couches and chairs for traces of gunpowder, property damages or any other signs of struggle. With nothing emerging, I dug even deeper, rummaging around the flat for signs of theft or burglary. Although the house was quite bare, it still seemed intact. So I began to probe her home for any personal belongings. Initially, it seemed as if all was lost, as her effects were quite ordinary. But as I spent more and more time inside, small logistical details began to piece together.

First, as I rummaged through Miss McCann's every day carrying bag. I gathered that she had not left her home since prescribed so by her doctor, as both her damp work uniform and miniature umbrella still lay inside. There had been no rain in London since last week, which if the reports were correct, was the exact day of her quarantine. A time frame began to develop in my mind, as I pressed further. I next explored her bedroom, uncovering a few particulars that demanded immediate attention. In specific, a collection of bloody coughing rags littered her nightstand. Intriguingly, the silk handkerchiefs were of exceedingly high quality, seemingly far too expensive for the wages of a nursemaid. They were made of fine white silk with what appeared to be an Eastern European design embroidered on the fringes. I recalled the description of a Russian man in her window, and looked for any clues that could tie the two. Stitched into the edges of the cloth were the initials, S.V.G.

After collecting the soiled rags, I made my way to her pillbox, which filled to the brim with dusty, untouched pain medication. It seemed abnormal that a carrier of tubercles bacillus, an overwhelmingly excruciating disease, decided not to take advantage of her pain medicine. Most victims like Catherine and myself, displayed quite the opposite behavior; becoming addicts to any sort of sedatives they could get their hands on prior to their inevitable demise. However, it was not until I went through the bedding of Miss McCann that I found the evidence I needed. Hidden in her pillowcase was a personal letter overlooked by the responding investigators. Folded two times over, the correspondence had already been opened - the wax seal, which also read SVG, was broken. It read…

My dearest Jacqueline,
I flatter myself to think, after all that has passed between us,
I might still call you dearest. In recent days I've found myself

humbled, for though I consider myself a fine judge at the fairest route to secure a woman's heart, you've proved me faulty. It would seem that fine clothing and lavish dining at the most opulent restaurants cannot move you to declare yourself mine. What more might I offer? I beg you now as I have begged before to secure your life with me. Yet the only answer I have received is a request for just "one more day." One more day? These days turn to weeks, driving me mad in the process.

Therefore, my love, it is with the deepest regret that I have arrived at my own conclusion. As my time in the city ends and you still question if you can pledge to join me, I must choose for us. I will not be without you when I journey hence. As surely as you received this letter from my manservant, tonight you shall hear these same sentiments from my very own tongue. It is my sincerest hopes to finally take you away with me thereafter.

Pray do not attempt to leave or design to be found with friends. This night shall be for you and I. Fear not dearest Irish Dove, for what I offer you is nothing less than a new life, free from hardships and pain.
Sincerely,
S.V.G.

S.V.G., it was the same initials sewn onto the bloody handkerchiefs and pressed along the wax seal. I stood up from the end of the bed, both excited and revolted.

"Davis," I hollered. James moseyed into the room with his half burned cigarette in his mouth and a slightly valuable looking vase in hand. He peered at the paper.

"What have you there Nathan, grocery list?"

"Hope you didn't want to get back to guarding the Thames anytime soon," I said elatedly and tossed the paper at him. He put down the vase on a dresser next to him just in time to catch the document before it floated to the floor. He then dug in his breast pocket and plucked out a pair of spectacles. Wiring them over his ears, he leafed through the page and envelope before looking up at me for explanation.

"What on earth does it mean?"

"It means," I said while snatching the cigarette out of his maw and taking a puff. "We may have a murder after all." James groaned at the thought of more work.

After a brief conversation about the letter, the two of us decided that we would visit the pub downstairs in hopes to confirm a few facts from the report. We were resolute to know more about Miss McCann's condition, the state of the witnesses that evening, and a better description of the nighttime visitor. After locking up the apartment, we headed downstairs, but unfortunately, found that the establishment doors did not open until midday. Davis wanted another fag, so the two of us loitered on the street curb, reviewing some specifics of the case. It was not too long after finishing my description to Davis on how consumption attacks the lungs that we spotted a queer looking gentleman behind us peering into the pub window from the walkway.

Initially, we hadn't noticed him approach the building, but once we did, I found it rather odd that he was so intent on inspecting the pub's interior. His hands were cupped over his eyes to block out the sun and his chin was pressed against the glass. He was a tall fellow with a skeletal build that arched forward like a wilted tree. He had a thin crooked face that drooped on the right side, partially paralyzed. His stringy whiskers hung down over the ends of his mouth, tracing his cheek creases, and his brows were dark and furry like wooly caterpillars crawling along his forehead. He wore a wide, glossy top hat that reeked of cloth polish and a sweeping long coat that dragged on the ground. The coat blanketed over a bizarre, mismatched ensemble. He had a blue and white striped shirt that dangled over a set of undersized tan trousers. He fashioned one untied boot on his left foot, and one elegant dress shoe on his right, both black, and kept a tanned leather satchel strapped across his chest that wriggled as if an animal were inside.

"Might I help you," asked Davis as we approached. The man pointed his gaze down to the ground bashfully.

"No helping me my friend," he said in a witty voice as he fussed with his palms, trying to clean them of some invisible stain. Davis looked to me for an explanation, but I could only donate a shrug.

"Had a rough morning?" I spoke up. "Not too many folks need a pint at this hour." The man directed the functioning side of his face to me, apparently straining to hear my words. He then took the time to swat at and capture a fly that was buzzing near his head, placing the insect in his mouth.

"Rather *good* morning actually," he insisted as he chewed. I could hear the muffled sound of a cat meowing from inside his satchel. Ignoring the animal's plea, the bizarre stranger stood for a moment as if to say more before irritably waving us off. He planted his face back on the window, ducking and weaving as he continued his inspection.

"I've been entrusted with a very important task. So if you'd please, I have plenty of work to do," he mumbled in frustration, fogging the pane of dirty glass as he spoke. He was clearly unaware that we were the policemen.

"Are you a private investigator," I asked bluntly. He groaned, then after a moment, gave me a fleeting glance, as if my query was rhetorical. He then skipped backwards and looked up. He was counting the number of floors between the pub and Miss McCann's apartment, using his fingers to keep track. An elated smile erupted from his face, as if he'd gathered some insight, but it quickly warped into an eerie moon-shaped frown. At first, I thought the stranger was purposely trying to be aloof, but after conducting some more math on his thumb and pinky, he finally turned back to face us.

"I am more of a *zoophagous-coadjutor*," he annunciated eloquently while pinching his fingers together and motioning them like a symphony conductor would his orchestra. Davis and I stared at each other with confusion. *Clearly, this man was as mad as a hatter.*

"A *what*?" hollered James, now clearly irritated. The suspect did not answer. Instead, he merely leaked out a raspy hum as if clearing his throat. "You know what, never mind. How about instead you guess who we are?"

The hatter moaned impatiently until James unsheathed his copper badge.

"Scotland Yard," Davis shouted. The stranger froze. His tired grimace quickly became smothered by a false, humble half grin that displayed his stained teeth. Extending both arms slightly outward, the hatter bowed his head anxiously as if he'd just performed a dance for us and was timidly waiting for applause.

"Now you lunatic," James continued, "I want some answers. We'll start with your name."

The hatter began to wipe his hands again, rubbing them together nervously. He looked from side to side frenetically as if expecting to find some inspiration for his answer.

"I have been called a great number of things," he brooded, "but most just call me Feld, Mr. Erni Feld to be precise." The name did not stand out to me, but what did was his resentful glare at my partner. Mr. Feld tried to mask his brief crossed glower by conjuring up a counterfeit smile. I'd seen the expression one too many times to be fooled. It was a face a young constable gave his superiors after a proper reprimand, cross, but respectful. I'd have to be the diplomat in this conversation from this point on, as Davis had lost all leverage.

"Well Mr. Feld," I said casually, as if I did not think him mad, "we are investigating a murder that took place here. I find it rather hard to ignore how interested you are in the crime scene. Care to tell us why?" Mr. Feld shyly shook his head no, seemingly ashamed of himself.

"Yes, I've heard of the murder," he answered. "I *too* am looking into the matter for my employer. He is...the landlord and owner of this pub, a one Mr. Goodwin." I immediately thought back to the reports Chief Inspector Swanson had given me. It was true that the landlord and barkeep, Giles Goodwin, did own the building. Reporting constables noted however that Goodwin seemed rather pitiless in the death of Miss McCann, instead placing emphasis on the fact that she still owed him rent. *Could he possibly have had a change of heart?* Mr. Feld cleared his throat to speak again, fingers contorting in rhythm as he sang out his words.

"So, yes," he slurred, "I guess you could call me an *investigator*."

"And do you have any identification Mr. Feld?" James continued.

"Um, no."

Davis removed his pencil and notepad from his pocket. He shoved them into Mr. Feld's hands indignantly. Feld stared at the writing utensils curiously, as if looking at foreign objects.

"Well, Mr. Feld, write down your address here in London incase we care to share notes," James said mockingly. "I will be talking to the landlord as soon as the pub is open and I *do* hope he corroborates with your account." Erni twitched his good eye and shoulders conjointly, then, seemingly aware of his lapse, hurried to scrawl on the notepad as though to distract us from his convulsion.

"Oh yes, he definitely will Detective," Mr. Feld garbled while scribbling down his information, "trust me. This is a big, big assignment."

The writings were meticulously defined, and near his name, *Mr. Erni Feld*, he carefully sketched the picture of a small fly. He then handed back the pad to James who squinted as he tried to read it without his glasses. Erni watched, as if he were hungrily waiting for James's approval. Davis tucked the pad in his coat and gave Mr. Feld one last look over before growing intolerant.

"Well, off you go then," James ordered while softly booting Mr. Feld's backside, "and take that for your manners." Mr. Feld stared at us with uncertainty. James growled, waiving his podgy hand. "You heard me, bugger off!" The madman scattered, scurrying down the avenue as if being chased by wolves. He turned down the first crossroad he came about, giving us one last seething glower before parting from our view.

"What a sideshow," complained Davis before tapping his walking cane along the cobblestone.

"We should make sure his story is compatible," I said, continuing to watch Mr. Feld cross the busy street. In my time as both a constable and a jack, I had met a great many crackpots. While you quickly find out that it isn't practical to handcuff and haul away every one of them that you meet, it doesn't mean that there isn't more afoot. For some reason Mr. Erni Feld left a foul taste in my mouth and I would be sure to double check our case files for any suspect fitting his name. However, at the moment, the fool was little more than a distraction.

"We still have a full day ahead of us Nathan and it doesn't look like the landlord is in. Let's comeback some other time to talk with Mr. Goodwin," said James. "He might be able to fill us in on a few facts that our constables left out of the reports."

"A few?" I posed flippantly. James grinned as he checked his notepad to see who was next on our list for questioning. I peeped over his shoulder to get a glimpse at our target address then with Davis at my side began walking in the intended direction. It was already turning into an odd sort of day, and it had only just begun.

CHAPTER 4

Davis and I traveled from the neighborhood of our murder scene to Miss McCann's doctor who'd been cited in the initial crime report. His place of work hid near Fleet Street by the Old Cheshire drinking house. After a good thirty-minute walk through the muck of London, we finally made it to his doorstep. Located discreetly in the basement under an old clock store, Dr. Timothy Guildford's medical facility did not quite mirror what one imagines when they think of a physician's office. He had no business signs, posted names or painted titles over his grimy entranceway. I began to lean on the assumption that Dr. Guildford was in fact unfit to legally practice medicine in London. I knocked twice on his rotted wood door and waited for the doctor to answer. To James and my salacious surprise, it was not Dr. Guildford who met us, but instead a scantily clad, flaxen young vixen.

Wearing a trumpet shaped skirt without any bustle, and a high collared top that cut just the right length to draw your eyes directly to her breasts, the beauty stared at us unwearyingly, giving enough time to take in each voluptuous curve. Trying to maintain the conduct of a gentleman, I removed my hat and bowed deeply. Davis on the other hand, lost all sense of propriety, and let out a perverted whistle before opening his fat mouth to speak.

"Well hello young lass, is your Abbess in?" Humiliated, I wildly backhanded my partner upon his arm. "Oof," he exclaimed, rubbing his bicep. "I mean, good day. I am Detective Sergeant James Davis and this is Detective Sergeant Nathan Brannick. We're here to see your father, Dr. Guildford."

The young girl let out the most delicious giggle while clinging to the door, embracing it flirtatiously as if to summon our most carnal desires. She fluttered her eyes and wrinkled her freckled cherry nose before answering.

"You are quite the joker, good detective." James straightened his tie lightheartedly. "Dr. Guildford is in his lab, but I'm not his daughter," she said in a sensuous voice. "I'm his assistant. I am studying to be a medical hand."

"Well," muttered Davis, "aren't you the little go-getter." I slapped him again and narrowed my eyes, sneering at him before turning back to Dr. Guildford's assistant.

"My dear lady, would you be kind enough as to show us to him?"

"Of course," she said pleasantly before escorting us inside.

I continued to glare at Davis as we entered, but it only seemed to encourage him. He chuckled proudly, unashamed of his conduct. Once inside, the young assistant offered to take our coats, scarves, and gloves. After she hung them, the three of us lingered in the confines of the dank front office to warm up, exchanging light conversation. The room was meagerly decorated with little more than an antique desk, crooked chair and patchwork sofa. There were blotchy brown stains on the floorboards, a rusty bicycle leaning on the wall, and drips of water leaking from the ceiling. I could *definitely* tell now that this was not an established place of business.

After a few moments, the assistant requested that we follow her to Guildford's office, and as we did, Davis and I found ourselves in a long, never ending corridor. James didn't seem bothered by the property's condition, as his eyes were fixed on our assistant's lovely derriere. Trotting along the passageway of what appeared to be a converted wine cellar, we reached the end of the hall that reeked of formaldehyde. We were ushered to a domed mouth entrance that led into the main chamber. The cold brick room was cluttered and unsightly, with cupboards, dusty bookshelves and a metal surgeon table. As we entered, a bulge in the floor caused me to lose my balance. Hurrying to regain stability, my bare hand inadvertently brushed up on a sheeted gurney, touching the naked arm of a small corpse I hadn't previously seen there. Suddenly, my vision started to fade.

It was a brisk morning on the streets of London, and a boy with a flat cap and oversized coat lifted his head to the sound of wind chimes across the street. An old chubby baker had rung the instrument, and was now giving out burned loaves of bread to nearby beggars. The boy's eyes lit up as he darted into the street, but unfortunately, he had not been aware of a galloping horse and rider that had just turned onto the road. The horse neighed as it crashed into the child.

When my vision returned, I noticed that we were surrounded by nearly a dozen other sheeted cadavers resting on steel slabs, their tagged toes protruding from the ends. *The echo had taken over.*

"This man is a monster," said Davis squeamishly.

"No you prat, he's an embalmer."

"That's quite correct," said a shrewd voice from the back of the lab. Climbing up from a set of subbasement stairs, a clean-cut man with greased raven hair wiped his hands on a towel. His oversized, dopey ears stuck out from a narrow set of cheeks that came down to a sharp point. Dressed in a ragged white lab coat, he calmly approached us, half amused with Davis who stared at the bodies.

"Don't mind them. They won't bother you," he chortled as he reached to shake our hands. I tried not to touch anymore of the nearby corpses, in case the echo triggered. I began studying Dr. Guildford as James shook his hand, and noticed neither of his eyes quite matched. One, a piercing grey, seemed to clash with the other, a dull blue that leaned lazily to one side. He was cleanly shaven with flaring nostrils and a cleft chin that he held up high. He wore a dark dress suit under his surgeon's apron, and had an expensive gold signet ring on his middle finger. Any man on the street would be able to tell that he was educated by his appearance and dress alone.

"Dr. Guildford," I announced with authority, while trying to shake off my vision, "Detective Sergeant Brannick, Scotland Yard. This is my partner Detective Sergeant Davis."

"A pleasure," he said diligently. "How may I be of service to you gentlemen?"

"Well doctor, we just have a few questions for you," butted in Davis, "about the death of Miss McCann." Guildford hummed insightfully then nodded.

"Yes, yes, I just buried her in Brompton Cemetery yesterday. What a tragic affair." *Damn, with the corpse gone, I'd be unable to utilize the echo.* Brompton Cemetery, also known as Westminster Cemetery, was one of seven large, modern cemeteries founded by private companies. I recalled reading a newspaper article about it some years back written after the death of novelist George Borrow. He had been buried there in 1881, and the article used his demise as a pretext to promote the garden burial ground for future prospectors. It was located near Earl's Court in South West London, established by an Act of Parliament and later consecrated by the Bishop of London for future burials. The site included large mausoleums, common graves, and small columbarium. I'd never visited, but The Daily insisted it was quite beautiful.

"*You* buried her?" asked Davis in an implicating manner.

"Yes, I'm an undertaker by trade, well…undertaker, mortician, embalmer, I do it all. It is quite nice for grieving families as they tend not know the first thing about handling their loved ones after they expire. I take care of it all *en règle* for a small fee of course."

"Ah, I see," said Davis suspiciously.

"Dr. Guildford," I spoke up, clearing my throat, "I understand by your title alone that you're a physician. Is it true you aided Miss McCann at the time of her illness?"

"Well, I give medical advice," Guildford said nervously. "My official status was revoked when I had a few mishaps sometime ago."

"Doctor," I said bluntly, "I'm not here to check your papers. I don't care if you illegally help ailing poor folk. I'm here to investigate a murder."

"Murder?" Guildford's grey eye grew wide with shock. He took a step back, rubbing his temple as if suffering from a headache.

"Yes murder," I clarified. "Perhaps you should take a look at this letter. We found it hidden in Miss McCann's flat." I turned back my lapel and removed the note discovered at Miss McCann's flat, handing it to him. His one good eye moved back and forth across the page, scanning the paper before handing it back.

"Impossible," he insisted. "She didn't show any signs when I treated her corpse."

"Nothing at all," I argued, "no strangulation marks or suspect wounds?"

"*Nothing*," he emphasized, "nothing at all."

"Doctor," called out Davis, "you originally gave Miss McCann the prognosis of consumption. What symptoms did she show?"

"Well, when the disease becomes active, victim symptoms include bloody cough, fever, appetite loss, pallor, and fatigue. In an additional quarter of cases, the infection moves from the lungs, causing extrapulonary tuberculosis. Swelling of the lymphatic system in the scrofula of the neck causes victims agonizing pain from mouth to lungs until their death. When I visited Miss McCann, she had all of these symptoms."

Well, at least I had something to look forward to.

"And doctor," I inquired, "When you visited Miss McCann, you suggested quarantine. Did you see or did she mention anyone living with her?"

"No," he condemned, "Miss McCann was a lovely bachelorette who lived alone as far as I know. The only other person in her life was the man she worked for. She tended to a wealthy elderly gentleman who suffered from a disease that left him crippled and weak hearted. I told her to keep away, as her disease could get him very sick. It was all very daunting for her, but she took the news as gracefully as one could. Why do you ask?"

"Well sir," blabbed Davis indignantly, "She had a visitor the night before her death. Some Pikey-Russian was seen in her home by eyewitnesses from the streets below. They say the man did not seem very happy with her."

"Oh, I see," considered Dr. Guildford. He gave a long pause and stared thoughtfully at the stone floor before suddenly squinting in revulsion. "Yes," he said thoughtfully, "now that I recall, she had mentioned a man, but it was an unsuitable courtship that she had insisted ended weeks ago. He wasn't Russian though. He was Romanian."

"Did she mention his name?" I queried.

"Yes," he murmured while biting at his inside cheek, struggling to recollect the name. "I only remember because it was very distinct. Vasile Ivanescu I believe is his name. He is a prominent man from a town called Sibiu if I remember correctly. He came here on his father's inheritance according to Jacqueline. She was very excited about him at first, could not stop talking about him in fact. Although during one of our last appointments, she indicated that the courtship did not quite work out due to his temper."

"And do you know where this man lives?" I asked while trying not to stare at Dr. Guildford's lazy eye.

"I have an idea," he said indefinitely. "She mentioned something about Tottenham. It's a dangerous area where foreigners stay. I don't have an address or anything, but at least that may be a good start."

"Anything else that she said that might help us doctor," I asked, trying to finish up our meeting.

"It might be good to know that this man is very dangerous. He was in the Romanian army according to Jacqueline. She said that he'd seen battle, so I'm sure he's no stranger to violence. Please, be careful."

"I think we can handle ourselves," replied Davis arrogantly. I smiled appreciatively, then placed my bowler back on and tipped it to Guildford.

"Thanks for everything doctor, we appreciate your cooperation. We'll see ourselves out now."

Guildford did not protest, wishing us well as we escaped from his morgue. Navigating through the cellar, we returned to the reception area and helped ourselves to the closet. I collected our effects while Davis gawked obsessively at the assistant. She tapped at the keys of an outdated typewriter, blowing a quick kiss to James before returning to her work. Davis nearly swooned as I shoved him out the door.

A storm of fire began to gather in my chest as we exited the building, causing me to cough up into the interior of my suit coat. Red mist dyed the wool, but I managed to hide it from Davis. I needed to chase the dragon again. It was the only way to deal with the pain. Finally, I gathered my wits and strained to rejoin James. He looked bored and unwary.

"Are you coming down with something?" he asked.

"Looks like it," I said as I continued to put on my long coat and gloves.

"So what do you make of the case so far?"

"You're like a cheeky parrot Davis," I spit, still frustrated by his behavior. I could feel the continuing need for a fix unravel my temper. "You just repeat the same questions over and over, not making any conclusions of your own."

"Uh oh," he spat sarcastically, "the old codger needs his pudding again. He's getting cranky."

I tried to disregard the taunts, slightly turning my back to James while I concentrated on the early facts. There were no obvious signs of murder, though we did have a particularly shady suspect in this Ivanescu character. *Was he a vengeful jilted lover? Is it possible that this suspect covertly killed Miss McCann, knowing her disease would cover up his tracks?* We would definitely need to track this Vasile down and question him. I turned back to Davis who was trying to get at me by obnoxiously imitating an old man, his walking cane tapping along the paved ground as he curled his lips inward.

"Well, if we can find this Vasile, perhaps we can learn if he's had practice killing before."

"Maybe he's an assassin for the military," plotted Davis.

"Targeting poor bachelorettes all in the name of a political coup? I think not James. Besides, we can not rule out the chance she *did* in fact pass from natural causes." Davis watched as I unconsciously struck at my chin with a finger. "However, let's say our suspicions are correct and she *was* murdered, it would have to have been by some sort of untraceable poison. I've seen it once before during the Bartlett investigation."

"Perhaps snakes venom?"

"James, how in the world did you become a detective," I asked blithely. "You could tell if it were snake venom. There is too much swelling and tissue damage." My thoughts built off of James's presumption. "However, it is conceivable that aconitum may have been involved, also known as wolf's bane. It's more common in Eastern Europe and nearly untraceable."

"Well then, now that we have a few guesses, what should we do?"

"Guesses are for fools. We need to keep collecting facts. Listen up James. *You* are going to return to the office and write the request to further investigate this case, personally handing it to Swanson. Try to avoid telling him that we do not have any real proof yet. Instead point out our new lead suspect, this Vasile gentleman, and be convincing."

"How am I supposed to do that?" he asked. But instead of giving him an answer, I only twisted my face into a sneer. Davis understood what I meant. "Alright, alright, I will figure something out."

He took a short recess to remove a homemade cigarette from the silver carrying case that his wife had bought for him on his birthday. Lighting the end of a freshly rolled fag, he breathed in the smoke, enjoying the taste of the tobacco on his tongue. Then, only after smiling at two young ladies walking by, did he return his attention to me, cigarette dangling from his teeth.

"And what will you be doing Nathan?"

"Tell Swanson I'm wondering through Tottenham in search of our suspect until the end of my shift. You and I will officially get started on finding the Romanian first thing tomorrow."

Davis clanked the gold metal tip of his walking stick along the street bricks towards the pedestrians, harassing some young girl as she trotted by with a basket of fresh flowers. He raised one of his bushy brows and gave me a suspicious expression.

"And what will you *really* be doing with the rest of your day?"

"Routine detective work."

After departing from Davis, it took all that I had in me to refrain from hurrying home to reunite with my opium. My body was tired and I now had a free pass to do whatever I wanted with my afternoon. But that didn't sit well. I was obligated to put forth at least a tad more effort towards the case in order to ease my conscience.

I intended on finding out more about some possible poisons that could have been administered to kill Ms. McCann and knew just the man to help me. His name was Timothy Dewhirst, but most people just called him the *Soldier*. He was a street gambler and artist who tried to assimilate the science of toxins and venoms for his trade. He specialized in the extermination of rodents, in particular rats, and leant his expert opinion to me on several previous cases. If I were to meet with him however, it would be quite the journey, as he resided in an old disabled schooner harbored inside the Millwall dock along the Isle of Dogs. He lived on the inherited boat and spent a large amount of time laboring over his art. Timothy was a painter, and when not killing rats, he sold his works along the wharf. He was strikingly abnormal, but a good man.

It took sometime to find a taxi that would make the trip, but eventually a carriage rider agreed and I began my journey eastward. After two hours time, I made it as far as the stagecoach driver would take me and walked the remainder of the way. I enjoyed watching the boatmen care for their vessels and reminisced about my time as a commissioned navigator. Finally though, just as it was becoming dark, I arrived at the Soldier's residence. The sky looked bruised with only an occasional wink from the stars. I found the Soldier painting on the main deck with a frayed blanket over his shoulders. He was middle-aged with long grey hair that he tied oddly in a bow behind his neck. He wore a tattered eye patch over his injured eye and a weathered red infantry jacket with rolled up sleeves. He had seen some dreadful things in battle and still suffered from the trauma. I felt bad for the bloke, but was always careful around him, as I never knew when he could snap.

He rested in an old whicker chair, working along a table made of cargo barrels and a single sheet of thin wood. He did not immediately take notice of me, so I knocked on the corner of a nearby moldy crate, grabbing his attention.

"Detective Sergeant Brannick, is that you?" he asked with his hoarse voice. I gave a half-smirk and tipped my hat, staring at him with my hands along my belt.

"Good evening Soldier. You look rather stoic this brisk evening. Mind if I come aboard?"

The Soldier stood up from his chair along the port side of the ship, dropping his blanket as he limped towards my direction. The hard beats of soft soles padded along the deck planks. Timothy peeked over the railing. He was aging, but his shoulders were still wide, and the muscles in his forearms were taut. He smiled at me while humming an old work tune.

"Allo' Nathan. I usually don't allow rozzers in my home, but I think I can make an exception. Come, I'll lower the dock bridge near the centerline."

He dropped a plank between the boat and the dock and allowed me to climb aboard. When I arrived on the ship, I couldn't help but notice that it was in a state of disrepair. It appeared as if an extravagant party had taken place sometime ago, as empty bottles of wine strew across the deck, dust settled across their surface. Red-stained glasses balanced themselves on top of the pulley block, filled with stale rain, and a smattering of playing cards protruded from the coiled rigging.

"You never have been able to pass up a good time," I said with a subtle truism to the point of praise. Timothy shuffled back to his paint station, looking over his shoulder at me as he simpered. I stepped over a few broken bottles as we made it to the table. The Soldier had been rendering a fairly morbid depiction of a rotted infantryman staring at the sunset. The ghoul's flesh was shriveled and his lipless mouth gave a ghastly smile.

"Very fearsome," I complimented. Timothy picked up the brush resting along the canvas.

"Now Nathan," said Timothy as he adjusted his eye patch, "I never knew you as an appreciator of the arts, so forgive me if I don't think you are here for a portrait." He sipped at a cup of sherry that looked as if it had been standing there for days, a dead spider floating in its red pool. He looked it over before raising it in my direction. "Care for a glass?" I shook my head briefly.

"I know it makes me sound like I'm a lushington and all," he sighed, "but it sometimes does the trick. Besides, we all need a way to deal with the atrocities of life." Timothy took in another mouthful, swishing the liquid between his cheeks before swallowing. "So then, if you ain't here for art, and you don't wish to drink, then of course, you must be here for my bloody opinion again."

I went to take a seat at an empty barrel near the table, but before I could, Timothy interjected.

"No, please don't sit there," he said abruptly, "That's Ravi's seat." I had no idea who he was talking about, but didn't question it. Looking for someplace to sit, I dusted off the upper torso of an old wooden figurehead nearby. Once, the proud decoration found at the prow of a ship, the face of the statue now seemed to be content with staring at me inquisitively, as if it too were curious why I had come. I sat upon its two large breasts, using them as a bumpy stool.

"Yes Soldier, you have proven *true hitherto*," I said in good humor. "I need your help." He curled his lower lip over his chin.

"Of course, tell me how I can help the pride of Scotland Yard?" he asked sarcastically.

"I am investigating the death of a woman named Miss Jacqueline McCann. She was found in her flat just a few days ago. On the surface, it looked as if she had perspired from a natural ailment, consumption. However, after police spoke with neighbors, there seemed to be more afoot. In particular, people living in the victim's building reported that every night for the entire week before she died, they could hear her crying in pain. In addition, hours before her body had been discovered, patrons from a pub on the lower level of the building reported that a very suspicious stranger visiting her flat. Still, with no signs of struggle nor any wounds on her body, I'm at a loss. Though her lips *did* have traces of blood on them, once again, the lungs tend to bleed with late stages of consumption."

"Do you still have the body?" asked Timothy in a quiet, well-bred voice.

"No, unfortunately I came across the case too late, after her corpse had been taken away for burial. While persons such as you or I have unfettered our bonds to the sanctity of the dead, most common folk tend to perceive the prodding of cadavers as unholy and a perversion of ethics."

"Christ man, I don't know how you do it? They want you miltonians investigating with one hand behind your back. Luckily, I am not as sensitive. Tell me, did you go into her flat?"

"I did."

"And when you did, were there any unordinary smells?"

"Unordinary smells? Hmm, well, it was a bit musty, but that's to be expected."

"No stench that might be similar to bitter almonds, fruit, garlic or rotten eggs?"

"Damn it Soldier, why on earth are you asking me such questions?" Timothy leaned back in his chair patiently, taking another mouthful of sherry.

"Cyanide tends to smell like bitter almonds, chloroform has a sweet fruity odor, phosphorus stinks of garlic and hydrogen sulfide reeks like rotten eggs. Now, did you come across any of these aromas?"

Damn it. Timothy was trying to help me and I spit on him, typical Nathan.

"My apologies. No, there were none of the smells you described. Are there perhaps any other symptoms?"

"Without a body, there ain't much I can offer. However, check in the report to see if her eyes had pinpoint pupils or if her fingernails had abnormal specs of white under the clear surface. Those are signs of poisoning as well."

"I *did* see her post-mortem photograph and unfortunately her eyes are closed. I'll check again, but I am quite sure that there were no discolorations in her fingernails."

"Well, that's rather disappointing. If you can't get to the body and did not smell hint of any poisons, then you came here for nothing I'm afraid. To my knowledge, those are the only signs. Apologies mate."

"No, don't apologize. I should be the one who is sorry for taking up your time. Besides, from what it sounds like to me, in all probability, Miss McCann has not been poisoned. I appreciate you helping me draw that conclusion."

I stood up from my improvised bench and went to shake hands with Timothy. He stared at my palm for a moment as if I had erred in offering it. Then, resting his glass on the table next to him, he took both hands to push himself up off his seat.

"Are you personally under the assumption that this was a murder old boy?" he asked frankly.

"I am just trying to understand all facts. Anything else would be groundless."

"Well, don't stare at your cards for too long mate," he said disapprovingly, "There's probably an ace in the next hand."

"Very deep," I chuckled, "I'll see you around old friend." Timothy gave a short grunt before pursing his lips. He then took my hand, giving it an old infantryman's shake before releasing me. I waived him farewell, then ambled across the ship plank back to the dock. I came away nearly as ignorant as I went in.

It was very dark already and I hoped to make it home before my regular return time. After hunting down a driver, I offered double the fare in order to get the cab to gallop west as fast as possible. My chest was burning and my muscles were sore from walking. Long ago, I'd come home to Catherine nestled in our bed with a book, supper waiting for me on the table. Now, the flat was lonely, and I'd be lucky if Ms. Abigail left me remnants of her own dinner.

I missed Catherine a great deal, but took comfort in knowing she was in a better place, especially after seeing all the agony she'd endured. We'd talked about me marrying again after her death, and she begged me to not wallow in my own pity. But I couldn't help it. I didn't want to be with anyone else. I don't think I'd ever meet a woman as unique as her, and part of me hoped I didn't.

During the ride back home, I took a long, much needed nap. Nightmares of the boy from Dr. Guildford's office, Catherine, and Miss McCann flashed through my mind. It was all very haunting. But, by the time I made it to my flat, I felt revitalized, ready for a good sitting with the opium pipe. I knew the narcotic would use up the rest of my night, *and* that I would pay the price in the morning, but I tried to block out those little wearisome details. I needed a break and a bit of tar was the answer. Besides, *we all need a way to deal with the atrocities of life.*

CHAPTER 5

Ms. Abigail was a sweet older woman who lived downstairs. She was the first to welcome us when we'd moved into the building, and later, when Catherine became sick, was the first to volunteer as caretaker. Even after Catherine's death, Ms. Abigail insisted on keeping a key to my flat so she could come in to clean up and feed my cat. She was a decent cook, and often left me breads and meats for dinner. Though she insisted that it was spare food from her own supper, I was fairly certain that she'd gone out of her way to cook it. She was a saint.

She'd been waiting in my flat when I'd arrived back home, a basket of sorted bottles in hand. Despite the fact that she was nearly twenty years older than I, she had a certain worn beauty to her. She had a youthful complexion with a stream of small wrinkles that creased near her mouth and eyes. Her salt and pepper hair was long and silken, and her clothes were modest, but fitting. I felt bad for the woman, because though we never talked about it, I assumed she'd had a tough go at life to be on her own so early.

"Nathan," she said warmly, "I'm so sorry to be a pest, but I had some things I wanted to bring over." Ms. Abigail began removing the bottles in her whicker container, spreading them across my table. "This one here will help your cough. I can hear you choking all night from my flat. Take it twice a day and you should feel better. This one here should help with fever, or at least, it should help you feel less miserable. Catherine rather enjoyed it."

I'd been very secretive about my consumption. All it took was one big mouth to ruin everything for me. Since I was to my ears in debt, getting let go from the force wasn't an option. However, Ms. Abigail seemed to see right through me. She was bringing me remedies that she'd used to treat Catherine. Luckily, she was a good woman, and I assumed that my secret would be safe. Nevertheless, a quick conversation couldn't hurt.

"Ms. Abigail, you're an angel," I said in praise. "You *know* though, don't you?" Ms. Abigail frowned.

"That I do Mr. Brannick, but don't you worry. I'll take great care of you. What we need to do is keep you in good spirits. I mean look at you already," she said while petting my arm, "You're not your usual self." She lifted her hand, placing the backside of it on my forehead, checking for a fever. "I know that you've been self medicating. I can smell the smoke from my flat. While I don't condone it, I would ask that you at least err on the side of caution when using that rubbish. And most importantly, don't hesitate to let me know if there is anything I can do?"

Let her know if there is anything she can do to get me to stop using opium is what she meant.

"Ms. Abigail, I know you worry about me, but don't. I'll get through this," I said while giving her a pat on her hand. "While we're on the topic though, I do need to emphasize that I've been keeping my illness a secret because I don't want anyone to be too concerned. Can you keep this little matter private?"

"Your secret is safe with me," she replied. "Don't worry." Ms. Abigail smiled at me in admiration. Though I didn't know much about her, I regarded her as a good friend. She cared for me like a mother would, which is comforting when you live the life that I do. It took a moment for her to wake from her trance. "Oh good heavens look at the time." She plopped down the rest of her basket. "Well, I'll be out of your hair then. Try to give some of these tonics a try if the pain gets too bad." She walked over to the front door and gave me one last grin. "Goodnight Nathan."

"Goodnight Ms. Abigail. God bless you." Ms. Abigail gave a pleasant little shrug then left the flat. I moved to the door and clasped it shut.

It had taken me less than ten minutes to prepare the opium. After removing my supply from its hiding space, I inserted two rubbery tablets into the round chamber of the bowl then hung it off my chest of drawers. I then retrieved a simple candle, and after lighting its tip, placed the stick under the bottom of the pipe's bronze lamp, cooking both pills. It felt as if some unseen force was timing me, and as I supervised the vaporizing process, I'd realized that I was still in my stuffy work attire. The opium was baking quickly and by the time I wiggled out of my suit, the dosages were already at a sizzle. Stark naked except for my socks, I decided there was little time to waste. I grabbed both my pipe and bowler while tottering back to my reading chair, placing the wood bore in my mouth while hanging the hat over my groin.

Opium, otherwise known as poppy-tears, latex, tar, or dope, feels lovely as a summer shower due to a chemical called morphine. I'd been introduced to the narcotic during my early years at sea, but learned more about the creation process after becoming a detective. One obtains the latex by scratching the immature seedpods by hand, causing the milky liquid to leak out and dry into a sticky yellowish residue that is later scraped off. From there it is packed and made into either a dust or malleable tablet that is vaporized and inhaled. Such has been the method since ancient times.

I began inhaling the bitter breaths, feeling the effects almost immediately. The opium smoke slithered through my body, unraveling the tight ropes along my chest, until finally nestling in my lungs. The cooling rivers and canals that made up my nervous system coursed sugary sweet blood into my ears, neck and lips. Phantasmal sounds began to swirl through the room and my heart beat like a drum. The hiss of opium continued to burn inside the draught hole of my pipe, singing its crackling lullaby. Sinking into the cushions of my chair, I watched as the tablet melted into a bead of foam, my body pulsating rhythmically.

The house stood eerily tranquil for sometime. I continued to suck at the white vapors fuming from the pipe, still contemplating the facts of the investigation. Then suddenly, a green twinkling haze surrounded my vision and soon a swarm of shooting stars bolted across the room like a hive of angry hornets. I must have smoked too much, as the visions were starting. My buttocks tightened and fingers coiled. Gasping for air as a storm erupted in my upper chest, I spit up a small spatter of mucus from my mouth, spewing drool down my face. Meanwhile, jumping onto the bed next to me was my housecat, Hades. He tilted his black head and purred in my direction. At first, nothing appeared out of the ordinary about the feline, but all of a sudden, two rabbit like ears sprouted from atop his head, as his whiskers spun clockwise like a windmill. I gave a dry, itchy laugh that caused smoke plumes to flow from my lips. The billows resembled a hand that I tried to chase with my eyes as it rose upward to the ceiling. My sight began to blur even worse as my hallucinations intensified, and after a short time, the entire room was throbbing.

My eyeballs rolled uncontrollably in my sockets as I peered around. The decorative vines stamped along my black and white wallpaper stirred up an unsettled dizziness, causing me to focus on any nearby object in order to avoid being sickened. I fixed my gaze on the beige drapes that flowed lightly from a wind outside. It took my mind a few moments to realize that the glass window behind the drapes had been opened. I was bewildered, as I knew I had clasped the lock shut before I'd left for work this morning. *Why was it no longer secure?*

My thoughts raced to Ms. Abigail. Outraged, I attempted to stand up in order to close the sliding glass, but my legs felt as if they were made of paper. I barely wobbled halfway between my chair and the casement before plummeting onto the floor. Crawling on all fours to the windowsill, I raised one hand in order to pull it shut. Just as I had, a large, ugly bat came soaring by, its wings scratching at the glass before it spun around and flew back towards the moon.

"Damn it Ms. Abigail," I said aloud, or at least I think I said aloud, "Bats make terrible house pets!" Had I not closed the window in time, the remainder of the night would have been spent with me, higher than the heavens, chasing a flying rodent around my house in nothing more than my stockings. Luckily, fate was momentarily on my side, though it would not stop me from having a serious talk with Ms. Abigail come morning, if I could remember. For now though, all I wanted was to continue relishing in my high.

The room began to rock and soon I felt that I had returned to the *S.S. Black Prince*. I could hear ghostly waves splash along the walls and the distant cry of bending wood as my apartment sailed across the shores. What a good ship she was. The third vessel of that name to serve in the Royal Navy, she had been the world's second ocean-going, iron-hulled warship. She was one-hundred-and-twenty-eight meters long overall and could displace nine thousand or so tons of hull. She had thick wrought iron armor and forty smoothbore, muzzle loading sixty-eight pounders. No ship could match it. I dug in my trousers that were resting along the floor, pulling out my pocket-watch. The clock had transformed into a silver compass, its imaginary dials spinning wildly.

"You need to go two degrees south sir," I said to Hades, pretending he was my old Captain. Then all at once, as if hearing my directions, the cat ran to the flat's entrance and started scratching. There was a buckling sound, and then the clasp from the front door's lock somehow became undone. Slowly, the door crept open, and along with the hallway's lamplight, a black shadow leaked in. It was a stretched female silhouette that painted my floor, her dress trim along the waste, with a flowing gown beneath. I followed the outline to its source, but found that the woman was just outside of my vision.

"Madame, this is highly irregular. Please come back in the morning." All went quiet for a moment, except for the ticker of my old wooden clock. The shadow stood stock-still, lingering along my floor.

"NATHAN," it whispered in a feminine voice, its pitch melodic and haunting.

"Catherine?" I called out wishfully, my body quivering from the drug.

"Sleep," the voice answered as its shadow whisked into the flat.

As if on command, my neck gave way, slackening from my body. I lay back my head and began blacking out from the overdose. *This was bad.* I gripped the arms of my chair, and though I could see nothing, I felt Catherine snaking her hands around my neckline. Her fingers were soft, but cold. My legs began to kick and my body convulsed.

"If only all this could be true," I murmured aloud before leaning back on the armchair cushion and falling out cold.

CHAPTER 6

D ays faded into weeks, then weeks into months. The illness had begun to take its toll, shattering my body and seizing my mind. It had struck suddenly in Munich, but I disregarded the nausea as womanly complications and continued traveling westward. However, as it worsened, I became more and more concerned. I began praying regularly to the Virgin Mary, wishful that this affliction was merely the stomach sickness Vasile had caught months ago. He'd recovered after several weeks, and I speculated that I would as well. We were brother and sister after all, of the same blood and body.

Though, as we made it to the outskirts of France, it became apparent how dire my condition really was. Queasiness, diarrhea and vomiting were every day occurrences. I could barely keep down food or drink. The first physician we visited suspected a rare form of cholera, a disease that had been plaguing this part of Europe for decades. He explained how incredibly life-threatening the suspected illness was. It claimed most of its victims rather quickly by drying out their bodies while lessening blood flow. I was given instructions and some sort of tonic for the discomfort, then left to fight the malady on my own.

However, by the time we arrived in *Le Havre*, I could no longer function. The pain in my bloated stomach was excruciating. Changes came over me. My drape of black hair both thinned and whitened while my eyes washed with yellow. The night terrors began, and it almost seemed better to stay awake and bear the physical agony than fall asleep to suffer the torment of my dreams. Brother was uncertain about what he should do. We had come so far, and to be defeated by a mere disease only made things worse. He blamed himself for allowing me to leave Transylvania, but in truth, he knew I would rather give my life to our great cause than shrivel from old age back in Sibiu.

Then, as if by the graces of God, Vasile stumbled upon a priest who offered us his help. This man of the cloth, Father Babineaux, had initially been summoned by my brother to simply bless me with the divine last rites. Save for when visiting my bedside, he declared that it was not cholera that had taken hold of me, but the king of hell himself. Luckily, the priest knew *The Rite of Expulsion*, a holy ceremony that can banish dark spirits and demonic forces from mortal flesh. Together, he and Vasile conducted the ritual over my crippled figure. It took them three full days and nights to complete, but finally, the demon had been driven out.

Though I do not remember a great deal, when I awoke several days later, my mind, body and soul were returned to me. God had lifted my curse, a gift I still am grateful for to this day. Nonetheless, the sickness had delayed our chase and we were now months behind. I refused to give myself time to physically mend, summoning what strength I had so Vasile and I could cross the English Channel. For once, I thanked the Lord for the pains that come with womanhood, as the suffering we endure helped construct a reservoir of equanimity that I used to get me across the waters.

Brother knew better though, and once we arrived in the eyesore known as London, he used what few pennies he had left to hire someone who could care for me. I slept in the attic of a husbandless Englishwoman, away from both her and her children. It was obvious that she kept me upstairs not just for *my* own good, but the good of her family. I was an ailing foreigner who could not be trusted. I didn't object because in part, though the worse had passed,

I was in need of uninterrupted rest. I spent most of my in bed, recovering from the possession with only occasional breaks for the privy or to eat. My body was famished and I had difficulty staying conscious for prolonged periods of time. In spite of this, it was during my recuperation that I underwent one of the most profound experiences of my life, an experience that would guide me towards God's vision for my future.

It started off subtly. I would wake occasionally to the sounds of a muffled clinking, as if chimes halfheartedly rang in a lazy summer breeze. It was barely audible and faded away just as quickly as it came. As time went on and I became haler, I could make out not just the chimes, but also a low whimsical hum resonating inside my tiny room, as if an opera prima donna had been fine-tuning her voice. The song echoed softly and was as comforting as a mother's laugh. It begged me to wonder if it were all just imagination, perhaps an after effect of the illness that produced vivid hallucinations. Thankfully, the vocalist soon helped dismiss my doubt, at last presenting herself.

It was early November and I had nearly completely recovered from my affliction. There was soreness in my ribs and stomach still, but otherwise I was in good health. It had been several days since my brother last wrote me and I began to grow worried. If Vasile were dead, it would be my sole responsibility to stop our prey before she left London. While I was fearless of my task, it did sadden me to think that my brother may have perished or perhaps worse. We had trained together our entire lives, and though he was too humble to admit it, Vasile was a stronger warrior than I. If he could not destroy the Bride, how did I deem that I could?

Restless, I decided to resume my neglected training. I conducted a number of exercises papa had taught me, including a particular exercise that involved suspending myself from the attic rafters to toughen my legs and lower torso. I strived to be more like papa every day. He was smart, cunning, and above all else, wise. If he were still alive, he would know exactly how to handle the beast known as Paraschiva. He had been a military man for nearly his entire young life, and even after he settled down with mama, remained capable and sharp. Nevertheless, as strong as he was, it was not until mama's disappearance that he evolved into the man of God that I would come to look up to. He focused his grief and anger into his work in order to protect others from suffering the same fate that we did.

I hung upside-down from the shafts of wood that held up my caretaker's attic roof, repeatedly reaching for my ankles. The activity caused my stomach and legs to burn with life. My skin poured with sweat and my mouth dried from exhaustion. The throbbing helped keep my mind empty. Then, when I finally felt tired enough, I crept down from the ceiling. It was upon returning to my feet that a great dizziness made me light headed. I grabbed at the bedpost, trying to remain upright. That is when I saw *her*.

She was a luminous figure with gold hair and a white gown. She looked to be no older than fourteen, with flushed cheeks and a chaste face. She carried into the room with her a scent of roses and a familiar toll of chimes. Her presence, though frightening, also put me at peace, and as I continued to study her, I prayed that this was something divine. *Perhaps she was St. Philomena?* She often cared for lost souls such as me. I opened my mouth to speak, but as I tried, only air came out.

"Save your breath my child," she said. I heard the words as clearly as if she was standing next to me, but her lips were as still as a church icon's. "I am here to guide you. We know what you and your brother plot." My heart beamed, for at that moment, I identified that the Lord supported our cause. "You will journey to the nearby district that favors your Eastern blood. There at an inn your brother awaits. He is in great danger, as Satan has impeded his path. Go to him. There, you will meet a man of the law, who has been hardened and weathered from the storms. He has been chosen by Samael, the angel of death, and will aid you in your pursuit. He will show mercy to you and even pave the way for the future, but only if you can broaden his gaze. Let him see the true design of God, one paved with many blessings. Take his hand and be his shepherd- for you are not twain, but one flesh. Therefore let not man put asunder which God hath coupled together."

After finishing her sentence, the angel dissolved into nothingness, fading away along with the chimes. I dropped to my knees and cried joyfully, thanking the Lord for his messenger. Then, all at once, I woke up slouched over the attic bed, just meters away from where I had previously felt lightheaded. My clothes, which had dried during my vision, were once again sticky with sweat. *Had I fallen unconscious? Was it all just a dream?* No. It couldn't be. God had sent his herald so that the path I followed would be clear. I could feel it in my soul. That night I packed all my belongings, ready to leave that very next morning. I did not have much except for a few changes of clothes, my mother's cloak, some knives, flasks and my *kilïjs'*, a family sword given to me by father.

The following day, I walked down the stairwell where my English caretaker and her family ate breakfast. They were nearly a half-dozen strong and sat around a table devouring some sort of caked slop. The household looked upon me as if I were a leper. I'd been their secret upstairs for so long. Now incarnate, they were unsure as to how they should react besides gawk. The mother fretfully ogled over my traveling trunks as she brushed her daughter's hair. I could see it in her eyes that she was afraid. She shook her head slowly; straightening her back and gathering what courage she had to confront me.

"G-Going somewhere are we darling?" she stuttered while straightening out a knot from her child's bushy mane. The young girl scooped up a spoon full of oats, jabbing them into her miniature maw. For a brief moment, I tried to hold my tongue in front of the Englishwoman's young ones, but knew time could not be wasted.

"Yes," I said with poise, "I feel much better. Thank you for your hospitality. I will take my leave now." The widow put down her horse haired brush and scurried in front me. She furrowed her brow, trying to appear fearless. I knew she didn't want to show any unease in front of her children. She bent down with her sweaty, stink filled head and whispered plaintively.

"But your brother will kill me. I gave him my word." I assumed that Vasile had given her stern orders to not let me leave without his consent, but my holy orders surpassed such desires. Moreover, any threats he may have suggested to the Englishwoman were hollow. My brother was a good man and would not harm the poor mother, even if he'd promised otherwise.

"I am sure he will understand. God has called upon me. Let him know that." I didn't want her, or anyone else for that matter, to know that I was on my way to find Vasile. Paraschiva was resourceful. The widow mumbled incoherently, trying to churn up something she could say that might keep me around. But before she could rally her thoughts, I put my head down and steamed forward, promising a collision with her if she did not step aside. She slipped into the short hall next to the kitchen and wordlessly watched as I exited the front door. I had much to do and little time to do it. There was no time to waste on social niceties.

The modest home I'd been staying at was located in the east end of London. I don't recall how brother found it, as my weakened state left me senseless upon our arrival. It was amusing to think that I'd been pent up there for so long, yet never caught a good glimpse of what lingered outside. It was overpopulated, filled with desolate workhouses and polluted by noxious factories. The broken streets and rotting buildings was an eyesore that drowned out hope in the faces of even the most innocent children wandering outside. Such was brother's modus operandi, cloaking us in the meager areas of towns to conceal our pursuits. It was easy to blend in with the poor and downtrodden, as they were deliberately ignored due to the weight they cast upon those more privileged.

Brother and I had read up on London before we crossed the channel. I had a good idea of where he was most likely staying, Tottenham. It was a considerable distance away and probably a confusing walk. I tried gauging the sky, hoping to plot my course by locating the course of the sun, but realized that it was too washed with filth to see directly. So I jabbed my knife vertically into the ground, stabbing it in a clump of dirt along the road. I watched as the sky painted a shadow from the blade. The line between those two points would be east and west.

Now confident in my direction, I continued towards Tottenham. The path was laborious and dismal, and I tired very quickly. I wanted to rest, but didn't trust staying still. Everything was unwelcoming. Every person was suspicious. Eventually, I made it to a point where I felt safe to take a break. It wasn't any less disconcerting than the rest of my trek, but for some reason, the little brick store that I hid behind felt comforting. My body shook from weariness and I began to question my hastiness in leaving the Englishwoman's confines. Then, as if to keep me headstrong, a whimsical clanking from across the street caught my attention. A bakery, no larger than a chicken house, kept a hung set of wind chimes near the main entrance of their establishment. St. Philomena, the angels and God were trying to get my attention.

There was a single set of windows built into the front of the bakery that allowed me to see the hearth of a cooking fire inside. I could see a chubby Englishman, sprinkled with flour along his brown shirt, raising his hands in the air. At first, I assumed that he was perhaps reaching for some pan or utensil dangling from a shelf above, but as my eyes focused, I took note of his panicked expression. He stood among three men, whose backs faced me. The trio, armed with metal pipes and knives, pointed their weapons threateningly at the old man. He dug into the drawer that he he'd been hiding behind, handing over a handful of coins. *I am the good shepherd. The good shepherd must always protect God's flock.*

I kept my hands under my black cloak, grasping the handle of my sword with one hand while fingering the end of a dagger with the other. I waited for the streets to clear of passage before crossing, scampering onto the outside wall of the bakery. I could hear pathetic pleas from the baker as he begged for mercy inside. Once enough carriages cleared the roads and the smattering of locals seemed distracted, I quietly crept to the storefront entrance and slipped inside. The thieves did not take notice me as I slinked behind them, my blades readied under my cloak.

"Come on now you randy old bastard," shouted a man with an olive flat cap as he wagged his finger in the baker's face, "We know there's more than this." His accomplices grabbed the baker's arms, tugging him over the counter. At first the baker resisted, trying to use his sturdy weight to counter them. As he looked up and took notice of me however, he surrendered, allowing his assailants to drag him over the table. They sprawled him out like a pig to be butchered while the man with the flat cap readied his metal pipe. The baker locked eyes with me, beseeching my aid. As he did, the thieves became mindful and turned around to follow his stare.

"Bugger off you damn whore," spat the man in the flat cap. His friends half snickered at their comrade's remark, as if obligated.

"A loaf of bread please?" I demanded. The three gawped at one another before collectively giving me a second glance.

"Alright, darling," said the man in the flat cap as he pulled his trousers up with one hand, "stay around and I'll give you a good loaf. When I'm done, Simon and Oswald here will have a taste of you as well." The two cronies hooted in unison.

"I said…a loaf of bread please."

The men's faces turned sober. The short blonde that had been holding half of the baker released his grip, granting his accomplice, a frail young man in blues, full control. The man in blue squeezed the pastry maker by the neck, slamming him back down onto the counter. Moving up so he stood shoulder to shoulder with his friend in the olive cap, the blonde removed a sizable knife from his coat. He was in a black mood, ready to stick me with either the weapon or the bits between his legs if I'd allow it.

"Now sweetheart," said the man in the flat cap as he tilted his left ear in my direction, pretending he was hard of hearing, "What was it that you wanted again? Cuz' I know you're not stupid enough to challenge the likes of us with your-"

"You bray like an ass," I interrupted. "Now give me my bread."

The capped man was taken aback. He seemed uncertain as to how he should react. He looked to his companions as if the answer might be written on their foreheads.

"Arrogant whore," he fizzled before shoving the blonde man forward. "Alright Simon, give her some bread."

Simon rushed forward, lifting the knife to stab me. However, I had already unsheathed a dagger under my cape, prepared to fling it at moments notice. Though my body was still weak, the blade glided gracefully from my hand as it had done so many times before. Simon grabbed at his abdomen as the weapon plunged into his stomach, cursing in pain. He fell backwards onto the floor, leaking red. The wood beneath him slowly drank his blood, creating a slippery obstacle for his capped friend to leap over.

Clumsily stampeding over Simon, the capped assailant wound his metal pole to strike, but by then it was already too late. The kilijs' was drawn and swinging flatly from my hip. With a kilijs', you don't need to be strong. The weapon does the work. The curved sword sliced through his pipe, throwing up orange sparks, and continued to carve downward until it pierced his ribs. I heard the bones crack and his warm blood sprayed upward, speckling my face with ruby droplets. Retracing the blade from inside him, I cautiously lifted it skyward so that the forte shielded my chest. But the man in the flat cap was no longer a threat. He'd fallen prone in a series of stages that started on one knee, then to the other, before finally he slumped flat on his side. His hands cupped the loose bits of meat dangling from his lower chest.

The frail man in blue seemed panicked. I flung the red liquid clinging to my blade at him before striding around the register to cut off his retreat. He released the baker and lifted his arms in surrender.

"Oswald is it?" I asked softly. The young man in blue began to shudder.

"Yes my lady," he said meekly. "Please, I didn't want to do it. They made me."

I plucked three English coins from my belt pouch, unsure of their value, and placed it on the counter. The baker slowly climbed up the table, purple in the face and still gasping for air. He glanced briefly at the two men bleeding on the ground before meeting my gaze. His expression pleaded for armistice, a request I fully intended to fulfill.

"A loaf of bread please?" I requested.

"Yes, of course," he replied. Hobbling to a shelf filled with breads, he picked out a round tan loaf and wrapped it in paper while I sheathed my kilijs'. He handed the package to me with shaky hands before collecting my coins, confusion still written across his face.

"I am trying to find Tottenham," I said aloud. Do either of you know if I'm I on the right path?"

"Hmm," the baker rasped through his tender throat. "You're going the right way, but Tottenham is awfully big. I'm assuming from your accent that you are looking for where all the Russians stay."

Everyone confused my people with the Russians, Germans, Polish and anything else that is not Romanian. Though we have protected Europe from the east for centuries, we always will be the forgotten children of Europe.

"Yes, I need to go where the foreigners stay."

"Oh, then you want north Tottenham," spat Oswald. "That's where you'll find what you're looking for. My cousin stays there. I can take you if you promise not to hurt me my lady."

"I can't promise anything, but your cooperation will be noted." Oswald nodded. The baker looked at the men squirming along his storefront.

"I'm grateful for what you've done," he said with a scratchy tone, "but you'd better get going my dear. It won't be long before someone comes in. They'll jail you for this."

I nodded in comprehension, pulling up my hood so that it shaded most of my features. I gave the two thieves fixed on the floor one last look over. The capped man seemed all but dead. Simon however, still showed promise. He held the handle of my knife in his trembling hands, coughing as he watched the ceiling. I wrapped my fingers around the handle and plucked the knife from his belly. Simon screamed briefly before falling unconscious. I waived for Oswald to follow me then withdrew from the bakery entrance. He fearfully obliged. We blended in with the other drab folk who made up London.

I don't know if God wanted me to simply deliver justice, or sent me inside so that I could narrow my search to northern Tottenham, but I was happy it happened. Though London felt like a lost cause, anything I could do to make it a little bit better felt right. It reminded me of a bible verse that father always read to us. "Not everyone who says to me, 'Lord, Lord', will enter the kingdom of heaven, but the one who does the will of my Father who is in Heaven."

CHAPTER 7

I woke in my chair, dried out and parched, to find Hades sleeping serenely on my belly. Last night was a blur and I had no idea what time it was. A raw headache split my brain in twine. My mouth was dry and felt as if it were coated in wax, forcing me to stumble from my seat in search of last night's water decanter. I lapped up the contents like a dog, extinguishing my immediate thirst. I hadn't realized it was morning until after taking a moment to catch my breath. It was time to start my daily routine. Washing up, I hurried to reshape my sideburns with a straight razor.

The blade had been a gift from Catherine. She'd teased about my scruffy beard, and convinced me to try sporting muttonchops instead. As always, she was right. The sideboards were much better. I thought back to when she use to help me shave. She'd lather my face with the shaving brush, and then draw funny pictures in the froth with her finger. She had a great sense of humor.

Unwilling to wallow in self pity, I pressed on, and after dressing in my favorite grey three-piece, I found myself yet again on the cold streets of London. The late night drunks and city whores still littered the roads. Smells of piss and moans of gluttony resonated over the dawn air. I staggered my way through the November brisk air, coughing up the spittle that had gathered in my lungs along the way. I decided to make one quick stop before navigating to headquarters.

There was one place in London you could always depend on being open no matter day or night, "The Exchange." It was a dolly shop tucked in the recesses of King's Road where one could pawn anything from jewelry to hobnails. The owner, George Evans, also known as "Cheese-Eater George," was a criminal informant for the Metropolitan Police who made a living by buying cheap and selling high, especially when it came to stolen goods. The few constables that were aware of his activities knew not to interfere with his business, as many of the more lenient Sergeants and Inspectors used him for information.

I rang the pull bell on his tiny store door and waited for him to answer. He lived in the rat-infested backroom of the building. I could hear him shuffling about from his folding bed to the storefront. The snap of several bolts and chains clang from inside before the door finally cracked open. George stood shorter than most men and had reddish dirty hair that clung together like yarn. He looked up at me with an unshaven face and his flat nose that made him look like an undersized lion. He stretched one stray suspender over his shoulder before scratching at his blemished cheek.

"What do you want?" he challenged.

A scorching anger came over me, flaring up heat in my face as my quiet seething boiled. *Clearly the boy needed to learn a little respect. After all, it was police like me who kept this snitch in business.* My fist balled up tightly before it launched uncontrollably at his forehead. I knew I had hit him hard because while stumbling backwards a few steps, George desperately grabbed at nearby furniture to keep himself upright. Finally he surrendered his balance and dropped into a sitting position. It felt good to let loose. I noticed the tense stress inside me release with the blow. I stepped within the threshold of his store and wrestled George by his collar, pulling him back to his feet.

"Good morning George," I said calmly, "did you forget your manners today?" George went into saying something, but before he could finish I hooked him in his stomach, a final warning that I was not fucking about.

"Christ, stop! Please," he begged. I stuck my head out and briefly checked the pathway to his store for any bystanders before shutting us inside. Once indoors, I made a point to clank my heavy soles on his dirty wood floor, before smashing George along the wall. His expression did the apologizing as his eyes swelled up in tears. Fluid leaked down his blushed cheeks onto my hand gripping his collar. The smell of tear salt burned at my nostrils.

"Now George, I know how regretful you feel for greeting me the way you did after all that I have done for you. I am however willing to look past this mild offense so long as you tell me what I want to know."

"Yes, of course. What is it that you are looking for? I am sure I can help," his voice yelped out agreeably.

Miss Jacqueline McCann, she lived on Curtain Road. Know who might have wanted her dead?" George shook his head no.

"I never heard of the girl in my life," he murmured. "Is she someone important?" I raised my fist again, threatening to strike like a hissing viper.

"Don't fib to me you little squealer." He winced, shielding his head with both arms.

"Honest, I don't know."

"Well then, did you have anyone come in recently who was trying to sell young ladies clothing or belongings?"

"No sir, but if I do have anyone who does, I will be sure to get in touch with you." His voice was squeaky and weak. I let him go by pushing him backwards, forcing him to crash into a collection of stacked wooden chairs.

"Good boy. Remember, I delivered you from the furnace. If you don't come find me as soon as you know something, it's back to prison with you." I straightened my coat collar and fixed my hat, staring at George with a hellish fury. "I'll see myself out."

The wind howled as I left the store, whistling in my ear with its tongue of cold. Though my visit came up empty, it was in George's best interest to get back to me if any suspect items came into his shop. Routine police work always seemed to start this way. Many empty leads, bated traps, and pointless inquiries. Sometimes, the investment paid off, but for the most part, you needed to let your lost efforts be forgotten.

I continued my walk to headquarters. After a hurried stroll that left me shivering, I'd finally made it to the warm confounds of the station. It always felt busiest in the morning, as most of the boys gathered around the compound as long as they possibly could before heading out collectively to guard the Thames. After signing in, I headed to my office. There in my spare chair sat Davis, crunching an apple that shed onto my desk.

"Morning old boy, how'd you sleep?" he asked, his bulb nose pointing out my office window as he stared at a young lady walking by.

"Not bad, not bad. Did Swanson take the bait?" Landing in my own chair, I browsed over James who was holding two shifts passes in his hand.

Permission to be excused from water guard duty, they read, hand signed by the Chief Inspector. Davis tried to tuck them below the desk, but his sausage fingers easily kept them in view.

"Afraid he said no," he fibbed, trying to tame his greasy twitching lips.

"Yeah," I said with smirk, "Then are those two tickets in your hand for the merry-go-round?"

Davis looked down at the tickets like a gambler with a losing hand then beamed with a jack-o-lantern smile.

"Heh, heh, eyes like an eagle Nathan. St. Swanson gave us two weeks to investigate without interruption. He hardly asked any questions either. He was too busy panicking about some dead woman they'd found in the Thames."

"Another murder?"

"Not likely. It was an older woman that they pulled out last night. She'd been dead for weeks, but the jacks looking into it don't think she'd drowned…well at least from water. Swanson is in a panic because the body was found with bloodstains spouting from her mouth, as if she'd been coughing out the red for weeks. He's worried some clueless family member threw her in the river after she'd died from consumption. In any case, if the public hears about this it would make all this guard duty nonsense for naught, and make the Chief Inspector appear quite blockheaded."

My mind grabbed wildly like a drowned sailor coming up threes. *Could this new lady of the Thames have any connection to the case? Perhaps she might be the latest of Vasile's victims?*

James looked bored. "So, should we head to the Tottenham?"

"That's the plan James. I know a Didikko named Nicolai who I work with occasionally. The gypsy knows everything that happens in that area. It'll cost us, but it's worth it."

"How much will it cost us?" questioned Davis.

"You and I, nothing, but the Queen will have to surrender a thing or two." Davis looked confused. "There are a few old jewels and a rusty pistol down in the evidence room from the Cuthbert murders. We'll offer him those."

"How in bloody hell do you expect us to get in there?"

I gathered an iron key from my drawer and commanded Davis to follow. We walked out of my office and into the hall, a devious grin squashed between my cheeks.

"Because I'm one of the five evidence trustees," I said, waving the key in his face. "Now let's go meet with my gypsy."

After a visit to the evidence room, Davis and I took a two-horsed cab to Tottenham. The depressing soot covered walls of the neighborhood were hardly ignorable, nor were the symphony of crying babies and smells of boiled cabbage. Women in babushkas hung up drab laundry, peering into our carriage as we went by. Sometime later, a pack of scraggly children came to our carriage begging for money. While I gave what little I could spare, Davis refuted, trying to chase them off by showing his badge. It wouldn't be but two blocks later that they returned with a volley of rocks that hurled towards James's window. Finally though, we arrived at my informant's deli, "Radziwonowicz's," and strolled inside.

The Polish-Russian establishment was empty save for Nicolai's tiny mother who cooked behind the counter. A hag of a woman, she had white whiskers growing from her chin and milky irises that followed us as we approached. She wore an ugly blouse draped over an unfortunate floral dress that she covered in gaudy Catholic jewelry that shined into my bloodshot eyes. She did not properly welcome or dignify us, instead only stirring her pot of shit-scented soup.

"Morning Madam," I greeted, removing my hat. "Is Nicolai here?"

The old crone slowly spun her bony nose in my direction. She pointed to a set of splintered stairs, and then hollered in some foreign tongue before returning a grey hand to her blackened pot. Her crusty, unblinking eyes eerily followed us as we ascended the steps, though the rest of her body remained statue still. Davis, unable to contain himself, waved his cane in false gratitude before we both stomped up the steps to the second floor.

We found ourselves at a paint chipped door of a private flat and after a series of knocks, were greeted by a gaunt, dark haired woman with a baby in her feeble arms. She owned a dopey face with a large overbite. We were wordlessly welcomed inside and shown to a patchwork couch as she went to retrieve Nicolai from a back room. The house stunk of cat, though there wasn't a feline to be found. After a brief moment, the woman came back out, still mute, with a slender man at her rear.

Nicolai, a cratered faced scoundrel with a thin goatee and grizzly scars, seemed unpleasantly surprised to see me. I displayed my offerings at once, drawing out a blue jewel bracelet and worn pistol taken from the evidence room. Nicolai's discontent dissolved quickly. He snatched up my bribes, slipping the bracelet in the pocket of his oversized black slacks, but pausing a moment to scrutinize the pistol, toying with the extractor rod. Apparently satisfied, he slid it into his coat and sank onto the couch along side us.

"Ah, my friend, how nice to see you. And how can I help today Sergeant?"

"Vasile Ivanescu, name sound familiar?" I asked.

"Hmm, I know many names," he answered swiftly, stroking his beard.

"He's from Romania," Davis blurted recklessly. Nicolai glared, sickened by my partner's informality. He studied James for a few seconds before returning his dark eyes to me. I began to fear for the worse. Nicolai was not the kind of man who cared about titles or laws, nor did he worry if you were a policeman on official business. I knew that James might get us killed if we were not careful. Clearing my throat, I tried speaking up, fighting for Nicolai's attention.

"It's true, he's from Romania and he may have killed an innocent Irish woman. Her name was Jacqueline McCann."

Tapping his fingers on the couch arm, Nicolai took sometime to think. I watched to make sure he did not reach for the firearm I had just gifted him with.

"Come downstairs with me," he said knowingly, "Mother will have an idea." Walking back down to the restaurant, we reconvened with Mother Nicolai in her boggy kitchen, still stirring up a pot of what appeared to be duck blood soup. Approaching her, Nicolai spoke in a thick throaty language while fingering the contents of her pot. The two conversed for sometime, occasionally glancing back in our direction. Eventually, Nicolai returned to our circle, boasting a satisfied shine as he licked the duck blood off his hands.

"Mother says he is Romanian immigrant. He and sister Vasilica come here a few weeks ago. She doesn't know where his sister is, but Vasile rents room at the Popescu Inn." Laughing to himself, Nicolai opened his mouth again to speak, but quickly swallowed back his words.

"What aren't you telling me Nicolai," I asked with worry, hoping for an answer. Men like Nicolai also didn't take well to commands or threats, so I could only pray he would reveal the pun.

"Mother says that the Ivanescu blood line is cursed. They consort with demons. She says you should be careful. Evil works above the law."

Nodding respectfully to Nicolai, I waived for Davis to follow and put my hat back on.

"Well Nicolai, thanks for your time, seems I have an inn to check into."

I bowed my head to Mother Nicolai who'd locked her eyes on my hand. I looked down to check what she was staring at and noticed that my birthmark was showing. I pulled the cuff of my jacket upwards, covering it, but it was too late. By the time I glanced back up at her, she'd clutched a crucifix hung around her neck and scowled. Uncertain how to respond, a humble smile was all I could muster. Hitting the streets of Tottenham, I could tell now that Davis knew all too well that we were in no-mans-land, as he endlessly looked over his shoulder.

"Know where this Popescu Inn is?" he asked awkwardly, gripping his cane as if to hit someone that might be sneaking up on us.

"No, but our cab coachman might."

We tried to hail down a carriage from the active roads, but instead only found a surly old cabby harnessing two mules and a rickety wagon.

"Popescu Inn," I said while holding up a silver sixpence, which was much more than the price of a typical wagon-fare. The driver took the half schilling with a consenting grunt, and then waited for us to be seated before beginning his charter. Traveling only a few blocks, we arrived in front of the Popescu Inn, which looked more like a two-floored stable. Paying the charge promised, we hopped off the wagon and entered the front of the crooked door, stepping inside the inn.

Reeking of horse piss, the inn's scented charm caused me to gag uncontrollably. Pulling out his handkerchief, Davis covered his mouth, leaving me to speak to the unsightly clerk staring at us from behind the desk, the taste of urine still swimming on my tongue. He was gangly with a cleft lip that permanently displayed his incisors. Reluctant to present my badge, I gave a simple nod to the young man and tipped my hat.

"A very good morning chum, I'm looking for a guest of yours. Name is Vasile Ivanescu." The clerk searched his record book, pressing down on an illegible name hand written in some sort of feathered ink.

"Yes, he stays here," he answered with his thick drawl.

"May we go up to see him?" I asked, looking for the stairs up.

"No, he pays extra to not allow visitors," he replied while scratching at his chest. I needed to think of a way to have access to Vasile's room. I picked from my pocket a leftover red garnet gem procured from the evidence room, waiving the cracked jewel at him enticingly.

"Might this do the trick?"

His tongue eagerly peaked through the gap in his lip. I watched as he stared at the rock, considering for a moment, before putting out his hand. He dangled his fingers as if in a hurry to see the jewel. Placing the garnet within his dirty palm, I watched as he examined it. His pupils shined with fiery red from the stone, seemingly excited by its company.

"Room fifteen, corner suite to your right," he muttered, eyes still fixed on his ruby.

Together Davis and I crept up the flight of stairs and finding room fifteen, stood outside the door, straining to listen. We took notice to the faded sounds of writing, as if a pointed pen or pencil was scratching on paper. There were no other people in the tiny hall, giving the two of us free reign. Overly eager, Davis raised his fist to knock, but before he could land his knuckles, I caught them and shook my head no. I then pointed at his shoulder; guiding the fleshy weapon towards the door while mouthing the words, *RAM IT*.

Davis nodded in comprehension, lowering his body and smashing through the cheap wood. The door splintered into dozens of pieces. Hopping from a bed of hay leapt a pallid man with a long handlebar mustache and flowing ebony hair. A book and pencil fell from his lap as he made it to his feet. He wore a puffy white shirt and black baggy trousers with a queer looking pair of knee high sable boots that tucked over his leggings. Readied in some sort of exotic fighting stance, the man brandished his fists in a guarded motion. Cockier than a rooster, Davis lifted his walking cane and rushed the suspect.

"Scotland Yard," he shouted in a spirited charge.

Dropping to his knees, the mustached fellow swirled in a whirlwind motion with one leg extended, hooking his foot on Davis's ankle. Off balanced, James fell onto his back, cracking his head along the floor. His eagerness had betrayed him. Blood leaked from the back of his scalp, but judging from the amount squirted out, it was by no means fatal. Grabbing at a brown sack near the foot of the bed, the stranger plucked out a scary looking sabre and held it waist level. Pointing it at me with one hand, he used his other to collect the sack. Hurriedly, I heaved out my revolver from its holster and blocked the doorway.

"Don't move Vasile," I ordered, "you are only wanted for questioning." Vasile estimated the length between himself and the window, which was covered by an odd wreath of garlic. He darted towards the casement, diving into the glass. I fired off a shot at his leg, nearly striking his knee before he shattered through the pane. "Not again," I groaned. Running to the makeshift exit, I looked outside and witnessed our suspect putting a great distance between him and the hotel. He had already passed ten or twelve homes down the street by the time I'd caught glimpse of him. I spun to Davis and found him rubbing the back of his head.

"Get up you nancy," I ordered. "Not so eager now are you?" Giving me an obscene gesture, Davis made it to his feet, and soon the two of us were racing down to the roads. However, with as quick as the Romanian was, the pair of us knew that checking alleyways and storefronts was futile, and we'd quickly given up. Reentering the inn, I slapped down the second, and final, cracked garnet, slipping it towards the clerk with an apologetic frown.

"For the window and door," I said regrettably. Returning to Vasile's room, we checked the entirety of his belongings. A single chest sat inside, filled with exotic items we had never come across before. Yoke shirts with woven stripes, wide dark trousers, and hard felt hats made up most of the possessions. However, digging deeper, we began to uncover more and more sinister goods below. A wooden mallet strapped in leather hid next to a sharpened bolt of twine handled wood. Flasks of water marked with hand painted crosses rested on top of a felt sack that was full of communion wafers. Chains, flintlock pistols, and climbing spikes, there was not an item inside we could imagine being put to good use.

"What in bloody hell was this man planning?" asked Davis, his temple spattered with blood. I handed him my handkerchief, which he promptly applied to his head, then shrugged.

"Don't know, but perhaps this will help?"

I held up the journal Vasile had been writing in during our unexpected visit, opening up the leather cover to find writing nearly on every page. Most of the inscriptions seemed to be in Romanian, but near the back of the book, there were a few dozen entries in English. I closed it back up, tucking the book under my arm. Then with Davis's assistance, I dragged the chest filled with torture equipment downstairs and headed towards the exit.

"Confiscating for evidence," I shouted to the clerk as we passed. He held up the two red jewels and smiled, allowing us to leave without protest.

We transferred between a few carriages, taking them as far as the drivers would allow until finally reaching headquarters. Davis and I decided to split up. He insisted on visiting someone who could take a look at his head while I began to tally the inventory of our confiscated items. Though the recovered pieces proved quite remarkable, they held little value for me compared to the journal. I felt like a child with a wrapped gift. It needed to be opened immediately, read from top to bottom. *Finally, routine detective work may have broken open the case.*

Rushing through my investigation report, I hurriedly added our new findings and went to drop it off at Swanson's desk. The room was vacant and the Chief Inspector was nowhere to be found. I could only imagine that he was off still stewing about the girl in the river. After neatly stacking the documents where he could easily find them along his cluttered desk, I dashed back to my office where I prepared a piece of scrap from the morning newspaper and a pen for taking notes.

The book looked old and worn. The entries were written with a carpenter's pencil and mostly illegible. I turned towards the set of scribbled accounts I'd seen previously in English and began to examine them. The lettering was quite difficult to understand due to phrasing and phonetic spelling. Not surprisingly, as I stumbled through the words, I made out gibberish of devils, lycanthropes, and witches. At first, I thought that the author must be a madman, but then all at once it occurred to me that what I read could very well be just the elaborate prop of a swindler.

I recollected a few years back when a similar conman from the honest town of Musselburgh went from city to city promising to chase away superstitious citizen's cellar ghosts. This scammer pocketed quite a bit during his short stint until he was apprehended on charges of fraud. Perhaps this Vasile had been manipulating the very ill and vulnerable Miss McCann in the same manner, using the journal as testimony to his false accounts?

Glued to the pages, I nearly forgot my shift had ended until Big Ben rang out the eight o'clock bell. This indeed had been an exciting day of work. Marking my spot in the journal, I packed the book in my coat and proceeded home. After another frosty stroll, I finally made it to the doorsteps of my building. I could see the gloomy window of my flat from below, pitch black as usual. *No one-armed boy this time.*

Hades meowed at my heels as I entered my apartment, following at my feet as I went to undress. After settling in, I ate the supper Ms. Abigail had left for me, and then squeezed into my night robe before turning off all the lights inside. The pain in my chest was sometimes unbearable, and I fantasized about the opium waiting for me nearly every moment of my work shift. Now nearly midnight, I wrapped myself in a blanket while enjoying some tea that I had made from the kettle. Crashing into my chair, I used the glow from my freshly lit opium to brighten the pages so I could return to reading Vasile's dog-eared journal. I flipped through the pages while alternating between small sips from my teacup and puffs of the pipe. The high did not allow me to concentrate for very long, but what I had already read seemed extremely elaborate...and beyond peculiar.

CHAPTER 8

December 23rd
*The wicked flee when no man pursueth but the righteous are
bold as a lion.*

~Proverbs 28:1.

Today marks my triumphant return from the Retezat
Mountains. For years a great malevolence has dwelled there,
one renowned by the Carpathian folk for her lust of human
flesh. This Strigoaica has concealed herself along the Vârful
Peleaga peaks, making a home beneath a gnarled tree that hides the
entrance of her cave. Its walls are adorned with the skins of children
who ventured too near, and her garden is littered with the bones of those
foolish enough confront her. The common folk whom she preys upon
have dubbed her Bolnak, Great Witch of Satan.

When my sister Vasilica and I received word of this hag's
cursed existence, we immediately set out to meet her. Traveling to the
village near her lair, we wasted no time in setting up camp deep inside
her ghostly woods. Together, sister and I organized a simple ruse taught
to us by father. Surrounding our encampment with a few buckets of
lamp oil, Vasilica disguised herself as a lost peasant girl, whilst I hid
in nearby. It did not take long for Bolnak to be enticed by our lure. Just
after nightfall the demon woman crept out from the wood line, her eyes
beaming a devilish red.

She crawled on all fours through the brush like some stalking tiger, her hoary skin and ragged dark hair smothered by night's shadowy cape. Her teeth protruded from a lipless mouth, all gnarled and grounded sharp as to better gnaw her prey. The only clothes she wore were blue tattered rags that barely covered her drooping shriveled breasts. She had begrimed children's toys tied to a chord that wrapped around her meager waste, smattered with brown and red. I must admit that she was indeed a frightful sight.

Regardless, I stayed true to our arrangement and watched from afar. Bolnak skulked closer and closer to sister until the hag's wretched claws were in striking distance, ready to grab at their next meal. However, just before Bolnak could sink her talons into my sweet sister's flesh, I sprung our trap. Leaping up with crossbow in hand, I fired a bolt, piercing the fiend's heart. Bound to a strong thread, the bolt kept her fastened while Vasilica and I struck at the witch with our kilijs'. However, much as expected, the hag used her hellish powers and changed into a devilish black owl, attempting to fly away while tearing at our binding with her beak. Except we were ready, and splashing the bird with our buckets of oil, we doused her feathers until they were too heavy for flight. We then hastily grabbed the soaked bird and threw her into our campfire, burning her once and for all into ash.

After word made it to the nearby villagers, we were rewarded with gifts of perfume, silver, and a pair of Furioso Stallions. The town elder was so elated, he even offered to slaughter a goat for our supper, as well as provide us with a nights rest in his sheepskin bed. While we appreciated all the offers, sister and I knew there were more folk who needed our help, and so we packed our things and left for home. Unfortunately for myself, during our long return through winter's worse, a terrible fever came over me and I have been bed ridden ever since. I will yield as many days as it takes for this great sickness to pass before continuing my ongoing training with Vasilica. With rumors of a Pricolici haunting a village just outside of Deva, I have little time to waste.

January 5th

Still I suffer from this horrid illness and still I am bed ridden with little more to do then write in this cursed book. Nevertheless, since my body must remain still in order to recover, I have focused my effort into refining my mind. I have always been proud of my ability to speak, read and write in Latin, Turkish, German, Spanish and Hungarian, but English has proven a bit more challenging. In her off time, sister *has been giving lessons while caring for me, and ordered that I continue practicing the language in everything I do, including this journal. Damn the English and their complicated vocabulary. I'd sooner fight a league of devils than try to learn it.*

It has been nearly two weeks since I last wrote, and much has occurred since that time. Sister and I were blessed enough to enjoy Christmas day together, though we needed to celebrate at our manor due to my body's weakened state. Together, we shared a meal in celebration of not only the birth of our Lord Jesus Christ, but Vasilica's recent conquest. We gorged on sausages strung from late last summer, delicious Cozonac bread, and freshly boiled white bean soup with lamb and onions. It was a feast fit only for a king. We then nestled next to the stone fireplace with some plum wine fermented by the locals before rejoicing with song that wore down the manor walls.

Sister had just returned from her hunt for an elusive Pricolici near Deva, and was very proud of her unaccompanied kill. After convincing me that she would be fine to do battle on her own, she set out by stallion to a secluded settlement where the beast was said to hunt. The locals were overjoyed by her arrival as the wolf demon had been continuously picking off solitary targets from the outskirts of town, including cattle, horses...and men. Since the undead canine was nocturnal, Vasilica knew she had little time for preparations before nightfall came and the beast struck again.

She spent the remainder of what daylight she had setting up another one of father's simple ruses. She purchased an inexpensive lamb from a Deva shepherd, and tying it to the bottom a pine tree, climbed above it, hidden amongst the branches. There with her musket and specially made bullets she lay in wait, ready for the hellhound's arrival. It took nearly all night, and Vasilica had nearly frozen to death when a shuffling came from the winter brush below. The monster stirred, and she could see a trail of mist from its heavy breath near some underbrush where the lamb slept. She said that it was at this moment that the woods went silent, as if the very forest was waiting in anticipation for sister to rid it of the horror.

Then, just as she pulled back the hammer from her musket, a sudden rupture from nearby bushes caused her to flinch. A flock of frightened blackbirds had scattered into the sky, giving away Vasilica's location as she leapt up from her hiding perch, startled. The Pricolici, a black furred monster with immeasurable strength, abandon all focus on the lamb, instead setting its sights on sister. It leapt from its nearby shrubbery and onto Vasilica's tree. The fiend clawed at the bark, making its way upward to Vasilica's feet that dangled from the tree limbs. Unfortunately for the lycanthrope, sister was far too well trained to panic. She fired a single silvered round bullet into the ascending Pricolici's gaping mouth, which traveled into its muzzle and out by its rear with a gruesome spray. The creature ceased at once, tumbling into the snow below with a thunderous crash.

Sister hurried down from her vantage point, wanting to ensure the Pricolici's demise so that she could collect her trophy. Only, what she'd forgotten was that such demons do not remain so for long, and after examining the beast she found that the creature had changed back to its human form. It was now nothing more than an unclothed man, unremarkable except for his fatal wound that colored the powdered snow. Along with her leashed lamb, Vasilica collected the body and walked back to Deva, where she reported her slaying. The town folk recognized the corpse immediately as a local hunter who sold pelts to nearby settlements. It was rumored that he was in league with witches. They promised to return the body to his family for a proper burial, but not before blessing it. Though they had little to give as a reward, the villagers did refund the coin she spent for the lamb and allowed her to keep the animal as a token of their appreciation. Needless to say, the lamb's meat helped serve for our Christmas stew, and we will spin the kept wool for clothes as well as shave down the bones for knife handles.

As for me, while I'm quite proud of Vasilica's accomplishment, I feel that it is vital that I get well soon. Sending her out alone is torturous and hiring someone trustworthy to assist her is not an option. Not to mention that our once proud estate is now nearly in ruin and we have gone poor from our exploits. Above all else though, I must get well because soon our trusted informant will arrive with new information about our nemesis. This informant, a mysterious, but trusted comrade of my father's, lives in a town near Bran Pass called Brasov. He is an expert occultist, swordsman and mountaineer whose dwelling overlooks in the sinister peaks, keeping an eye on our ward. Hopefully the abominations that live up those foothills have remained dormant, but only my scout will be able to tell me for certain.

January 21ˢᵗ

Today I embark on my most perilous pursuit yet. Vasilica and I will be making our way to Munich, where it is said that one of the three brides of Vlad Tepes has arranged to travel. Vlad the Impaler, also known as King of Wallachia, Vlad III, or his patronymic name, Dracula (son of the Dragon, after his father Vlad II Dracul), was a three-time Voivode of Wallachia, ruling mainly from 1456 to 1462, when the early

Ottomans were in conquest of the Balkans. His father was a member of the Order of the Dragon, a sect who not only protected Christianity in Europe, but also inspired the Kaziklu Bey (Impaling Prince) to follow in their footsteps. During his lifetime, Vlad reputation for excessive cruelty spread abroad, from Russia to Spain. He gruesomely tortured enemies, dined on their flesh, and devised horrific displays of intimidation with their corpses as a warning to others. The total number of his victims was estimated in the tens of thousands- however, little did anyone know that in death, those numbers would swell even greater.

Over the centuries after his false death, Vlad has insisted on keeping three brides to fulfill many of his most ghastly and clandestine wishes while he hides safely in the shadows. These three women are the only ones allowed to drink his unholy blood. They gather wealth, protection, and most importantly, sustenance for their dark King. None are safe from these wretched souls, as we learned through the sacrifice of our own mother. So, in hopes of trying to counteract his tyranny, our father made it our sworn duty to impede Dracula and his brides at any costs. "I am the good shepherd," father use to say. "The good shepherd must always protect God's flock."

It was but a few days ago when our informant arrived. The cliff scout, who I will not name for his own welfare, made a special trip into Sibiu solely to report his findings in the mountains. He had learned that one of Vlad's brides, known only as Paraschiva, had been dispatched along with new orders, and left Bran Castle but four moons ago. From what my informant has gathered, which has always been accurate, Paraschiva is charged with collecting a special servant for her master. This servant, which Vlad Tepes has foreseen through a very dark ritual, is known as a necromancer, and will heighten the dark prince's power. The Bride will travel west in search of this mortal, but to where exactly, we do not know. Without the safety of her master or her sisters, Paraschiva will be forced to face the might of the Ivanescus by herself, if only we can track her.

Certain to be more potent than any undead or witches we've encountered before, the four hundred year old bride will possess abilities never documented. The trip will be both arduous and expensive and I am forced to use the last of our family's inheritance to fund it. Come tomorrow, sister and I will go to our priest for one final blessing before departing on the following dawn. Father watch over us, I beg you. We will need you. Let not the wicked damn us with their spreadable curse.

February 23ʳᵈ

It is with great sorrow that I must report that sister and I will be leaving Munich sooner than planned. This great ivory city, filled with an inspiring mix of historic buildings, impressive architecture and landmarks, has treated us kindly within our short time here. We arrived several weeks ago, hungry to find our bride, but after searching for days, learned that she no longer was present. She stopped in Germany very briefly under false name, departing only after collecting a retainer to assist her. She lived lavishly through the wealth of her blood slave, using the poor soul's riches to plot her safe charter west to France.

Meanwhile, Vasilica and I have grown low on resources. We will need to be more sparing as we follow our mark to the French city of Le Havre, the town where Paraschiva has arranged for travel. A port town, Le Havre is a sailor's highway to all of Western Europe, and assumingly, this will be where Paraschiva will depart by boat to reach her next destination. She will most likely trek west by carriage, as she is untrusting of trains. Riding through the roads of France will take time if she wishes to remain discreet. If we make haste, Vasilica and I may be able to catch up by cutting northwest.

While my English has strengthened, I know little of the French language. Fortunately, Vasilica is well versed, and will be our translator while visiting Le Havre. Tonight we will board a steam train traveling from Munich to Caen, then purchase a wagon-pulling horse with our belongings to Le Havre. I must keep my body, mind, and spirit sharp, continuing my daily conditioning. It will take all that I have to end the bride, especially now that Vasilica has fallen ill. It began in Romania with nothing more than dizzy spells, but has rapidly deteriorated. She spends most of her time in rentable beds, occasionally leaving only to interpret for me. I fear more and more that her fever lacks resemblance to the minor illness I only recently recovered from back home, as her symptoms have ripened into a paralyzing affliction.

April 12th

Three months have gone by since I last wrote and still the nightmare known as Paraschiva lives. She has eluded us once again, if only by chance, and crossed the English Channel from Le Havre. Along with her blood slave, they have headed to London, but we are unable to pursue. For you see, Vasilica has fallen victim to her human frailty and the sickness she's been battling has nearly killed her. We've taken shelter in an inexpensive inn with little more to do than pray. When not caring for Vasilica, I have made it my obsession to research anything on both *nosferatu* and *necromancy. Though I'm quite familiar with the abilities of the nosferatu, the western records I've translated have given me even more insight on what such abominations are capable of.*

According to regional folklore, while most of the damned are as strong as ten men, it is only when they get older that they become implausibly frightening. Not only are they more cunning than any mortal, but they can direct the elements themselves, be it a storm, fog or thunder. They can control meaner beasts of the wild, such as rats, owls, bats, moths, and wolves, sharing many of their keen senses. Ancient nosferatu have been known to evaporate into a cloud of steam, traveling this way at short distances. Then there is Vlad himself, who much like the biblical Witch of Endor, can use his rare evil gift of necromancy to communicate with and control the dead. This, in part, is most likely why he wishes to find the mortal who shares his talents. If there is someone besides himself who could control death, then they would hold domain over nosferatu, who are nothing more than the living dead.

As for Paraschiva, she is the most alluring of Dracula's brides, and is said to possess nearly all these powers and more. Although she is unskilled in the art of necromancy, she is rumored to be able to influence the minds of men with her beauty. Rumors persist that even before her change- she had charmed the Impaler himself during their courting. Unlike her dark haired sisters, Paraschiva has locks of gold like the sun, claret lips, and eyes so blue they can instantly freeze a man's heart. Her chalky skin covers an enthralling shape only comparable to Aphrodite's. She fashions herself in clothing that reflects the current trends, but is said to favor her beloved Cămașă cu platcă, a dress worn on the night she was changed.

While she will feast from most anyone when desperate, Paraschiva tends to favor males, as she takes pleasure in the game of seduction. When feeding, she furtively drinks upon her unwary lovers until their death, but most often uses them to cater her lavish needs beforehand. Unlike the other brides, Paraschiva is said to be fearless of Vlad Tepes, engaging in quarrels with him from time to time, and according to some books, even rivaling him in strength. Lamentably for the bride however, even the darkest creatures must follow the laws of their nature. Nosferatu are unable to disobey commands from their creators, for reasons unknown to the living. And so Paraschiva must carry out Vlad Tepes' instructions if he so wills it. Such may be why she may be so eager to find the mortal necromancer. If she can seduce this warlock, she may be able to use their dominion over death against her domineering master.

I beg the Almighty to forgive me for admitting to an odd admiration for her methods. She is clever, inventive, and devoted, submersing herself in whatever she sets out to accomplish. She will be my most formidable foe. After learning what I have about her, it's my fear that she may already know of our pursuit, and has already begun planning our demise. She will have traps and distractions waiting for us at each turn. Nevertheless if God favors us, who can be against us?

May 25th

For too long now my good sister has endured this terrible sickness, withering her body into nothing. Her hair has atrophied from a proud mane of Romanian black to a thin blanket of snow. Her skin has paled, her eyes have sunken, and her body has thinned to bone. Any food she eats is quickly spat back out and any medicine she takes does not cure her. Dreadful night terrors come each eve, causing her to tear at her flesh. She must be tied down each time she sleeps in order to keep her from harming herself.

Fearful for her salvation, I arranged for a Le Harve priest to give Last Rites. Father Babineaux came at my request, and upon meeting sister, instantly recognized the symptoms of evil. He performed the Rite of Expulsion, and after days of blessings, somehow broke her fever. I can only assume that Paraschiva has had some part in this. Such considerations provoke me with a well of bottomless fury, only amendable by Paraschiva's death. Fear not, bride, we will not bend or stray. One of us must perish for this conflict to pass. I take great comfort in knowing my death is but a doorway to eternal salvation, unlike you, who must spend the rest of eternity as Satan's whore.

I have organized for Vasilica and myself to boat to southern England, where we will hike our way to London and finally destroy the bride. We have but a short savings left and I must spend the majority of it to hire someone that can nurse Vasilica back to health. I will need her at full strength in order to help slay the bride before she can find the soul that her master has ordered her to recover. While sister is busy recuperating, I'll begin my search, pinpointing Paraschiva's whereabouts. Each day I grow more and more understanding of how she operates. It is only a matter of time before she is cornered. I will not fail.

July 9th

It was just a few weeks ago when we arrived in London and already the place sickens me. Expensive inns, overpriced meals- it is a wonder anyone can manage the cost. Fortunately, I succeeded in employing a desperate widow and mother to care for my sister at a reasonable cost, allowing me to focus my attention on the bride. My own living arrangements, a tiny hay bedded room inside a rundown inn, is ran by a Bucharest man who often houses Easterners looking for work. It makes for the perfect cover.

Safely camouflaged under this ploy, I can continue my hunt without worry of gathering unwanted attention. Regrettably, even with this concealment, it seems that every time I draw closer to cornering the bride, her trail runs cold. I suspect she must possess some supernatural ability that has allowed her to walk plainly before me, as I've had testimony from witnesses who state that we've been in the same room together. Namely for this reason, I have abandon hunting for _her_ and instead began tracking her mortal slave from Munich.

The thrall is clearly not as clever as his mistress for it is with the greatest ease that I discovered his location. I'd learned his Christian name, Sebastian, in Munich, and since then, the fool has made several reservations to exclusive restaurants and hotels across London. Following his paper trail, I located the hotel where he, and hopefully Paraschiva, are hidden and have decided to pay a visit. Arming myself with only concealable equipment, I managed to slip into his hotel by acting like staff. It wasn't before long that I was at the doors of his hotel suite, breaking in by pry bar.

When I entered, the air seemed stagnant and foul. The earthy, miasmic odor became stronger as I neared the parlor where a beautifully crafted coffin of white marble awaited. I was but precious moments away from banishing the bride to the hell she belonged. However, before I decided to pry open the coffin lid- I thought it best to first ensure that we were alone in the suite. While it seemed that her servant was out on errands, as the room was mostly empty, I did take note of a set of bloody surgeons tools near Paraschiva's tomb that I could only imagine were used to dissect her prey.

However, when I pried open the cover- I was aghast to find that it was not Paraschiva resting, but instead her blood slave, Sebastian. His skin was no longer natural looking, but a mixture of dead grey and putrid green that clashed with his scarlet stained mouth. His lips had narrowed and his fingernails were now long and sharp. She had changed her vassal into one of the damned, now forever cursed to the hunger for flesh and thirst for blood.

The monster, now lying alone before me, was entranced in his daylight hibernation. His eyes stayed open, milky and lifeless. I aimed the point of my wooden spear at his heart and lifted my hammer to strike. However, in a moment of avarice I would later regret, a foolish idea came over me. I'd become greedy and decided to first interrogate the demon on Paraschiva's whereabouts. Only after he gave me my answers would I deliver him to his final judgment.

Tying up his cold arms, I used a trickle of blessed water to wake him. He reared up, hissing like a snake. Bound and tethered, the blush color came back to his flesh and his voice sounded almost human as he pleaded for me to spare him. But I remained deaf, instead ordering him to tell me more about his master. He refused. Instead, he surprised me by gnawing at his hands and tearing the flesh from his bindings as to loosen the grip around his arms. Stunned, I hurried for my other weapons while watching as he wiggled free from the ropes and raced to a nearby dumbwaiter with unnatural speed. Diving inside, he plummeted down below.

Though I tried with all my might to get down the stairwell with haste, the six floors were enough to allow the monster to get away. By the time I reached the base of the dumbwaiter's mouth, to my horror, I found only a young porter who must have been cleaning out the hoist when Sebastian leaped down. He lay prostrate, one arm cleanly cleaved off by the fiend. A pile of bloody table clothes cluttered next to him and a set of red footprints trailed to the doorway leading outside. The creature must have glided down to the first floor, used the boy's arm to feed on and restore his power, then taken one of the table-cloths to repel the sun while escaping. I immediately called off my chase, tending to the young man until staff arrived. When the crowd of confused people filled the room, I then slipped out of the hotel's backdoor and returned to my inn. I had failed, perhaps costing an innocent boy his life in the process.

September 18th

Dearest Journal,

After several weeks of deciphering news clippings, I have confirmed that Paraschiva has severed all ties with her progeny. For days now, locals have described a repugnant creature lingering in the confines of London catacombs and sewers. Though the authors of the short accounts mostly write in farce, those brave enough to describe the beast have depicted it as severely scarred with barbed teeth and candle light eyes. Dubbed "Spring-heeled Jack," this monster I assumed to be Sebastian, has attacked several caretakers and city workers over the last *week. It seems the child of Paraschiva, wounded from our encounter, is desperately trying to regain his strength while searching for his abandoning maker. Though I feel no pity, I am disheartened at their separation. With no new direction, I find myself adrift.*

Why would Paraschiva discard her loyal minion? My guess is that Sebastian was not only ever of value to her, but has risked her safety. As punishment, he must fend for himself. For that reason, I must continue my search. First I will finish the feral minion. Once I'm through with him, I'll return my focus on his mother who still searches for her necromancer. Where has she gone and what is she plotting? I suspect the worse.

November 10th

Excelsior! Victory is at hand! Last night, I not only found the hidden location of Sebastian, but the trail leading to Paraschiva as well. It seems that the two nosferatu have indeed split, but luckily-

CHAPTER 9

ot, smoldering smoke- If forced to describe how an opium hangover felt, I would say it burns like hot, smoldering smoke, wafting upwards from your chest and into your brain, as if trying to find it's way out. Some people have been so bold as to tell me that opium has no hangover. *Those* individuals are liars. Any night I've ever chased the dragon always follows with a sufferable morning that includes soar lungs, nausea, blurred vision, and itchy, burned fingers that are shriveled as dried pork. Ah yes, nothing better than noxious, acidic, hot smoke to remind you of your evening sins. It is quite painful.

I peeled myself from my chair and headed for the washbasin to clean up. As I splashed the tepid water across my face, I noticed that the liquid ran off me and into the bowl with a pinkish hue. Before long, the entire basin's pool was rose in color. I looked into mirror along my wall and found the part of my neck between the collar and nape had a large gash. Blood had trickled down sometime during the night, drying along my skin. I tried recalling when I might have cut my neck, but my overindulgence had made the entire evening a bit of a blur.

After cleaning up the blood, I took my straight razor and fixed up my sideburns. I thumbed the shaver's handle, rubbing it gently like I use to with Catherine's ear. Her smile rang through my mind, taking me back to our early days. Catherine and my relationship had lived as briefly as Macbeth's candle, ignited by a series of cheerful moments that were quickly snuffed out by death's eager finger. I met her on Boxing Day when I was but a London alley cat searching for someone to scratch behind my ear. Fortunately for me, Catherine did not approve of strays and she had quickly bent my will towards domestication.

It seemed to come so easily for her. Not only was she beautiful, with a statuesque figure and fashionable tastes, but she also possessed natural warmth that one can't fake or feign. Simply entering a room made all the ladies pout and chums whistle. Her parents, horse breeders from Suffolk, paid for their precious daughter to study in London, allowing a dozen dolts, including myself, a chance to pretend we were worthy of her hand. At first, I competed with an assortment of simpletons from her university, but as time went on, Catherine narrowed it down to some cocky little horse rider that her mother had introduced to her and myself. So, it was only natural to believe that fate was on my side that day when she accepted my invitation to the Policemen's Ball.

Oh what a night it was. I had been dreadfully nervous during the festivity, and it didn't help that Catherine had captivated nearly all the blokes on the force. Every fool with a badge tried to dance with her or get a moment of her time. Nevertheless, she stayed on my arm the entirety of that eve until that fateful moment when I gathered enough courage to ask her to walk with me on the grounds outside. I was so frightened that we only took a few steps along the path before I hurried to one knee, begging her to be my wife. At first she went quiet, staring at me blankly. Those few seconds of silence might have been the longest of my life. Then, with a smile sweet as honey, she slipped into my arms and whispered yes.

For one year, and not a day longer, we enjoyed the wonderful bounty of married life. We dined together, danced together, and bed together. We were so happy. Then suddenly, as quickly as it struck so many before her, Catherine was ambushed by her illness. She had gone to her physician with pains that she hoped were from being with child, but returned only with the grim news of her tuberculosis. At first, we tried to ignore it, pretending the disease was nothing more than a common cold. But in time, it became obvious. She had withered as quickly as a rose in the winter, and before long, we were writing out her will.

I swallowed the lump in my throat and made way for work, shaking off the haunted memories. The pea-soupers outside weaved in and out of the main roads. I hated breathing in the disgusting fumes and tried avoiding the poisonous cloud by taking a short cut along a series of back alleys. I began to focus my attention towards the case. I thought back to Vasile's journal. It still struck me as odd that he would put forth such an effort to write his absurdities if only to use them as a prop. That would surely mean that he planned on someone coming across it. I wondered if he intended on using it as evidence within the courts to prove his madness. It seemed completely illogical, unless perhaps, he really was a madman.

As I continued to brood, I thought back to Vasile's remark on a select individual who this "Paraschiva" was commanded to retrieve. *Could it be that Miss McCann was possibly the individual he'd made mention of?* Perhaps the writings were all some sort of metaphor or code that was meant to be deciphered by his sister, Vasilica. If so, then I needed to find motive as to why the pair wanted to kill Miss McCann in the first place. I needed to know why anyone would want to kill a young woman who was both sickly and vulnerable. Regardless of what the journal said, it wasn't going to be enough to break open the investigation. This only meant one thing. I'd have no choice but to collect more facts, question new suspects, or find another clue. Hard work, perseverance, this would be my methodology.

I arrived at the station, signed in for my shift at the front desk, and waited for Davis. The constables gathered near the front doors, readying for their patrol along the Thames. They looked particularly exhausted today. It wasn't easy going up and down that river every day, and most times, it was as dull as dishwater. I wondered if the boys would be drawing a line in the sand any time soon if they continued to guard the waters much longer. Not soon after the patrolmen left did Davis mosey in, lugging a picnic basket in his hands. I shook my head in disbelief as he approached.

"Christ Davis, are you really that fat?" I laughed while poking at the whicker container.

"Hey," he moaned, his porkpie hat squeezed over fresh bandages, "and here I was about to offer a kindness. The wife made you and I some breakfast, but it seems I'm too *fat* to share it with the likes of your highness." My stomach rumbled, crying out for something more than the bread Ms. Abigail had left me to eat when I first awoke.

"Well easy now, don't get hasty big boy. Didn't your mother teach you to share?"

We grinned at each other before weaving through the halls, until finally landing inside my office. Pulling out an assortment of fresh bread, marmalade, blood sausages, pears, milk, and a cold kettle of tea, Davis spread out our breakfast across my desk. Meanwhile, I prepared the small coal furnace in the corner of my office to warm up anything that needed reheating. After a quick kiss of the fire our breakfast was ready. We feasted on the meal rather quickly, and after only a short while, I could feel my spirits beginning to rise.

"Tell Martha I say thank you," I spat out along with a morsel of marmalade-smothered bread.

"Ah no problem," said Davis through a juicy pear, "She's worried about you. She says the market grocer near you, who's her cousin, hasn't seen you in their store in ages. What are you living off of?" Digging out Vasile's journal, I plopped it on the desk, rippling the surface of our leftover tea and cream.

"Mystery, I've been living off of mystery", I said hoarsely. Confused, Davis blinked at the book for a few seconds before returning his focus on the more appealing blood sausage squeezed between his fingers.

"What on earth are you talking about Nathan?" he asked flatly.

"Vasile Ivanescu, a self proclaimed witch hunter, was kind enough to scribe some of his adventures in English for us. There's a lot of nonsense in there, but not a lick of it gives mention of a Jacqueline McCann." Sipping at his saucer overfilled with milk, Davis gave a moment to swallow before speaking again.

"So, he didn't court her?"

"My assumption is that if he did indeed know her, it was short lived. So short in fact that he didn't write about it inside his journal. Unless of course, he made mention of our victim in the Romanian portion of his book, as only a quarter of the pages are written in English. I'll have to have Falamas translate the Romanian half. I believe he speaks their language." Falamas was the station bookkeeper posted at what is dubbed the "Back-Hall", a simple reception area. He was a police officer in his homeland, wherever the hell that was, but escaped to London after political infighting became bloody on the streets.

"That is a capital idea old fellow," said Davis, "and what should we do in the meantime?"

"After breakfast, we'll split up briefly. You'll go to the nearest seamstress or clothier and find out anything you can about these handkerchiefs," I said while balling up one of Miss McCann's bloody rags and tossing it towards his lap, nearly missing his toast and preserves. Davis swiped it away, insulted that I would risk his precious bread and jam. "Meanwhile," I lied, "I'm going out to see if I can't find any street folk near her flat that saw Miss McCann the night of the murder." Davis nodded in agreement before waving me off, focusing on his wife's homemade fruit spread.

Shortly after we ate, I headed to the Back Hall to meet with Falamas about translating the journal. He was an interesting looking bookkeeper to say the least, with sad eyes, a broad face, dark hair that he always combed forward, and a clean short beard. He had a slight limp that caused him lean forward and some sort of fungus that grew out of his green fingernails. He barely ever spoke, and when not inscribing records, interpreting telegrams or cataloging evidence, he kept his nose in a book. As quiet as he was, make no mistake that the man was vicious as a whipped lion. We had broken up numerous scuffles between him and some of the more discourteous policemen after they ran their mouths off a bit too long.

"Falamas, I need your help with some evidence please." He looked up from an electric telegraph message he'd been deciphering, unmoved, and waited for me to continue. "I remember you saying you are fluent in Romanian. Any chance that you can translate parts of this journal for me? It's part of the McCann investigation."

I slipped the book onto the counter in front of him. He turned it over once before thumbing through the pages. At first I thought all was lost as he gave a discomforting groan, but then as he began to read the inscriptions, a faint glimmer of interest flickered in his eye. He said not a word, but rather turned to the front page and began sweeping his eyes back and forth. I took this as him accepting my request and tiptoed off before he changed his mind.

Not much later, I was back on the streets. I took to the Limehouse District in a hurry, needing to pick up a bit more opium for my night. Most naïve Londoners stayed away from the area, fearing that the Chinamen living there would capture and enslave any English folk daring enough to come near. Truth be told, there were only a few hundred Chinese in the neighborhood and most were quiet, peaceful, and guiltless. It was the morning papers and fictional literature that were to blame for the nasty reputation that came with the Limehouse District, a reputation that most of the Chinese didn't object to, as it kept the white men at bay.

The den always kept itself shadowy and poorly lit. The rules were simple, but stringent. You would enter through the front of a shabby restaurant and after reporting to the elderly woman at the counter, I believe her name was Xiao, wait until she guided you down to the basement. There, ornate rugs and cushions sprawled across the floors for customers to enjoy while being hand served large bowls of opium by the owner, Mr. Cheng, and his family. Luckily, I had already bartered a deal with Cheng and only needed to stop by for a few moments so he could weigh and pack up my opium, tablets which I was specially allowed to take back home.

Following the protocol, I found myself in the basement amongst the handful of hypnotized patrons who mostly ignored me as they engaged in their tar. Cheng had gifted me with a wooden scaled down pipe which was much different than the hookahs that the customers huffed at. I considered myself fortunate because the apparatuses were at least a meter long with winding chords and lamps that jutted from every end. The entire basement looked like a row of factory chimneys with long protruding tubes puffing out halos of smoke.

Eventually, Cheng came out to collect my money and I noticed that the usually stoic little den master appeared unhappy to see me. He glared bitterly, and though I tried to overlook it, was forced to recognize his peculiar behavior when I handed over my half-shilling. He had quickly latched his squat rough hand around mine, pulling me closer so he could stare into my eyes.

"Bad chi," he grumbled with his broken eastern accent. "You bring bad chi into my den." Ripping my hand away, I balled it up into a fist and waved it at his nose.

"Men have been punched for less Mr. Cheng. Don't do that again."

Cheng rubbed at his inflated belly, mulling over our trade before finally taking my money. He motioned me to stay put while he retrieved my pills. I stood between a few ornamental rugs covered in smokers while growing increasingly impatient. In part, my intolerance had been sourced by the uncomfortable stares of sedated regulars that pressed at me. Each of their faces was sunken and pale with vacant expressions painted upon them. Their eyes followed me shamelessly and without reserve.

I took special notice of a young girl across the room that slightly resembled Miss McCann. She had russet undone hair and a simple face. She sat languidly among the other smokers, and as I continued to watch, I was appalled to see her stab the tip of a hookah's mouthpiece inside an unhealed gash along the center of her cheek. Smoke curls coiled ever so slightly out from the cranny as she inhaled, then after a few breaths, barreled back out in a shower of silver. She was sickly, with ribs that could be seen from beneath a tight tattered shirt. The girl must have detected me watching, because she lifted her chin towards me and attempted to smile. I nearly lost my breakfast when she did so because a line of hemp stitched between her toothless gums, keeping her mouth roped shut. I cringed briefly before looking away. My conscience told me to try and have another glimpse without recoiling, a silent attempt to mend my rudeness. But before I could, a ragged voice called me by name.

"Detective Brannick," said a lean hoary man from a dark corner of the den. It took me a moment to recognize the face, but once my memory made the connection, I knew it was time to go. The man went only by his street name, Ballister. He worked as an informant for Davis occasionally, but was not to be trusted. He was an outlaw who gave your everyday criminals a bad name. He allegedly enjoyed the raping of prostitutes, burglarizing of homes, and occasionally, slitting the throats of important men among the criminal Underworld. He was a reputed knife fighter who was said to have claimed the lives of several dimwitted challengers, and had the marks on his face and neck to prove it. Though James and I believed him to be in his early sixties, the man carried himself like a young stag, strong and arrogant. He always had an intense expression about him that made you feel as if he were trying to stare a hole straight through you.

"Detective Brannick," he repeated, "Is that you? What a coincidence. An associate and I were *just* talking about you," he said while looking back at a stranger cloaked in shadow. "How funny it is that you just- *poof-* show up." I could only imagine what he meant, but knew if I wanted to come out of this conversation unscathed, it would have to be thoroughly cunning. Ballister tended to challenge folks, getting his pleasures out of their discomfort. He knew I had much to lose by coming down to the den and was going to try and make me squirm. I could not show weakness, nor could I lose face, as the criminal world tended to act like wolves, eating up the weak. Even as I opened my mouth to speak, a plan already formulated in my mind. I'd stall until Cheng came back out.

"Oh? Unless it has something to do with the bastard who stole my hairline, I'd rather not know what it is you two were talking about."

"Really?" he rattled deviously, "because I think it might be a terrible surprise if you have to find out later." He was either trying to intimidate me, trick me into paying him for information, or both. I didn't understand how Davis could do business with the likes of Ballister, but wasn't going to use this opportunity to bring it up. I checked my pocket watch, pretending to focus on the dials before needlessly winding it. I then put it to my ear, listening to its ticks before faking a smile. After putting the clock back in my pocket, I finally turned my attention back to Ballister. *Where the hell was Cheng?*

"I rather like a good surprise ole' boy. I think I'll pass." Ballister snarled then suddenly thrust a hand in his coat pocket. I quickly imitated him and swung my hand into my own, gripping the handle of my revolver.

Just then, Mr. Cheng came stomping out from his storage area. He mumbled incoherently while pushing one of his little daughters standing in his way. Waddling towards Ballister and myself, the Chinaman forcefully handed me a small package wrapped in brown paper with a single thread of yarn tied around it. He then pointed to the stairs, grunting irritably as he glowered.

"Go!"

He must have still been seething about my threat to punch him in the nose. Little did Cheng know that his intolerance was working in my favor. Taking the package, I turned to Ballister and gave a disappointing frown before shrugging.

"It seems I have worn out Mr. Cheng's hospitality. Good day to you Ballister."

Ballister tried grabbing me as I paced quickly past him towards the staircase. Even after I escaped his grip, he continued to follow me with his yellow eyes, watching as I carried up each step. He shook his head and smirked before losing me from sight.

"That was close," I whispered under my breath as I made it through the upper restaurant and out into the streets.

Unnerved, I hurried into the labyrinth of winding pathways and twisting lanes, trying to get to the main roads. It was no easy task getting out of the den, even for a man who steered ships across the oceans. There were small markets, animal pens and religious processions that seemed to just spring up from nowhere in the Limehouse District, forcing you to constantly stop and change your route. It was during one of these brief pauses, while redirecting my course, that a tugging on my sleeve caught my attention.

It was a young Chinese boy, no older than eight. He held onto my coat and stared at me blankly. He was round faced with a single rope of hair that swept over his cleanly shaven scalp. He wore a pair of matching olive pants and shirt under a dirty white tunic. I looked around and saw that he had no parents or siblings nearby. I crouched down so that we were at eye level, then removed a leftover breakfast-pear from my pocket and offered it to him.

If there was one thing that could always pull on my heartstrings, it was the tragedy of a destitute child. It didn't seem fair that a little chavy was forced to survive on the treacherous streets through no fault of their own. I'd caught a few young palmers in my day, and truth be told, I very rarely ever took them in. They didn't have a choice. It was steal or die.

In spite of this, the boy didn't take my offering. Instead, he poked at the small bulge along my breast where my revolver rested, and then with his same finger, pointed behind him. I looked past the child and studied the crowd. There were a few celestials exchanging money, a small band of men praying, and a single spice salesman peddling on a crate. But I knew what the child wanted me to see.

Just past the small crowd was a small clearing where heaps of discarded wood remained. There, between the piles of timber, waited Mr. Erni Feld. He was covered with more than a dozen onion colored moths that fluttered there wings along his shoulders. His half-face gave a slouched grin, as if he were amused by me spotting him. I pushed the boy aside and charged at Mr. Feld. But just as I drew near enough to grab him, the madman lifted his chin and looked upward, triggering the swarm of insects to fly off into my direction. I shielded my face long enough for the moths to disperse. When my sight returned, Erni Feld was gone. *Had my careless use of opium triggered some sort of delayed hallucination?*

I tried hurrying to make sense of it all, studying the ground where Feld once stood. Unfortunately, I'd only just traced the brick floor with my eyes when a pair of thick fingers clasped onto my shoulders. The owner must have been a heavy handed bruiser because his palms squeezed tightly over my entire shoulder with ease. Without hesitation, I quickly stabbed my elbow into the assailant's gut, causing him to loosen his grip. However, as I spun around to see who had been so bold as to lay a hand on me, I found that not only did my attacker have two partners with him, but he was a hulking giant of at least seven feet tall.

All three ruffians were dark haired, donned in fisherman attire. The man to the colossus's left was squat bloke, fat with a patchy mustache while the one to the right was young and frail. The colossus on the other hand was of a different mold entirely. He ran at least three heads taller than myself and was twice as wide. He had slicked back curls that matched an oily goatee that drew a sharp line down his scarred cheeks. Half of his right ear was missing and he had fresh scratches scattered all across his chin and nose. I was fairly certain that this man fit the description of Samir Samwell, a Turkish bare knuckle boxer wanted for questioning in the murder of Harold McCormick.

I went for my iron, but Samwell's hand stopped me at the wrist. I responded by rotating my arm clockwise until it twisted from his grip before once more trying for my revolver. It clumsily slipped out of my hand and bounced down onto the brick. Smiling with his remaining teeth, Samwell gave a quick guttural laugh before punching wildly at my head, nearly landing a devastating haymaker. I dodged the blow before throwing a swift knee into his private stash. Bellowing in pain, he dropped to the ground while his accomplices rushed me. Swinging a wooden board with a nail in it, the fat thug grazed my left bicep as I stretched out for an uppercut to his mouth. Ramming my fist into his jaw, I could hear the fracture of teeth as he spiraled to the floor.

Hurriedly, I squared up with the fragile looking boy, whom I could tell didn't know the first thing about a street fight. Raising my fists, I faked a right-cross then let loose three left jabs, each landing between his eyes. Blood spurted from his nose and I knew I had broken his bridge cleanly. Grabbing at his face, he went to one knee, moaning in agony. Meanwhile, Samwell lurched back up and limped towards my direction. Holding my knuckles high, I planned on feigning a blow to his chest in hopes to distract him long enough to boot him in his bullocks again. However, just before I could throw another stinger, what thin hair remained on my temple was pulled back cleanly, and a knife held to my exposed throat. A thin set of arms curled around my shoulders and I could smell a sweet hint of jasmine.

"Enough Mr. Brannick, I'm not here to kill you," said a woman's voice firmly. I held my hands up in surrender, standing as still as possible. I then watched as the thugs made it back to their feet and approached, securing my arms. The three turned me around to face the woman holding the knife. She was a tiny little creature with snow-white skin and hair to match. She had buttoned sized eyes, pinned up hair and a pair of ruby lips. Her doll face hung over a sleek body adorned in slate leathers and an obsidian cloak. Her knife, held in a gloved hand, curved like a crescent moon with a rim of rust around the edge.

"I'm here to warn you," She announced with a heavy eastern brogue. "You tried to arrest my brother, but you are a fool. He is here to help."

"Ah, then you must be Vasilica," I challenged. Vasilica's eyes widened with surprise. She sheathed her dagger in a snake-skinned case along her belt then tucked her arms under the cloak.

"Bravo."

"So," I said daringly, "if your brother didn't murder Miss McCann, was it you?"

She cocked her head back before shaking it, clearly annoyed. Then, with a bird-like flutter, she hovered alongside me, tilting her face at me as if studying a piece of art. "Come now darling," I added, "you honestly have me stumped. I just want to know how you did it."

"You are not listening!" she shouted. "Miss McCann is not dead and I can prove it. Tonight, I challenge you to go find out for yourself. Go to her grave during the witching hour and my brother's innocence will be proven."

"Oh please," I sighed. "So you can bury me with her?"

"DO IT," she roared, mad as a wet hen, "*do it* or I will kill you now." I weighed my options and decided for the sake of my throat, which I had grown quite fond of, to cooperate.

"Fine," I said before taking a minute to think. "I'll go, but if it's a trap, you'll find that I'm a blimey mad dog when it comes to a fight."

She belted out a clumsy chuckle then picked up my revolver from the gravel and tucked it back in its holster.

"I can see that. And make sure to arm yourself with this," she said while patting the gun, "but not because of Vasile or me. There are worse things that linger in the night." She pointed her chin at the men on each of my arms, directing them to release me. "Oswald, get your friends and let's go. I believe I promised dinner."

Samwell gave a suspect look to the frail boy who was catering to his broken nose. The young man spoke through his fingers, cupping his face.

"Cousin," he said to Samwell, "Don't forget what I told you about Benny and Simon. Listen to her and let him go."

Samwell nodded before driving an anvil shaped fist into my gut. The pain was overwhelming. I fell flatly onto the cold alley floor, coughing up watery vomit as he and his mates joined Vasilica. I could hear the group snickering as they walked away, but my teary eyes couldn't focus. After taking a minute to recover, I managed to regain my senses, and after making sure my opium was still intact, stumbled towards the main avenue.

I returned to headquarters, trying hard not to hold onto my stomach as I limped to Falamas. My ribs were tender and I knew that they'd be giving me hell for the next several days.

"What can you tell me about our book?" I asked with a wince while bracing myself along a wall. Falamas picked at a scab on his ear and flicked it off his finger before pushing the journal onto my side of his desk.

"Mostly ghost stories," he said frankly. "This man who writes is of the old ways."

"Elaborate please," I sighed.

"He believes in specters, hags and devils. Much of Eastern Europe is like this, very superstitious. Their culture openly accepts such creatures as everyday life. He even goes so far as to claim that his family specializes in the disposal of such demons, going from town to town and saving locals. The author calls himself," he paused, "a witch hunter."

"That's it? No mention of Miss McCann or anything involving my case," I pouted while rifling through the pages of the journal. My stomach throbbed, causing my frustration to intensify. I had high hopes for the book, but it was nothing more than scribbled rubbish. I was back at square one.

"Yes Sergeant Brannick," bit back Falamas, "that is it. Most of the pages contain techniques on how to defend against these nightmares."

"God damn it," I growled, balling my fist angrily. Falamas cocked his brow. I must have looked like a lunatic. Embarrassed, I took a moment to breathe deeply before straightening out my tie. "Sorry Mr. Falamas. I appreciate your efforts." I handed him the ripe pear I'd kept in my pocket, and then once he'd taken it, slowly hobbled away. "I really do appreciate it mate," I added over my shoulder as I made towards the hall. *Nathan, stop making a fool of yourself.*

Shuffling back to my office, I threw my hat on its rack then painfully removed my coat so I could comfortably take refuge in the comforts of my chair. Most of the force was out protecting the Thames, so the building kept quiet. I took a moment to settle, thinking about Erni Feld and Vasilica. As I did, my eyes began to wander around the papers on my desk and I noticed a single, unopened telegram near my typewriter. Someone must have dropped it off when I stopped at the den. Usually, deliveries such as this were held at the reception area with Falamas. Someone must have either snuck past him or insisted that they personally deliver the message. I collected the correspondence and broke the official seal. It was from Cheese-Eater George, one of the few low lives who could read and write.

Dear Detective Sergeant Brannick,

I hope this message finds you well. True to my word, I write to report that there have been some suspicious sales in my establishment this morning. Specifically, I believe I now am in possession of some belongings that match the description of your Miss Jacqueline McCann. There are a few dresses, an umbrella and one handbag with the name Jacqueline sewn into the rim. I did not think with great askance until the man selling me the items refused to give any background on the pieces he offered. He appeared to be younger with an odd face and long mouth. He wore a black long coat and refused to give me his name.

He has informed me that he may return tonight with some additional jewelry that I fear may be more of your lady's property. I invite you to come if it suits you, in hopes that you can root out this murderer and send him to justice. As always, I am happy to help you in anyway possible. This is not solely because of our agreement, but because it is also my civic duty. Please keep this in mind if my name ever comes up at Scotland Yard.
Sincerely,
George Evans

I laughed, knowing why George was so willing to aid me. He was nervous because of my visit and scattered to help in anyway he could. Once again my rat was willing to give up anybody he could in order to protect his little business. *No honor among thieves.* Now that I needed to stopover at George's establishment, I ventured it would be a busy night, as I also was determined to visit the graveyard in the late eve. Perhaps I could make a quick trip to The Exchange beforehand. Thinking back to what Vasilica had said, I wondered if perhaps it all *was* just a trap. It didn't seem logical, as she could have easily murdered me in the den's alley, disposing of my body with ease. But then again, who knows.

Suddenly, from the confines of the silent halls, a gentle wrapping came at my office door.

"Come in," I shouted.

The door slowly pushed open and waiting in the hall stood Lord Wilhelm Frederick, detective-consultant for the Metropolitan Police Department, Prussian war hero, and my former crime investigation instructor. His presence was as wanted as pissing your trousers, as the two of us differed in methodology, and more importantly, manners. In short, I cringed whenever he spoke as he had a painfully maddening habit of insulting me in the most polite way possible.

"Young Nathan," he said through a toothy grin, "It is wonderful to see you friend." As usual, he paraded in his coat adorned in awards and metals, as if the entire world were required to know how important he was. "The years have been cruel to you Nathan," he remarked in an upbeat, teasing manner while inspecting me, "but let us hope that like a bottle of good wine, it has only enhanced your flavor."

I planted both my elbows on top of my desk and massaged my temples. The extent of my patience was radically shrinking. I looked him over, trying to find some fault in his appearance that I could fire back with, but Wilhelm did not age nor did he appear messy or unkempt. Though he was mostly bald, the grey hair around his crown always appeared flawless and his white beard, mustache and sideburns were trim and orderly. Ten seconds into our reunion and he was already winning.

"Fancy seeing you around Lord Frederick, to what do I owe this honor?" Wilhelm looked at the open seat across from me.

"Aren't you going to invite me to sit?" he asked. I bit at the tip of my tongue while giving a false smile and waving to the chair.

"Oh yes, please sit." He pulled out the chair, then, after looking repulsed, dusted off the surface with his hands before lowering himself into a cross-legged position.

"I have sojourned here in London for only a short time. I am on business as usual," he said conceitedly. "As you may know, they are looking to relocate your headquarters and I have been asked to give my professional opinion on the matter of design. They wanted something both elegant and intimidating. A rare balance to be sure, but I have a few ideas." Wilhelm's words rattled my spirits. I had not previously been aware of Scotland Yard headquarters' plans to relocate. He studied my face and began to snicker. "Oh dear Nathan, you did not know yet? Well, I'm sure they would tell the lower ranking men eventually. Just consider it a gift from me and keep it as our little secret. They won't even break ground for another year or so." I didn't know if I could keep from leaping over my desk and strangling him.

"So, you felt obligated to come and visit your failed student?"

Wilhelm continued to beam proudly. "Now Nathan, you did not fail. If I remember correctly, I awarded you with a passing mark. I just made mention to your superiors that there was room for improvement. From the looks of things, it seems you have not furthered your pursuit to use of science in the field. A shame, it might help in your murder investigation with this Miss McCann. Now, I can tell you did not conduct any sulfuric acid tests for arsenic in her lungs and stomach like I taught you, but did you at least have the decency to let someone examine her neck for broken cartilage in case of strangulation?"

"How do you know about the case?" I hollered, but no sooner than I had, did I notice my reports resting face up on the desk. I wagged my finger at him condolingly. "Tsk-tsk. It's not nice to look at things that aren't yours now Lord Frederick," I said mockingly, pretending to scold him like a child.

"Nor is it nice to be so contemptuous with an elder. Now please listen, you may learn something after all these years." His words were impressively wounding. I thought about drawing my revolver and shooting him, but doubted self-defense would hold up in court. "I am sure you have already thought of this," he continued merrily, "but the photograph of the victim shows that her eyes are closed. Studies, which I have shared with you in the classroom, have proven that eyelid closure at death suggests a peaceful closure of life. If the victim were aware of her immediate death, the eyes would have most likely been drawn open with alarm, staring into nothingness. Have you ever considered that your victim either died willingly or under the influence of some soothing narcotic? I would have demanded the body be exhumed for examination if I was in your position, but I'm sure you already tried that. Besides, these are only my thoughts after a mere minute of reading your case files. I am positive you have immensely progressed beyond my initial conjectures in this case of yours."

"Lord Frederick," I said raucously, "Where has the time gone? Are you not late for one of your very important dinners with Queen Victoria?" Wilhelm went quiet and stared at me endearingly. He took a moment to savor the last seconds in his chair before arising and straightening out his extravagant coat.

"Oh Nathan, I always thought you were so bright for an uneducated man. You have the determination of a Greek protagonist of old, but the rationale of a stampeding bull. Logic is only as obliging as men allow it to be. Give some of the scientific methods I've taught you a chance." He bowed briefly before making his way out. The tart had managed to win again, making me feel dim-witted and imprudent.

He had a point though. My usual approach of persistent fieldwork, zealous scrutiny and relying on sensible probabilities was not working. I needed to go about this one differently. I began to tensely go over possible new scenarios, but nearly leapt out my seat when Davis abruptly came crashing through my door.

"Nathan, good news!" he hooted.

I took a moment to allow my heart to sink back into my chest. "Did you find something about the handkerchiefs origins?"

"No. The bloke said the handkerchief could be from anywhere in Eastern Europe," Davis answered uncaringly, "*but* there is a new sweets shop next door to Gabriel's Tailoring." Stealing a laugh from me, James grinned while removing his hat as I pointed at the open chair.

"Sit," I requested. He plopped down his rear. I could hear the wood whine as his weight crushed it.

"Find anything out old boy?" My mind retreated to the hallucination of Mr. Feld before jumping to the encounter with Vasilica.

"No…well sort of. I was at a dead end when I was suddenly attacked."

"Attacked, what in the blazes?"

"No, no, it's alright. I am fine. Well, mostly. Vasile's sister, Ms. Vasilica Ivanescu, paid me a visit on the streets with a gang of misfits. They subdued me so she could have a little chat."

"Attacking an officer- preposterous!"

"Would you shut it?" Davis quieted himself before settling back in his seat. "She's proclaiming her brother's innocence and guarantees that she can prove it if I just visit Miss McCann's grave tonight."

"Well it's a trap Nathan, surely you won't go?"

"Yes I will. It is not a trap," I said while staring out at the white and tan buildings erected along Whitehall Place. It was peculiar, but a loud, overbearing voice inside me that insisted that I be at that cemetery tonight. "I have a feeling that I must go. It's vital."

"Feeling," rebelled Davis, "I thought we deal in facts?"

"Just hear me out Davis. Ms. Ivanescu could have killed me this morning, but she didn't. I do not know what she plans to prove, but if she wanted me dead, she would have already done it. Besides, this case has a different feel to it then the ones we usually investigate. Our approaches so far aren't working. I'm going to go."

"Then I'm coming with you," he said. "I'll even bring the hunting gear." Firearms in London had been outlawed for sometime. Getting an official document to carry my revolver alone had been a difficult task, involving copious amounts of paperwork and registrations. However, hunting in the countryside was different, and owning a hunter's rifle was a nice little trick to weasel through the regulations if you insisted on having a ranged weapon. Most police ignored a collection of hunter's firearms so long as the owner either came from upper class or legitimately tracked game. Davis, who wasn't of any line or ever hunted in his life, owned multiple rifles and long barreled shotguns.

"I would admit your company would be nice, but this could be dangerous."

"I thought you said you don't think it's a trap?"

"I know, but she did mention I should arm myself just in case."

"Well," he said before pausing and tightening his head bandage, "I'm still coming."

"Fine, then we'll meet at the gates of Brompton Cemetery at eleven tonight."

"Eleven?" Davis was a glutton, worshipping of all things desirous, including food, stout, sex, or most importantly, sleep. He sounded appalled. "Why eleven?"

"Because she said I needed to be there at the witching hour. That is anytime from midnight to three o'clock."

"I hope this cockamamie idea of yours works Nathan. I require a great amount of beauty rest to look as magnificent as I do," he muttered in amusement with himself.

Leaning back in my chair, I paused shortly to think of the peaceful night I would be missing with both Catherine and the pipe. This entire plan gave me a bad feeling and I hoped I would not live to regret it. "I hope it works too old boy...I hope so too."

CHAPTER 10

I hurried home to ready myself for the visits to both the Exchange, and more importantly, Bromptom Cemetery. I put on pair of grass colored knickers, long leggings, and a rough set of work boots, preparing for a muddy march through turned cemetery soils. I continued to get dressed, wiggling out of my work shirt and into a comfortable wool sweater, when suddenly, a rapping came at my door.

"Nathan?" called out Ms. Abigail. "Nathan, are you in there?" I answered the door and found Ms. Abigail holding a tray with baked mutton and a bowl of steaming flour-soup. "Nathan," she said surprised as she looked at my clothing, "If I weren't certain that it was foolish, I'd say you were planning on going out somewhere."

"Ms. Abigail," I snorted, "You're a wonderful woman, but you worry too much. I'm as healthy as a horse."

"Like hell you are," she said while shoving the tray in my chest, "Now take this and eat. You have to have your strength, especially since you're fighting the," she looked both ways through the hall, and then mouthed the words *consumption* so that none of our neighbors could hear.

"I'll tell you what," I said while letting her in my flat, "Put the food on the table and I'll eat it up as soon as I get back. I have some things to look into for work."

"What kind of things?"

"The foolish kind," I laughed. *But it wasn't foolish.* In fact, since my thrashing in the Limehouse district, a sudden unrelenting anticipation had come over me. It was an unexplainable urge that firmly insisted I see this whole Brompton mess through. Grabbing my effects, I went to the door of our apartment, pausing at the egress. I took one last glimpse at Ms. Abigail. She was fussing with her hands, staring at me with worry. "Come now Ms. Abigail, I'll be back soon, and when I do, I'll eat all of your delicious food, take all of your remedies, and whatever else you'd like me to do. I promise." Ms. Abigail smiled.

"Oh fine then, off you go." I gave a quick waive and then made it down the stairs.

The veiled moon lit up like a dirty lamp in a lonely home, and the sky lay dark with gleams of starlight between dents of clouds scudding across the black canvas. I strolled to the Exchange to meet with Cheese-Eater George and whoever might be selling him Miss McCann's possessions. The cab had made it to the store rather early and I could hear George's low, monotone voice speaking to someone inside. I gently placed my fingers on the door handle and tested to see if it was locked. It wasn't. *That a boy George.* He must have assumed that I'd come by and left it open for me. Quietly, I drove the door forward and crept inside.

When I first received my telegram from Cheese-Eater, I speculated that he invented some false lead in order to convince me that he had my best interests in mind. However, it became undoubtedly obvious that his convictions were legitimate once I caught sight of a suspicious looking man's backside inside the store. George stood at his cashier table, casually negotiating with the peddler who was covered in black from head to toe. The stranger's face was cloaked by a tight topper hat and stiff jacket collar that rose upward towards his cheeks. His empty coat sleeves hung loosely along his side, giving him the appearance of a man without arms. *Could this be the young hoodlum who perpetrated the break-in at my home a few days back?* George caught me in his view and gave the slightest wink before motioning with his nose towards the mysterious man. My temper began to boil over with each passing second as I studied the one armed thief. This black swaddled boy was bold enough to not only intrude on my home, but the investigation as well, all in a single week.

I slunk behind the suspect and viciously clutched the rear of his neck, tugging him backwards in order to get a better view. George gasped, feigning surprise. Shockingly though, as the fellow's spine hooked abaft, it was not the youthful glare of the one-armed boy that I was staring at, but the panicked expression of Constable Harper. His bulky horse teeth and enormous chin unbolted to release a fear driven scream. At first, he must have thought it was a setup, as his hands quickly sprouted from under his coat, guarding at his neck. However, as Harper stared into my frown, his senses returned, and the frightened look he sported shifted into a laggard smile.

"Brannick, I mean," his face sobered, "Detective Sergeant Brannick, sir, what are you doing here?"

It all made sense now. It wasn't the one-armed boy or Vasile I should have been expecting at the Exchange. Constable Harper, who had been charged with guarding Ms. McCann's flat, was pawning her items off for gain. This was a serious offense, as the young policeman was still in his probationary period and would not only be released from the force, but detained for corruption charges. Scotland Yard had already worn its numbers thin, and losing another constable for such a petty crime, stupid, but petty, felt wrong. So, with yet another hopeful lead coming up short, I decided that instead of exacerbating the situation by detaining the young constable, I'd put the fear of God into him, and then be on my way.

I kicked my leg behind Harper's thigh then pushed him against it, tripping the policeman onto the floor. Spittle sprayed out of his mouth due to the impact. He rolled to his side, gasping for air. Once his groans stopped, I kneeled down to his level, waiving my taut finger in his face.

"Are you stupid Harper? What the hell do you think you are doing?" Harper gave a stricken looked, fearful that I would bring him to proper justice. His lips began to quiver and he wrapped half of his face in one hand to cover up his glossy eyes. Then, as if some impalpable pain had stabbed at him, he wailed desperately before gagging out a few words.

"Sir, please no. I only did it because my mum is sick. She…she," he stuttered, "Has consumption you see? I have no way of paying for her doctor bills on my salary, *but* I needed to do something!"

Tears rolled down his cheeks. I turned my head sideways to break from flustering sight. Only my superiors knew about Catherine, and no one knew about my own illness, so I doubted he was trying to use his mother's plight to gain my sympathy. Yet it did. I knew how hard it was to care for someone with the illness. I would have done anything to help Catherine. Unfortunately for her, there was little that could be done. Maybe Harper would be different? Maybe his mother still had a chance? I couldn't be certain. Taking him by the hand, I brought him back to his feet.

"Good God Harper," I said disapprovingly, "pull yourself together." He wiped his eyes with one sleeve before meeting mine. "Now listen to me. Go sell whatever George here will buy from you and then do not touch another thing inside that flat. If I find out you've continued to sell Miss McCann's possessions, I'll make sure that you are put away for a very long time. Here," I added while taking out my money purse and giving him half of what was inside, "take this too." Harper reluctantly pinched the handful of money I put into his hand, a puzzled expression spread across his face. "And George," George looked at me fleetingly, undoubtedly confused, "you did right by sending me that telegram. Buy what you want from Harper and never speak of this again. Your business will continue to be overlooked by the Metropolitan Police so long as you do. Now, I have other matters to attend to, so if you would excuse me."

I trampled outside, brushing off the incident. It bothered me a bit how stupid Harper was, and if I'd caught him on a normal day, things might have been different. But at the moment my sights were set elsewhere. Since making Vasilica's acquaintance, somewhere deep inside my conscience, a voice cried out. It told me that the cemetery would be different, more helpful than any clue I'd yet come across. I walked a bit of the way to Brompton while counting my leftover money, calculating the cost for a lift. There was still enough for a carriage ride. So after finding a carriage for hire lingering along the streets, I left for the graveyard.

I decided not to tell Davis about what happened at Cheese Eater's store, as James had it out for anyone he could safely make an example of. It wasn't that he was righteous or moral. No, it was quite the opposite. He was selfish and self-centered, eager to offer up any guilty party on the force as a sacrificial lamb. So long as he was convinced that Harper didn't have any dirt on him, James would happily turn the constable over in order to decrease any suspicion leaning his way. *Davis you nasty shit, you'll do forty-nine things right only to commit fifty-one wrong.*

The stagecoach rocked endlessly. I rested on one of its soiled couches, looking outward from behind the glass as we closed in on the cemetery. Finally we arrived at the entrance, and after paying the spooked cabbie, I hurried along to the barred entrance. The thick iron poles looked like a row of metal spears fixed threateningly between a large stone arch. My senses were on high alert, and peering into the grounds, I spotted several eerie silhouettes of statues strewn across the property. They were masked in shadow and seemed as if they could come to life at any moment.

The area was abnormally hushed except for a light autumn breeze that made the nearby tree branches clap. Not a living soul could be found, from late night workers to midnight drunkards. I began second guessing my gut feeling, still hoping that this visit would not be folly. Pulling out my revolver, I checked to make sure that the cylinder was properly stocked with bullets then patted my pocket to recheck the extras I'd put aside. The metal clinked together.

As I continued inspecting my weapon, I heard a faint, but distinct clopping of horse hooves. I quickly returned my revolver to its holster. Not soon after, the silhouette of a two horse carriage came barreling from behind a corner. James's head peeked from the side window. He blew me a mocking kiss as his driver steered the cab towards the gates. Once they reached nearer to me, the horses stopped and James hurriedly climbed out, a massive burlap sack in tow.

After handing the driver his fee, Davis waved him off, watching anxiously as the wagon galloped away, slowly being swallowed back up by the darkness. James shuffled over to me in his saggy outdoor trousers drooping at the waste. He took a moment to catch his breath, steam billowing upwards.

"Good evening Nathan," he greeted while wiping the wet droplets hanging from his reddened nose. "Have a couple of presents for us." He shook his bag and the rattle of heavy steel rang from inside.

"Did you find where she was buried?"

"Oye," he hooted while sniffling up a bogey. "Have it right here." Crumbling out a sheet of paper from his coat, he handed me a primitively penciled map that he'd copied from the station's archives. I looked it over and could see that Miss McCann had been buried near the back of the graveyard near the northwest plots. I tried to memorize as much as I could, examining the paths and picking out emergency escape routes if necessary. Afterwards, I folded the paper and drew my attention back to James.

He was posed enthusiastically with a massive unwrapped rifle in each hand and bobbing his signature brows. One, a classic hammerless hunting rifle, had a long wooden stock with gold metal inlay along its side. It was long, but manageable. The other, a more imposing weapon, was a silver double-barreled shotgun that looked to be far too much for one man, even in the grips of Davis's thick hands.

"Well cock-a-doodle-doo James," I shouted, "we're not going to war." Davis, still elated, maintained his childlike grin.

"Never know Nathan."

I rolled my eyes and took the fancy looking hunting rifle, allowing Davis to have his silver ship cannon. He loaded a shell in each barrel before examining the iron lock fastening the cemetery gates.

"Want me to blow it off?"

"No!" I barked. "Don't be silly. We are not looking to use these damn rifles unless absolutely necessary." I removed my knife and dug into the keyhole, pushing at the pins. It was a quality lock, but after a few moments, I managed to release the miniature joints from their bar clasp, releasing its grip. I then thrust the gates wide enough for Davis and me to squeeze through before securing it once more behind us. "Come on, follow me."

Weapons pointed, the two of us stepped off the path and scurried through the slippery grass. We hurried between yew trees feeling like men on the battlefield, though in truth, most likely just looking like a pair of blind fools. Nevertheless, with the help of the map, we finally stumbled near Jacqueline McCann's burial plot. The pitch-black atmosphere made reading grave inscriptions impossible and after a brief debate, we decided to light one of the candlesticks I had brought along. Using its dim glow, we sorted through a few headstones before finally finding a fresh patch of soil perched under a grave marked *Jacqueline McCann*.

"Well, now what?" asked Davis as he leaned on the butt of his gun.

"We wait."

The two of us parked ourselves on the damp soil near the grave and tried to warm up, scanning the horizon for anything suspicious. The leafless grey trees swayed back and forth from the winds like stiff corpse hands waving farewell. Dogs barked in the distance and a single raven cawed aimlessly in the chilled air. I didn't let the eerie sights and sounds bother me much, but I couldn't say the same for Davis. He aimed his barrels at every falling twig and scurrying rat that clamored.

"Don't like this Nathan, not one bit."

"Here, take some of this. It'll calm the nerves." I handed him a flask of whiskey I'd packed and watched as he urgently drank up the contents. After a few wincing sips, he screwed the top back on. His puffy cheeks flushed a rosy shade of cherry and his posture loosened. "Better?" I asked.

"Much, thank you."

Together we lingered in the dark, our candle slowly burning down to the bottom, smoldered into a heap of wax. It had been almost three hours and still nothing. I reached for my final candlestick and attempted to light the wick. My shaky cold hands fumbled with the matchbox, but eventually I managed to pinch a small wood stick from the package. But as I searched for a surface to strike my match on, a sudden scratching sound grabbed my attention. It was coming from beneath us. The strange muffled thumps drummed wildly below, as if something were scraping violently at the earth.

"What's that?" cried Davis. I couldn't see much more than his inked outline so I inched closer, feeling about for an arm. The wool from his sleeve was cool, but it kept us together. I began to wonder what was worse, the mysterious clamor below us or the torturous chill.

"Don't know," I said quietly, "give me a second to light this."

I struck the match on the bottom of my boot, sparking a flame that I quickly brought to the taper wick. Now lit, the candle illuminated the immediate area, revealing what had been rustling nearby. Rising from the grave was a mound of dirt that spewed upward, unearthing a slender female hand. The clawed fingers grabbed at the topsoil, tugging at the surface until finally a shaggy head emerged. Covered in puce dirt, the ghastly face was crowned in a bushel of webbed hair, sickly skin, and most frightening of all, a fierce set of beady glowing eyes. As terrified as I was, I couldn't help but notice that the face strongly resembled the likeness of Miss McCann.

Davis, jaw dropped, squeezed the trigger of his shotgun, firing a rumble of thunder that shattered granite shrapnel from Catherine's headstone. He had missed the bobbling head by nearly a foot. Hastily, I tried to make sense of the grisly scene. Somehow, someway, Miss McCann must have been buried alive. It was the only logical reason. And now Davis was trying to kill her.

"Hold your fire damn it!" I demanded while lowering my rifle. Miss McCann continued to drag herself from the grave, her glare fixed on the pair of us. "Jacqueline," I called out, waving a free hand near her face. She snapped at it violently, nearly biting off my finger. Her entire upper half was now exposed, leaving only her waist and legs in the soil. She was but mere moments away from digging herself out completely. "Stop, please! My name is Detective Sergeant Brannick and this is Detective Sergeant Davis. We're the police."

Jerking her legs from the mound, Jacqueline rose to her feet, taking us both in with her bright, illuminated pupils. She licked at her lips with a wormy purple tongue, opening her mouth wide enough to reveal a pair of grisly fangs.

Whap! The butt of Davis's shotgun slammed into the back of Miss McCann's head, sending her to the ground. She dropped facedown from where she'd been standing. I glanced back and forth between the two, completely stunned.

"Oh Davis, What have you done?"

"I panicked! Did you see her? She's a loony."

"She was delirious," I said in as rational of a tone I could muster. Jacqueline laid spread out with her arms and legs outward, showing no signs of life. "Jesus, Mary and Joseph, I think she's dead James."

Brompton remained still beyond the moan of the wind. We glanced at each other, frozen in uncertainty. Then suddenly, horribly, Jacqueline flew to her feet, rising effortlessly as if lifted by the very winds themselves. She hurtled at me with lightning speed, grabbing at my throat and gripping it with surprising strength. I could feel a burning within the muscles along my collar. Then shockingly, she lifted me up and tossed me backwards. My stomach dropped as I sailed over a neighboring plot, until finally, I collided with its grave marker. My head had taken the brunt of it, bouncing off the stone and causing my vision to blur.

Gliding to Davis, who held up his shotgun like a cricket bat, Jacqueline reared her talons, cackling sinisterly. Davis swung his firearm and cracked her on the elbow, causing it to bend backwards like a bird leg. Unaffected, she used her good arm to tug the weapon from his grip, throwing it over her shoulder. She then grabbed onto his jacket, dragging him downward until they were pressed face to face and rolling in mud. Jacqueline sniffed at James like a dog before opening her mouth and unhinging her jaw unnaturally wide. However, before she could sink her large canines in James, a primitive wooden bolt suddenly soared downward from the heavens and into her inner shoulder.

She hissed and released her hold on Davis, searching in a panic for her attacker.

Meanwhile, I was still seeing double. Sluggishly, I lifted my rifle and aimed between the pair of lit eyes, chasing the spinning images with my barrel. I fired a volley, and watched as a few bullets managed to find their target, ripping through Miss McCann's torso. She stumbled back a bit, but kept her footing. Then, miraculously, Jacqueline rose from the ground and levitated towards me. She closed the distance between us almost instantly. Drawing my revolver, I squeezed the trigger rapidly, driving several bullets into her chest. Still she persisted, grasping at my outstretched leg. I kicked at her hand while clumsily slipping into my pocket for spare ammunition. The bullets poured out onto the grass in every direction. I dazedly felt around for spilled pistol rounds until a paralyzing feeling came over me. Jacqueline tried grabbing at my foot, but instead brushed her palm on the naked skin between my boot and ankle. Then I felt it. For some odd reason, the *echo* was taking over.

I was back in Miss McCann's flat, only now, it was night. Jacqueline sat in a chair near where her body had been found. The room was unlit and encompassed in shadow. She wheezed with a pain ridden grimace, holding her palm to her breast.

"Look at you my Irish Dove," said a deep voice with a thick accent. The square silhouette of a man lingered in the darkness, "You're falling apart. Come- let me at last alleviate your pain." Jacqueline nodded, prompting the figure to stand up. He drew near her, embracing her in his arms as his lips parted. His jaws locked onto her neck, and suddenly, I could feel an excruciating pain above my own collar.

Then, unpredictably, Jacqueline let go of me. An abrupt shattering of glass erupted from her back. This time, a flask had been hurled from the bushes, cracking and drenching a steaming fluid all over her. Howling in anguish, she scratched at her smoldering spine, chipping off chunks of skin. A mist bubbled from the surface of her flesh, causing Jacqueline to whirl in circles from the agony. Davis, still on the ground, attempted to blind-side her, aiming the shotgun he'd recovered at hip level. Firing a shell into her side, his firearm violently brought her down. Shockingly, even with the gaping hole in her torso, Jacqueline promptly rolled onto her belly and crawled relentlessly towards James.

She pried at his boot, dragging herself on top of him. Now smothering him, she opened her mouth and sank the set of frightening teeth into his flabby chest.

"Gah!" he yelped. Wobbling to my feet, I charged at Jacqueline with my lowered shoulder, slamming into her fizzing back. All at once, the air in my lungs was stolen, and I staggered back to my prone position. The entire front half of my arm felt as if I had ran into a wall, numb from the collision. Ignoring me, Jacqueline continued to suckle on Davis. Her wounds somehow slurped closed. I watched with disbelief as a hundred days of healing were restored in seconds. Davis cried out, begging for help. I strained to make it to my feet again, but try as I might the lightheadedness anchored me to the grass.

Then, all at once, leaping from the shrubs, a mysterious black figure emerged. Jamming a wooden spike through the center of Miss McCann's back, the cloaked stranger pushed at the dull end until Jacqueline slid off Davis's belly and onto the ground, paralyzed from the blow. Our rescuer followed by unsheathing a menacing curved blade, raising it above them, then swinging it downward, lopping off Jacqueline's head. Though my vision still spun, I tried to steady myself, watching as the cloaked phantom removed their hood.

A bundle of white braids fell around a delicate, but intense looking face. It was Vasilica Ivanescu. Her cheeks were painted with mud that blended in with a smattering of fresh blood. She went to Miss McCann's decapitated head, taking out a handful of strong smelling cloven vegetables from her pocket and shoving them into the dead woman's mouth.

"Are you injured?" she asked. I was mute, too dizzy to speak. Vasilica looked into my eyes. Then, as if recognizing my wooziness, she came over and helped me to my feet. She let me to lean upon her for balance as we wobbled to Davis. "We must get your friend help quickly. I'll need your aid in lifting him, but we may still be able to save him."

"I think I've cracked my skull," I mumbled, the taste of iron in my mouth. The two of us loomed over Davis, who pressed a blood-covered hand over his clavicle.

He studied me a bit, giving a slight cringe as his eyes fixed near my brow.

"Looks like you sprung a few leaks too," he said through his gritted teeth. I could feel the warmth trickling down my temple. Davis extended his uninjured hand and used me to pull himself up. Wearing matching grimaces, the two of us painfully hobbled to the body of Miss McCann. Her two halves were shot, stabbed, and leaking crimson. Smoke still rose from cooked skin that was now turning slate grey.

"We are in a lot of trouble now aren't we Nathan?" asked James.

"More than you both know," Vasilica interjected. "Your friend here has the curse," she said while pointing to James. "It will not be long now before he takes his last breaths. Soon, the blackness will take his soul, condemning him to the unlife. We must act quickly."

"And who the hell are you lass?" spat Davis. He used the shotgun as a crutch, removing his copper badge and presenting it to Vasilica threateningly. Vasilica seemed uncaring, shrugging briefly before wiping off her blade with her cloak.

"Vasilica Ivanescu, sister of the persecuted Vasile Ivanescu, and hunter of the damned." She returned her sword to its sheath, shaking her head at Davis as he continued to present his policeman emblem. "Your laws and authority do not concern me, however your lack of urgency does. We will need to get you to a holy man now, one who will know the old ways. Come, we can leave her body. It will take care of itself shortly."

"Vasilica," I spoke up, "we do appreciate your aid, but you need to understand we have all just partaken in a murder."

"Murder, no," She said in a sterile voice. "The abomination who created this poor girl murdered her. We have just liberated her soul from committing countless unforgivable acts. Hopefully Satan cannot claim her spirit. Now quickly, we must get your friend aid."

"Now listen up," shouted Davis. "I'm not going to any holy man and neither are you. You are coming with us to the station to be processed."

Vasilica sighed, hesitating for a moment, then without warning spun backwards into a somersault, kicking Davis in the chin. The blow knocked him backwards onto the twitching torso of Miss McCann. Vasilica returned full circle to her feet before darting out of the candlelight and into the unlit surroundings.

"Stupid men," she blurted as she barreled between mausoleums and headstones until disappearing altogether. Maybe it was because I had been in far too much discomfort, or perhaps it was because I secretly was grateful, but for whatever reason, I did not try to pursue. Instead, Davis and I trudged back to the exit, desperate for medical attention. While I had only been trained to administer to the most basic wounds in the navy, I assumed that I had at least suffered some sort of bruising of the brain. Davis meanwhile would definitely need to be stitched for his gaping wound. We made it outside the gates and tried to hail a carriage to the best of our ability. Because of the hour, it took sometime for anyone to pass by, but eventually a lovely couple on their way home from a social gathering pulled over to see if they could help us. Upon presenting our papers, we were raced to a nearby cholera infirmary free of charge.

If for a moment I had considered the cemetery bleak and depressing, such thoughts were quickly washed away when we arrived at the medical center. I was quickly reminded of the epidemic at hand as we passed the rooms crammed with moaning men, screaming children and crying widows. Eventually though, we met with a medical hand, and after a grueling hour of stitching, were on our way out.

Night gave in to dawn and the two of us traveled back to Scotland Yard, exhausted. James reported our evening to the Chief Inspector, who'd just arrived for his morning shift. He listened to the vague and somewhat altered account. He was perturbed, but applauded us for our efforts. He insisted that we take the remainder of the day off, returning for mid-shifts on the morrow. Davis had pinned the entire disastrous account on Vasilica, and though I tried to argue, I was too worn out to properly defend her. Swanson then gathered a unit of constables and ordered them to comb Brompton for Vasilica, Miss McCann's corpse, and any other evidence they could find. Though my conscience weighed heavy, I relished in the thought of returning home, and hurried to catch a ride from one of the morning patrol carriages. A sudden rush of excitement drowned out the trauma of what had just occurred, as my thoughts were drawn to the opium.

Once home, I nibbled at the food that Ms. Abigail left, and then prepared for bed. I wrestled out from my dirty clothes like an escape artist, and then slid into my sleeping robe. Afterwards, I collected my tar and packed the wooden apparatus with two doses. I lit the lamp and let my afflictions melt away. My eyes grew heavy, buckling into a senseless torpor. Before fading off, my mind flashed to the ghastly scene just hours ago, tainting my high with Jacqueline's ghoulish visage.

CHAPTER 11

"**W**here's she gone?" I asked in my clumsy English. Mrs. Edith stared at me blankly, rocking an infant in her arms. She was a ragged Englishwoman with unkempt hair, buttered teeth and a pink skin rash, who I learned had become desperate for money after her husband's death. She had agreed to watch Vasilica for sixpence a week, but according to Mrs. Edith, such payment was far too little for her to try and stop my unruly sister from leaving.

"I haven't a clue Mr. Ivanescu," she said sheepishly, her cheeks suffusing with color. "Just came down with her bags packed yesterday morning and said she was off to give London a go. I tried to talk her out of it, but she wouldn't take. She said something about God's will, but I don't know what she meant. I even warned her that you'd threatened to harm me like you said to do, but she saw right through it. As stubborn as a wild horse that one is."

I'd just identified the whereabouts of Sebastian, child of Paraschiva, and now needed Vasilica's help in stopping him. But before I even had a chance to retrieve my sister, London Police chased me out of my quarters in Tottenham. I'd been traveling covertly ever since. It had taken some effort, but I found myself back at Mrs. Edith's home with little more than the clothes on my back. It was only by the graces of God that I was fortunate enough to make friends with a pack of travelers who, for the last day and a half, allowed me to blend in with them until I could make it back to sister. Digging in my money pouch, I handed Mrs. Edith my last schilling, placing it in her hand like a Eucharist wafer. Here eyes grew big as she stared at the generous payment. Grabbing her clammy hands, I squeezed them firmly adding, "Take care of your young ones, and remember, tell not a soul of our business together."

"I'd never Mr. Ivanescu. What sort of creature would be so nasty as to break their word?"

"Thank you Mrs. Edith. Oh, and if my sister *does* return, please inform her to leave a message at the inn we first visited upon arriving to London. She'll know where it is."

"Of course," she clucked while slipping the schilling in a pocket under her apron.

The streets were bitterer than in days past. I tucked into the warmth of my cloak and exited the confines of the caretaker's modest home, concealing myself amongst the soot-covered cityscape. Not moments after stepping out though, did the heavens opened up, crying a harsh rain. A crack of electricity filled the sky, and soon I could hear only the tapping of heavy droplets along my hood. Still, duty called. I needed to rush in order to make it on time to the Prospect of Whitby, a pub where a contact of mine requested to meet.

I clung to the sides of the streets, keeping a guarded eye out for police whom were posted along the river. I'd arrived at the pub fairly early and waited patiently under a flower box that hung out from the second floor window, taking shelter under the dry spot beneath it. With nothing else to do, I curled into a ball and dozed off, awaking only shortly after because of the wet clattering of hard soles along the slippery stone walkway. It was the nameless Irishman I had been waiting for, donned in an olive caubeen hat that matched his soaked wool coat. He kicked the mud from his boots onto the threshold of the establishment door, oblivious to me thanks to the thick drapes of rain. I waited for him to enter before slinking closely behind and tailing him inside.

The pubs hearth was burning bright, illuminating a flagstone floor with a stretched pewter counter atop of several barrels. The large timber beams appeared to be long forgotten pieces of a mast, taken as spare wood after some poor ship was scrapped. Just past the open fire was a seating area near the river where the Irishman made his way. Settling at a booth overlooking the waters, he removed his wet coat, still unaware of my presence. I weaved between patrons until I was but an arms length away before sliding onto the bench opposite him at his table. I waited quietly as he absentmindedly shed his scarf, gloves and hat, piling them into a wet mound as he sat down. Finally, once comfortable, he set his eyes upon me inadvertently, leaping up with a startled gasp before coming to terms.

"Scared the devil out of me, ya' did!"

His patchy red scruff littered a pair of chubby cheeks like weeds in a garden. He was a round man with a broad, pink nose and widely spaced eyes. His top was mostly bald with an unkempt patch of hair near his forehead that curled forward close to his brows. He calmed himself before snickering from the excitement. Once he was composed, he called for the barman, who was worn to a whisper, and waited for the old soul to limp over before ordering a pint of grog.

"And for you?" asked the server, but the Irishman cut off my words before I could answer.

"Nothin' for him. He's a prig."

I was unaware what he meant by *prig*, but assumed it had a wounding quality to it. Once the barkeep returned with the frothy dark liquor, he went back to his post while the Irishman devoured his drink. After a few sips, he looked up at me, a foam mustache pasted across his satisfied grin.

"Ah, like mother's milk."

I'd known the Irishman was a rogue, the worse kind of scoundrel in fact, but he had served me well during my short time in London. I had met him through a network of travelers in Tottenham who promised he could provide the information I was looking for. He'd proven his value after selling me the names of several different people and places imperative to my hunt. As our relationship developed, I decided to take a chance and share some of the more protected details from my crusade in order for him to have a better understanding of my directives. Two weeks later, I'd received a letter declaring he had attained facts paramount to my pursuit. He provided a time for us to meet at the pub, emphasizing the importance of discretion.

"Now, let's get to business," he blubbered in a singsong voice. "I have a rare bit of details at hand for ya' that might help with your…goals. You see, I know a fellow who lives a wee bit away, perhaps a stone throw from Piccadilly, who confided in me about a *very* peculiar happening near his neck of the woods. Now at first I thought it was all just hogwash until I recalled our conversation about your *night people*. It seems my friend's young neighbor, a porter at a local hotel, had been tragically maimed in a dumbwaiter accident and perished from his wounds."

His words struck me like a blow. I briefly lost all awareness as my mind flashed back to the day of the failed hotel ambush, the poor porter flopping armless within the back hall. Self-resentment overcame me. My teeth gnashed together and a stinging sensation stabbed at the core of my chest, punishing me for my part in this boy's fate. Sebastian could wait. I needed to make this right.

"What was his name?" I blurted.

"Huh?"

"The boy's name, what was it?"

"I don't know," he bellowed, "Sam I think. Who cares really?"

Sam, the boy I had condemned to death. Not a thousand years of repentance would ever clear my conscience. I wondered if the Irishman could sense my troubles, but judging from his dazed expression, it was not so.

"Now here is the part that will get your prick hard," he continued. "This honest friend of mine told me that he's frightened to death because every night since the boy was buried, he claims to still see him. In particular, the spooky little bugger keeps showing up on the rooftop where he once lived, just gawping down at the folks below. Now I'm not much of a believer in ghost stories, but I know you take the subject very seriously, so I thought this one couldn't wait."

God have mercy on my soul. The boy is one of them. When the tragic incident at the hotel first occurred, I'd presumed that it was the dumbwaiter that had claimed the porter's arm, only to be stolen by Paraschiva's offspring as a future meal during his escape. However, if the story was true, it must have been Sebastian himself that gnawed through the boys shoulder, blighting the young man's blood and body with the curse.

"Do you know the address?"

"Aye, that I do," he replied, pulling out a piece of manila parchment from his satchel. A mischievous smile smeared across his face. "Have it right here in fact, but it'll cost ya'."

With nothing to spare, I looked up to the ceiling, begging heaven for guidance. *I needed that address.* My mind went blank as I squeezed my eyes shut. I could hear the tapping of an impatient finger on wood from across the table. Then, as if answering my prayers, the sting from the crucifix around my neck pinched at my chest hairs. Unhooking the chain from my collar, I raised it to the Irishman, offering it to him for inspection. The gold cross was encrusted with rubies and sapphires, the last of my dear mother's possessions. Though it was highly valuable and extremely sentimental, I had to remind myself that it was only a material possession. Its worth was incomparable to the good it might do.

"Will this suffice?"

"Aye, that'll do," he said excitedly, licking his lips. We traded our gifts simultaneously, he tugging at the cross with one hand while I snatched the note with the other. "Don't worry," he jawed with false sympathy, "I'll pray with her every night." I read the address and tried memorizing the numbers before finally folding the paper back up. "You don't plan on looking into it *tonight* do you?" he added inquisitively, as if my expression had given something away. I stroked at my mustache.

"Yes," I said while promptly recollecting a related quote from Proverbs. "Boast not thyself of tomorrow; for thou knowest not what a day may bring forth." The Irishman pretended to reflect deeply, appraising his new crucifix all the while. Draping my damp cloak back over my body, I once more prepared for the outdoors, squeezing from the stall with purpose. "Enjoy your drink."

The rains continued as I followed the roads to the given address. It had taken me some time because of London's vastness and complexity, but eventually I figured out where I was going. I hadn't much time to spare before nightfall, but decided to make a quick stop at a local park I'd stumbled upon, gathering three sturdy branches from an oak tree. Afterward, I found an empty walkway between two unoccupied homes and nested under a set of stairs to hide from the weather. Sharpening the branches on a cobble stone pathway, I brought the ends to sharp points, creating a wooden arsenal to defend myself with. Thereupon, I took out my last molded biscuit bequeathed to me by the travelers, and begged God to bless it. After eating the bread, a renewed vigor surged within me, driving me to continue my undertaking.

It had always mystified me that the world of men occupied their time with ambitions of wealth, influence and science when the zenith of all pursuits stared them directly in the eye. Religion told the history of our great creation, explained why our lives have been spared and promises a future of everlasting salvation. Phenomenon so profound, that their simple ceremonies like receiving the Lord's blessing could inspire a man such as myself to walk a thousand men's journeys. I use to feel a sense of isolation because of my enthusiasm, but father encouraged me not to.

"Do not hide your love for God," he told me, *"For he will never hide his love for you."*

I arrived at the house of the porter with an overwhelming sense of urgency as the sun began to set. The gothic four storied building, singed black from the coal stoves inside, had been well secured, with doors and windows firmly locked. Nevertheless, my will was unbendable. I inspected the facility with a more scrutinizing eye and found that the eroded backside of the structure created a set of rigid depressions within the bricks. A rather fortunate coincidence as father had trained sister and I in the coveted Romanian climbing technique, *Calcai-Carligului*, also known as the "heel-hook" technique.

I rubbed my palms in a nearby dirt patch and made sure they were gritty enough to cling to the slippery surface. My hands clenched at the sharp, hardened clay while my legs pushed upward, fueling the climb as I slowly ascended higher against the slick wall. Two scraped knees, seven bloody fingers, and an hour later, I'd finally reached the rooftop. The showers seemed to pickup, and after catching my breath behind the roof's fire-bell shed I decided to conceal myself. A large puddle collected on the roof's flat surface, and reluctantly, I submerged myself in the freezing water.

The bitter chill of the small pool instantly cooled my skin. It was agonizing and painful, but I'd hoped that it would be enough to mask my body's temperature from the eyes of the bellhop. The curse was different for each of the damned, but most often, Nosferatu were gifted with the ability to see warmth like mortal men do colors.

"Incalzeste-ma Iisuse," I begged aloud to Jesus, in hopes he would protect me. I began using a set of meditative techniques, concentrating on my heart's fire, focusing to keep my insides warm. It seemed like forever, as my teeth chattered and body numbed, but finally the drowning sun completely plunged under the skyline. *The night had come.* The heavy rains grew into a torrential downpour. The wind's insufferable lashing made my wait almost unbearable. I lay prone, inspecting the rooftop, nearly ready to call off my search before I froze to death. However, just as I was about to give up, a flash of lighting lit up the sky, assisting my eyes in spotting the silhouette of a figure leering over the roof corner.

He was lanky and skeletal, resembling a perched vulture hooked over the building's crown. Squinting, I made out that was wearing a leather long coat tied up along one arm. He had stringy dark hair and a youthful shaped face. *This was my boy.* He gazed down at the city, allowing the drops of rain to pour off him without so much as a cringe. His unlife had granted him immunity from such hardships that mortal men must endure.

I removed two of the wooden daggers and held them low while crawling towards him. *It was time to end what I had started.* I followed the shadowy outlines of rooftop chimneys and shingle stacks, drawing nearer. As the devil would have it though, just before I could make it within striking distance, the unmistakable sound of a firearm hammer clicked abruptly behind me.

"Don't move lad," called out a familiar voice. I remained as still as my shaking body would let me, eyes still fixed on the boy. The porter twirled around and glanced at me briefly before securing his focus on the man with a firearm behind me. The boy nodded with approval. I had fallen into a trap.

Like most undead, the one armed boy's appearance had been corrupted. Purple veins pulsated around a pair of pea-sized eyes, their surfaces a glowing dull white. I could tell from how the monster studied me that he was starved. It was like looking at a lion. *I cannot let him take me alive.* I turned my attention to the heavy breathing from behind me and readied my wooden darts. I tried to calculate the distance before slowly rotating to face my ambusher. My suspicions were confirmed. The soaked Irishman held a large caliber revolver at my head.

"Nothin' personal mate, he just offered me more."

With no time to waste, and a starved demon at my back, I took action. As rapidly as my stiff arms could muster, I elbowed my cloak upward, releasing one of the miniature wood spikes towards the Irishman. Perhaps it was my lack of focus or numb fingers that worked against me, but as I let the oak dart go, instead of landing straight in his chest, the sharpened point jabbed into his shoulder. As fortune would have it, the wounded arm was the very one holding the pistol, causing the Irishman to drop the gun while screaming. He splashed onto the ground with a hard thump. *Now my opponents and I were even, each with only two good arms.*

Whirling towards the bellhop, I readied to hurl my second dart, but the monster's supernatural speed allowed him to escape my sights. He'd disappeared into the inky background, now stalking me in the safety of the darkness. Holding up my weapon, I readied for the creature's attack, franticly searching each corner and crevice. To my misfortune, the monster had managed to creep up behind me, and soon his uncanny strength was hammering into my shoulder. I collided with the floor. A current of pain pounded through my body, stupefying me as I rolled along the roof. My nose sprayed with blood and a few of my teeth wiggled loose. My wooden weapon violently flew out of my hand, far from my reach. Facedown and lightheaded, I rolled my eyes wearily and caught glimpse of bone protruding through my forearm skin. Pinkish muscle jutted between spurts of scarlet. My mind began to stir in panic.

Picking me up by the waist of my trousers, the porter lifted me above the ground before twisting my dangling body until we were face-to-face. Steam from my breath rolled off its nose.

"You want the necromancer too, don't you?" he wailed, his voice shrill and deafening. Wiggling my good hand to my belt, I furtively clutched the last wooden spike and hid it behind my forearm.

"Sam, you've been cursed. Let me end your suffering." He looked to me befuddled, twitching irritably before shaking his head.

"Cursed?" he laughed. Without warning, I jammed the wood into his chest, but to my dismay, the branch cracked in my hand from impact. The boy whipped me to the ground, rolling me in the Irishman's pool of blood. I looked to the stub of timber in my hand. It was shattered, the tip now completely dull. Sam growled. "You fool. Do you think I wouldn't have prepared for that?"

Opening his coat, the young Nosferatu displayed a rusty steel breastplate that covered his front torso. *Someone had taught him well.* He shook his head at me disapprovingly before raising his leg and kicking me directly on top of the sobbing Irishman. "I know your plan," he screeched. "You wish to use the necromancer against the master."

Why would he think that I, a man of God, would use the necromancer? The Lord only granted Samael, and Samael's chosen, divine rule over the death. Anything else that dabbled with unlife was pure evil.

Meanwhile, the Irishman squeezed feebly at the spike sitting in his shoulder, wobbling in pain. He had been too wracked in his own torture to acknowledge anything else around him, ignoring even the cocked pistol sunk in water nearby.

"Sebastian said that you'll try to help the necromancer develop his gifts," squealed the porter like a wild boar trying to sing. "We can not allow it. No one should have power over the dead besides *our* kind!"

I inched my good hand towards the wood dagger jutting from the Irishman and gently began to tug at the end. His eyes flashed in anguish, but he said nothing. Gradually, the bellhop closed in on me until I could feel him blocking out the incoming winds. Somehow, I needed to pluck out the stake from the Irishman then get close enough to the bellboy for one last blow with what little energy I had left.

"Your master is lying to you," I belted, gripping on the stake. "I don't want any necromancer. Whatever you've been told is a deception. Sebastian is manipulating you in order to stop me from slaying him. You're just his pawn my child."

"No!" he exploded, spit launching from his mouth. "*You lie!*" The boy took me by my throat, drawing me towards his jaw that unhinged to twice its natural size. Using the monster's strength to help me draw the wood from the Irishman's bicep, I flung it above the beast, bridging my arm over his shoulder. With every ounce of strength left in me, and supported by the Sam's momentum, I rammed the weapon into his back. The force of my blow not only pierced through his back, but also jetted out from his armored chest, gouging lightly into my own belly.

All stood still. The boy looked down at the tip protruding from his heart, horrified. He glanced back up at me, staring with betrayal. His hand let go my neck, allowing me to land on my toes.

"I've failed him," he sniveled. Buckling to his knees, the porter looked outwards across the skyline before finally plummeting face first onto the roof. Then suddenly, the muffled wails and roars of Hell came from under his corpse. I had seen Nosferatu deaths before, but always recoiled at their violent end. *The fallen always come to collect their prize.*

His flesh began to smolder and before long, a large unnatural bonfire reached to the skies from atop of his carcass. As cold as I was, I dare not get closer. This was hellfire. It took but moments for his body to wither into nearly nothing. Only a shrunken carcass covered in ambers remained.

I turned back to the Irishman and watched as he drew a serrated boot knife. He held it up at me pathetically, too weak to try and use it.

"Please, no. I didn't want to fella', honest I didn't." Lashing at his wrist with my good hand, I squeezed with pressure under his palm, taking the knife away. I then used the heel of my foot to boot him back on his side. Grasping the knife, I returned to the boy's charred body and carved at what was once his neck. The gruesome act was exhausting, but when it was done, I spread the two parts out for the sun to claim. I then turned back to the Irishman, pointing the blade at him. I contemplated killing him outright, but could see that he was desperate. He continued to babble, trying to invent an excuse so that I would spare him. "Honest lad, he offered me ten pounds, I couldn't refuse." Kneeling beside him, I reached into his coat and drew out both my crucifix and his money purse.

"This will cost you your thirty silver pieces Judas," I said condemningly.

"Course, take it."

Placing the money in my wet belt pouch, I continued to aim at him with the knife.

"Tell me how you made it up here," I commanded. He pointed behind him, guiding me to a rooftop hatch cracked slightly open. "I'll be locking the door behind me. If you're resourceful enough, you'll find a way down." I hobbled to the hatch, then after entering, closed and latched the lock behind me. The building stairwell felt warm. Though it was soothing, by the time I made it down the four flights of stairs, the feeling in my body had returned. A deluge of pain sent me into convulsions.

"Lord, guide me," I pleaded, my arm and belly scorching with intense heat. Staggering into the streets, I dragged myself to the first inn I could find. I slammed a pound on the clerk's table, raising my eyes pathetically to an elderly woman working the counter. She was frail with a puckered mouth and aged spots along her skin.

"Please Madame, one night room and board?"

She gawked at my wounds, then nodded and took the money. She then removed herself from behind the table and hooked her body under my good arm, helping me up a set of wobbly stairs. She had brought me to the first room in the hall and laid me down on a bed. She then left momentarily before returning with a pair of dry men's work clothes, bandages, and a pail of water. Wordlessly, she helped me out of my drenched garments and into the dry ones. My mind flashed to my childhood, and for a moment, her touch felt like Mama. After I'd dried off, she bandaged me, using a moist towel to clean my wounds before tightly swathing them in dressings. Later, as I rested, the quiet innkeeper revisited with a hot kettle of tea and bread, feeding it to me slowly. After I'd eaten, she tucked me in before leaving, closing the door behind her. After hearing the lock click, I stumbled up and barricading the door with a dresser. It took sometime to relax, but as I did, questions began to swarm over me. *This night all came to pass because of my sloppy performance at that hotel. What would I do to repent?*

More worrisome still were Sam's last words. Sebastian had known he'd cursed the boy's soul and came back to claim him as a servant. He deceived the poor porter into setting up a trap for me, feeding him lies about my need for the necromancer. *Perhaps he knew about mother?*

Just like that it dawned upon me what was at hand. Paraschiva had been ordered to recover a servant that would tip the scales of power in her master's favor. If there *was* a rare mortal who could control the dead, he would have authority over all nosferatu. If Vlad recovered this human, the dark prince could expand his influence over the damned. However, if I knew Paraschiva like I thought I did, she would instead turn this necromancer against her master, finally freeing herself from his will. With my body shattered, I could only think of one way to stop this. I'd need Vasilica.

CHAPTER 12

My exhaustion had sentenced Vasilica to death. It always astounded me how fatigue influenced a man, but never in a million years did I think it would drive me to abandon my principles. Nevertheless, after a full day of investigating, a graveyard skirmish and visit to the infirmary, I'd been too fatigued to stop Davis from reporting his inaccuracies. By the end of it, we'd woven a tale that protected James and I from sounding like madmen, but condemned Vasilica to the gallows. I was ashamed, but unsure how to repair the damage.

Davis was infamous for letting others take the fall. Some of the detectives had warned me when I first partnered up with him, but I was too dyed-in-the-wool to heed their claims. Besides, I had quite the reputation myself. Certain policemen at the station had labeled me as a recluse and loner, so by no means was I going to allow gossip to sway my better judgment. Instead, I let James confirm his faults first hand, watching during our cases as he revealed his true nature.

It initially seemed innocent enough. He'd blame a thief of pinching more than they had or confiscate the belongings of a crook in favor of his own pockets. I mostly overlooked his trivial misdeeds, as his cheery demeanor was a breath of fresh air. Yet, for as much as he'd charmed me, I became a bit reserved once he'd been caught red handed taking bribes. Luckily for him, the allegations were eventually dropped and Davis was allowed to continue his crooked ways. And although he always claimed his innocence, I had developed a knack for discerning his lies.

A blistering beam of sunlight fought through the overcast of clouds, slipping between my curtains and onto my face. The heat kept me awake, boiling my skin and drying my throat. I rolled out of my chair and was assaulted by a stabbing pain in my chest. The sting quickly escalated into coughing, and before long, I was on my knees spitting up blood. *How did Catherine get through this pain?*

After pulling myself together, I checked my pocket watch and found it was nearly time for work. Hurriedly, I dressed in my camel haired suit, which was my least favorite, then ate a leftover supper from Ms. Abigail before heading to headquarters. I slipped out the gloomy building and onto the even gloomier streets. The sky wore a coat of heavy rain clouds. I tried to hurry to the Yard before the storm poured down, but it was too late. The deluge made my umbrella-less walk that much more wretched. It was a rotten kind of rain, one that stung your face and froze your body. I sprinted to the station and hurriedly signed in to the log book before sneaking to my office. I began wiggling out of my drenched clothes, freeing myself from their misery and hanging them near my office stove. Now only in my undergarments, I took a moment to check myself in the mirror. The site made me recoil.

Catherine use to claim that it was my handsome face that won her over, but I never saw it. I knew that I wasn't repulsive, especially because of my bright green eyes and strong jaw line, but never did I think that I was strikingly attractive. Today however, not only was I unsightly, but I looked more like a ghoul than a man. My bloodshot eyes blinked over a pair of plum half circles that clashed with my sallow skin. My teeth bore specs of yellow from opium and my lips hued a lurid blue.

"Ghastly," I said to myself.

Digging out a bulbous jar of *Bovril* meat paste from my desk, I spooned the meaty globs into my mouth, hoping food would bring a bit of life back into me. The taste made me gag, and I had to make a strong effort to hold it down.

Returning to the mirror after a couple more bites, I straightened my sideburns then smacked my cheeks for a bit of rose.

"My word," Davis snickered from my door, "you're hideous. " Walking in with a handful of papers, he took the liberty to welcome himself to both a chair and my meat paste.

"Don't you have an office of your own?"

"Yes I do," he said in high spirits, "but then I couldn't poke fun at you Nathan." I scampered to the coal register in my leggings, throwing another nugget of coal inside. Meanwhile Davis choked up the Bovril, spitting it into his handkerchief. "Nasty, he said between coughs. "So old boy, how do you feel today?" I rubbed the back of my head, letting the tender flesh send a scream down my spine.

"I am about as good as a worm between two bird beaks. What about you? Why are you so merry this morning?"

I briefly observed him and found that Davis had removed his bandages. He looked a bit tired, but was otherwise unchanged. I couldn't imagine how he was getting along without his bindings after all that we'd suffered through at Brompton. I'd taken half the beating that he did and felt as if I'd been ran over by a carriage. He gave me a drunkard's smile while looking down at his reports. I knew right away what he was thinking. He was proud of himself for clearing us of any misconduct, instead blaming it all on Vasilica. As far as he was concerned, the case was nearly closed.

"Maybe I met a new mistress," he suggested good-humoredly. I rolled my eyes. Davis, detecting my impatience, gave a false chuckle. "Oh come on now Nathan. You and I narrowly just escaped death. Doesn't that make you appreciate life a bit more?"

"Mmm, no," I said flatly. "Might I remind you that we have an entire day of follow-up reports and a botched investigation to continue? May I also add that we've condemned an innocent woman to death, the *very* woman whom we owe our lives to?"

"That Romanian lass?"

"Yes, Miss Ivanescu," I said while flipping my clothes on the hot metal.

"Oh, to hell with her Nathan. We had the situation handled. Moreover, allow me to refresh your memory. If it were not for her, we might have Miss McCann in custody instead of dead. The integrity of this entire investigation was nearly destroyed had we not pointed a well deserved finger at her."

"Ah, that reminds me," I cut in while putting on my damp trousers "let the boys know I'd like to take a look at Miss McCann's body before they rebury her." Davis froze, his feathers clearly ruffled. He shoved his papers onto my side of the desk before crossing his arms tightly.

"What body?" he hissed through his locked teeth. I scanned his report, rereading it in disbelief. According to the information, it seems that after we'd returned from the graveyard, Chief Inspector Swanson had sent a unit of constables to gather evidence. They arrived at the grave just after dawn only to find mounds of ash where a corpse should be. From the constables' point of view, it appeared that someone had tried to incinerate the body.

"Impossible," I muttered, "simply impossible."

"No Nathan," Davis ridiculed, "You're little Romanian lass came back and cleaned up the murder scene. Can't you see that it was her and her brother this entire time? They're murderers, and they've tried to sell us some silly fairy tale in order to get away with it all."

I remembered the vision I had because of the echo during the run-in with Miss McCann at Brompton. The man in the shadow at Jacqueline's flat was square shaped like Vasile and he'd also had a thick accent. Still, I wasn't positive that it was definitely him. I didn't have any proof, nor could I find any motive for the Ivanescus to put forth this much effort to cover up a murder. They were foreigners. All they'd have to do is leave town and we'd never be able to find them. But still they lingered.

"That's absurd," I hollered while shooting out of my seat. James clearly believed that the Romanians killed Miss McCann, proof or no proof, but I didn't know how to tell him what I'd seen in the echo. I didn't know how to tell him that I had some witch-like curse that allowed me to see into a dead person's past. Davis and I heatedly locked eyes. "None of it makes sense. There's no motive James."

"Facts, we deal in facts Nathan, remember?" I broke free from our face off and moved to my window, pacing back and forth. There was a momentary pause as I absentmindedly watched a unit of constables marching for the city. "Think about it," shouted Davis at my back. "The fact is that we have two Romanians linked to the murder of an ill young lady. One was seen in the victim's flat the night before her supposed death and the other foreigner beheaded the victim right in front of us. Both of them claim to be *witch hunters*, who according to Vasile's journal slay the wicked to protect the innocent. As far as I'm concerned, they're either really good con artists or lunatics. Either way, Miss McCann is dead because of it." Davis stopped, trying to gauge my reaction. "Tell me why that sounds absurd Nathan?"

"Now listen Davis, if we are going to investigate together, we need to be on the same bloody page. Miss McCann wanted our heads last night didn't she? I say there is more to this than we think. I do not know what yet, but it is not some damn con. Miss McCann was not just *delusional,* and our rescuer is not a murderer. Say what you will, call it a hunch, but I cannot believe that Vasilica or her brother have heinous motive. Davis, please…you have to trust my gut on this one."

"Trust your gut?" Davis contested.

"I know, I know. It is something I would never support if you argued the same, but you have to support me. Please mate, I need your help." Davis inspected me like a counterfeit coin. He seemed disgusted with me and I think I knew why. I'd made a career on hard work, details, and facts, and was now risking it all on a simple hunch. Shaking his head, he quietly chewed his lip, humming in skepticism.

"Fine Nathan, we will do it your way. I'll give you the investigation, because you've never lead me astray." I sighed in relief. "Let it be known though, if this comes back to bite me on me rump, it'll be you I blame when Swanson calls." I understood his apprehension and nodded in thanks. "I mean it Nathan, you spoil this investigation and it's you on the noose."

As exhausted as I was, an undeserving surge of determination filled inside me. Maybe we'd been too proud to indulge in the idea that this murder might actually have some bizarre roots in the unnatural. If that were the case, I knew just the person to talk to. I redressed myself in my mostly dried out suit then went to my hat rack and crowned myself in my bowler. Davis, seeing my readiness, buttoned up his coat and grabbed his cane. We gathered at the office door, my resolute glare and James's worried expression plastered to our heads. Davis tapped the tip off his shoes with his walking stick before addressing me with his stare.

"So Nathan, where to now?"

"An old friend," I said resolutely.

CHAPTER 13

I had known Marcos Bianchi II for nearly ten years, or as he liked to be called, "The Great Mago." He and his father had developed a street act in Milan, and were doing quite well for themselves until Marcos Senior lost it all in a bad hand of poker. Shortly after, the pair, who now owed a considerable amount of money to the local crime syndicate, decided that it would be in Marcos II's best interests to leave for England. He started off in London as a petty thief, using sleight of hand to steal wallets, purses and jewelry. I would occasionally bring him into the station when his robberies went sour and enjoyed his banter during our brief encounters. Soon, I began to use him as a contact on the street, a resource to help solve some of my more significant cases. Ultimately, through time, the two of us became good friends. He had an admirably dry sense of humor, and though he could sometimes be a bit too cheery, he always knew how to steal a laugh from me.

Luckily for Marcos, he was more than just a talented magician. He was also handsome and charming. I can still remember being amazed by the swarms of young lady admirers willing to bail him out of trouble whenever he needed. Ultimately, he'd used his influence over them to live a more lucrative life, graduating from petty theft to leeching off of lonely widows. To this day, I still can't understand how no one ever figured out that he was a mandrake, hiding his favor of men behind the backs of all those English women. It genuinely baffled me, but then again, I never cared one way or another so long as he didn't try to get bold with me.

Nevertheless, as time went on and fate would have it, one foggy evening, an old theatre owner down on his luck caught wind of Marcos's act and decided to join the audience. Marcos had been performing on a little stage inside a dingy brothel owned by one of his lady suitors, and acted mostly as a pleasant distraction for customers waiting on their turn with the ladybirds. Except, during this particular night, the theatre owner was mesmerized by Marcos's show and offered him a few acts a week. That was three years ago, and now *The Great Mago* can be seen twice a night in front of a packed crowd as he conjures magic and awe.

I knew very well that Marcos not only was a master of illusion, but an aficionado of the occult, and decided it would be best to catch his act before getting his opinion. We had made it for his five o'clock show, and I had hoped that the quiet time during the performance would be enough to ease the tension between Davis and me. Marcos's act took place on a dilapidated stage within the theatre district of central London. He demonstrated a number of his trademark tricks including a flying act, straightjacket, and a disappearing routine that freed him from a flaming coffin. His audience was mostly made up of young children who oozed with delight as they questioned whether somehow magic really existed. The funny thing is that was the same reason I was here.

After the show, we crept backstage, slipping by a custodian who halfheartedly guarded the breezeway. James followed behind me like a bored child forced to shop at the grocer with his mother. We knocked on Marcos's obnoxious looking door etched with a bright yellow star and waited for him to answer.

"Come in," cried out a voice with a jovial Sicilian accent. Pushing inside, Davis and I went into the dressing room where a jacketless Marcos slumped on a wooden stool. He was fixed on his shirt, yellowed with sweat, attempting to undo a cufflink marked *M.B.* with a single hand. He was black haired with stage makeup smeared across his face that made him appear exceedingly youthful. His face was thin with high cheekbones and a trademark smirk. Most fascinating however were his eyes. Deep as a well, and dark as one too, they never stood still, always nipping at their surroundings.

"Ah Nathan, I saw you in the crowd *amico*. How have you been?"

"Well enough Marcos. Thanks for asking," I said while examining his mysterious mechanisms and bizarre apparatuses resting along the walls. His dressing room had everything from iron maidens to guillotines, all of them resembling torture devices more so than props. Nearer to his dressing mirror in the back of the room however, a much different side of the *Great Mago* took shape. There was a frameless painting of a patron saint and large sermon sized cross decorating his wardrobe. I was never much of a believer, but kept it to myself in order to avoid any annoying conversations about my salvation. Marcos however, was fervent devotee, even though he'd always be considered an outcast by the church.

"And how is that wife of yours? She should be mine you know?" he teased, unwilling to disclose his true nature amongst the likes of Davis. I felt uncomfortable having to darken the mood with Catherine's death, so I did my best to downplay the bad news.

"Well, these are trying times for everyone right now Marcos," I said while trying to sound sensible. "She passed not too long ago from her consumption." Dropping his grin, Marcos leapt to his shoeless feet and embraced me, slapping my shoulder a few times before kissing each cheek. Tears shimmered from his eyes, drawing lines through his caked makeup. He drew back his head, shaking it. He must have been resolving some sort of bleak conflict in his own mind, because his expression went from gloomy to confident in seconds.

"You poor, poor man Nathan. I am so sorry."

Pulling away from our grasp, Marcos finally dignified Davis, who appeared taken aback by the Italian's flamboyant demeanor. Marcos recognized James's repugnance but offered up his hand anyway, almost challenging. With a bit of trepidation, Davis examined the open palm, eventually shaking it.

"And you must be his partner," asked Marcos.

"I am," said Davis smugly, tucking his walking cane under an arm. "Detective Sergeant James Davis." Davis only used his full name or title when he wanted to impress or strike fear in someone. It wouldn't work with Marcos.

"Well Detective," Marcos replied, undaunted by James's behavior. "I hope Nathan's the punctual one out of the two of you, because I've noticed that you don't even carry a watch!"

Marcos lifted a pocket watch with the initials J.D. etched along the back, dangling it like a pendulum. Goaded, James ripped the chained clock from Marcos's hand and tucked it in his back pocket. I tried not to titter or smile. Returning to his stool, Marcos perched on its end like an amused monkey, his knees tucked upward above his shoulders. "So, tell me why you're here Nathan, besides wanting to see the greatest magic show in London?"

"Right, let's get to it then Marcos. I need to ask you a few odd questions that I'm hoping you'll have the answers to. We are investigating a woman's possible murder and I need your advice on how she might have deceived authorities." Marcos raised a single brow.

"Go on."

"You see, the victim was pronounced dead by responding policemen, and then further examined by a physician before finally being lain to rest. Yet, just the other day, both Davis and I personally witnessed her climb out from her own grave." Marcos's eyes went wide. "She had been under the soil for days, so a simple misdiagnosis is highly unlikely as she'd have suffocated." The Great Mago tapped his groomed fingernails together, pondering over my question. This brings us to why we're here. Have you, or any of your colleagues, ever performed a magic trick like this before?'"

The Great Mago tapped his groomed fingernails together, regurgitating my question under his breath. He sat silently for a moment, apparently pondering. Then, like an oncoming train, he began to hum, slowly letting the volume grow more intense. James stared at him coldly.

"Diavolo," Marcos finally spat out.

"I'm sorry," I asked.

"Diavolo," he repeated with conviction. "Many great magicians have tried the *Buried Alive* act," he said before pausing, "All have failed. I knew a few of these men personally, top minds in the world of magic. Each of them perished one-by-one, undertaking the impossible in hopes to achieve eternal glory. For such a feat would put you on the wall of legends, immortalizing you throughout illusionist history." Marcos leaned his elbow on one knee, lamenting as he studied the floorboards. "No my friend, I know of no one who has buried themselves alive and lived."

"So it's impossible," asked Davis.

"I did not say that," Marcos bit back. "I said no one has done it and *lived*." Walking to an old bookshelf along his dressing room wall, he harvested a single green tome, bringing it to us. Flipping through the stained pages written in Italian, he pointed at a depiction that looked as if it were rendered during the Elizabethan era. It portrayed a man dressed in red robes with long blades of black hair and beady white eyes that glowed similarly to Miss McCann's. His face was hard, cruel and sensual. "Baron Victor Romero, also known as Baron Diavolo," whispered Marcos. "He was not an illusionist, but a true magician from Madrid. It is rumored that he could transform his appearance, charm the minds of men and even employ the dead."*Could Marcos be talking about the echo?* "He never aged nor did he grow sick. For it is said that this wretched man sold his soul to the devil himself in return for eternal life."

"Poppy-cock!" spat Davis. "Come on Nathan, we're wasting our time."

"Shut it," I gurgled through a film of spit in my throat. "Please Marcos, continue." Davis gave me a hard look, but I tried to ignore it, refocusing on the pages. Marcos waited for us to settle and then continued.

"But the devil never plays fair you see, and in return for such power, Victor was taxed with many great burdens, including an eternal hunger. He no longer desired the appetite of common men, instead craving the blood of other humans. He was forced to devour a pound of men's flesh each night in order to sustain his gifts." Turning the page,

Marcos's finger darted to a specific passage he must have been looking for since opening the book. "More importantly, he also needed to sleep under the earth, and is said to have ordered his men to bury him each night in the soils of Spain, only returning after the sun had settled."

A single hand painted picture hung under the foreign writing. It illustrated several wiry men all uniformed in matching tunics, lowering a rectangular coffin into a hole with vine-like ropes. It was a simple piece, most likely drawn by an untrained hand, but it told an eerie visual tale. It reminded me of the grisly scene uncovered at the gravesite and I wondered if Baron Victor Romero suffered the same fate.

"So, what happened to this Baron?" I asked apprehensively

"Unfortunately for him, the church received word of his frightening acts and commanded a pack of loyal zealots to hunt and slay him."

"But how?" I asked eagerly, half embarrassed at my own question.

"First, they pinned him to the earth, binding him to the soils with a shaft of wood. Once he was immobilized, they showered his body in the blessed waters of Jesus Christ. Afterwards, they removed his head, and then dragged both parts of his corpse out into the sun which charred his flesh to ash." My mind went back to Vasilica as she cut down Jacqueline. I glanced briefly at Davis who did not seem to share the same enthusiasm as I. He began to clap his shoe sole on the floor, bored. Marcos's eyes did not leave the book, though he obviously recognized James's impatience. My interest on the contrary, was at its peak.

"Marcos, you made mention of this Victor being able to speak with the dead. Do you know anything else about that?" James gave me a suspect look, but Marcos simply nodded.

"Of course," he said while flipping to the back of the book. "There are a few different practices, but I never took you as a man to believe in the supernatural Nathan?"

"I'm not," I defended, "But we *did* come across our lead suspect's journal which made mention of dealings with the dead. I'm curious if there's a connection."

"Ah, the legends of magic are a favorite subject of mine. Allow me to do some research. I can start tonight," he said excitedly. "I'll send you what I've found right away. Perhaps it will help you get in the mind set of this suspect. Are you still living in your old flat?"

"I am," I answered, "and it would be much appreciated."

"Can we go now Nathan?" James begged impatiently.

"Fine," I uttered, rolling my eyes. "Sorry to be brief Marcos, but it's time for us to go. " I reached to shake hands with Marcos, who scoffed at my offer and violently tugged me into a hug. He then leaned his head into my ear to whisper.

"*Sometimes there are things in this world we aren't made to understand. When that time comes, follow what's here,*" he suggested, tapping at the side of my chest just over my heart. I smiled and waved him farewell before leaving with Davis through the skinny dressing room door.

I followed James through the auditorium, taking notice of a new weight along the left side of my jacket. I dug into my breast pocket and found a compact bundle crammed between my shirt materials. Jerking it out, I discovered a hand-sized bible, no doubt smuggled into my clothing by The Great Mago.

"Now can we do some real detective work," blabbered Davis, breaking my concentration. He was prickly and petulant. I didn't know how much longer I could tolerate his snappish behavior, but I tried reminding myself of how peevish I could often be. I would need to just grin and bear it.

"Very well Davis," I said while scanning through the verses of the bible before returning it to my pocket, "You've been patient enough. I appreciate your tolerance. Now we can do it your way." James eyed the bulge along my chest, shaking his head disdainfully. Then, as if seemingly relieved that I had finally come to my senses, he eased his scowl. "So, what is the plan then?"

"Well first off, let's return to the pub under Miss McCann's flat like we had planned. I am sure if she was moaning and screaming every night for an entire week, chances are someone on the property complained to the owner. Maybe the landlord can tell us more about what tenants had to say beyond what was in the initial report. And even if he can't, maybe he'll at least confirm who that nutter, Mr. Feld, was why we found sitting outside the pub door."

Davis had always been a difficult person to deal with, but never like this. He was bitter, ego driven and confrontational. Perhaps his injuries from Brompton had caused him to become more irritable. Or maybe it was the stress of the case. Regardless, his resentment and my quick-temper were a recipe for disaster. I'd need to gather all the restraint I had in me to not shoot him. *Come Nathan, you can do this.*

"Suit it yourself Davis. You lead and I'll

CHAPTER 14

I could tell James was still frustrated by our visit to Marcos, as we'd wasted a good part of our day on my inclinations. Truth be told, I was starting to not care anymore. We were going two different directions on the case, and while I knew my theories were starting to sound flimsy and impractical, Davis's stubborn speculations and finger pointing didn't resemble detective work in the least. It was clear that all he wanted to do was mold any evidence around the Ivanescus' guilt, as if they were architects behind some grand plot.

James and I avoided talking about the case during our walk, as the tension between us had already become a bit too much. We kept the subjects of our discussions trivial, trying to mend our rapport by criticizing articles in the morning newspaper. By the time we arrived at the pub it was early evening. The establishment was already busy with workless men, their mollishers and even a few children that the factories used to squeeze between tight machinery for repairs. We bound for the bar immediately, paying no mind to the rowdy looking crowd and asked the middle-aged fellow behind the tavern-wood if he knew Mr. Giles Goodwin, landlord of the building.

"*I* am Giles Goodwin," replied the barkeep matter-of-factly. The man had a sort of facade about him that heralded *old soul*. He had grizzled blonde hair that receded partially up his scalp, making his jutted forehead appear powerful and large, like a ram. There were thick, deep creases along his brow and a pair of crow's-feet that raked along his light blue eyes. He was clean cut with a double chin and smooth rounded nose. As intensely palpable as his features were, he was still rather handsome for an older man and moved about with a refined poise. Though he dressed in black laborer's clothes, they were custom tailored, and fit rather well. He came across more as a traveling musician than a barkeep.

"Well Mr. Goodwin," said Davis, taking the lead in our conversation, "I am Detective Sergeant James Davis and this is my," he paused, "this is Detective Sergeant Nathaniel Brannick."

Now he's refusing to call me partner? Clearly, there was a larger breach in our relationship then I had presumed. I tried not to give notice as James continued.

"We are investigating the recent murder of Miss Jacqueline McCann and were hoping you could help sew up a few unanswered questions."

"What type of questions?" asked Mr. Giles briskly while flipping a wet rag over his shoulder. The cloth was smattered with what looked like brandy. I peaked behind us and noticed we were getting more of the patrons' attention than I was comfortable with. They looked frustrated that a couple of policemen were in their place of refuge, and threatened James and I with hostile glares. I tried to act indifferent, returning my interest to Mr. Goodwin, but truth be told I was a bit nervous. James removed his porkpie hat and continued to speak, unknowing of the growing danger behind us.

"I am sure that the days before her death," James said to Giles, "you received a great many complaints about the victim's obsessive wailing from other tenants. Was there anything in particular that seemed out of the ordinary in their claims?"

Mr. Goodwin took a moment for himself. I could see the gears grinding inside his head, but he didn't care to share with us exactly what he was thinking. He watched Davis as if the two were playing one another in a chess match, each carefully choosing his next move. However, instead of giving a direct answer, Mr. Giles just crossed his arms and winced.

"Well, if you're going to ask such an intimate question, don't be rude about it. Order a drink first. What can I get you?" James looked to me. I waved my hand, passing on the offer. As I did, Giles regarded the birth mark on my arm, following the red cross with his eyes. Meanwhile, typical Davis, as anticipated, accepted.

"Do you carry William Younger and Co.," he asked. Giles gave him a nasty glower before shaking his head no. "Fine, whatever stout or grog you recommend then."

Mr. Goodwin took a tall glass and put it under a barrel tap. Pouring out bronze ale, he waited for the foam to settle before putting it in front of Davis. James slowly went for his purse, delaying his action a bit while waiting for Mr. Goodwin to offer it up free of charge. Giles smirked as he watched James's hesitant hand reaching into his coat.

"First one is free," he said with an amused snicker. I could hear the regulars stridently murmuring behind us. Their voices were angry and sharp, whipping at our backs. "And so is the answer to your question. *No*, there was nothing obvious that stuck out about the many, many stories I heard from my tenants. However, I did put a few things together myself. On the final day she was seen alive, a few of my tenants confirmed that Miss McCann had been visited by not one, but two separate men, neither whom looked familiar. The first was an odd young chap who came just after dusk. According to some of my customers, this boy was dressed all in black with a telegram in hand, which is funny, because it was the only hand he had. The youngling had one arm you see, and used it to deliver Miss McCann a message."

My heart dropped. The one armed boy from my flat had been here. I thought back to the letter found in Miss McCann's bedroom.

"As surely as you received this letter from my manservant, tonight you shall hear these same sentiments from my very own tongue."

We must have been onto something. I looked to Davis who had a bemused expression on his face. He refused to dignify my stare, but I knew he sensed my ogling.

"Who was the second person," he blabbed, trying to move along the conversation. The screech from a drawn chair along the wood floor cried behind us. One of the brawnier men in the pub had stood up a, as if infuriated by James's question. He had massive arms that bulged out of his pulled up sleeves and gritted coffee teeth that matched his suspender fastened trousers. Luckily, his lady friend took his hand and pulled him back down. Giles seemed to take notice, but paid the incident no mind.

"The second," he said, bringing his interest back to us, "Was some sort of foreigner. He wore a silly fur hat and had a large mustache. He was seen yelling at the poor girl from the window side. I tried telling the constables that both the visitors were equally suspicious, but they did not want to listen to me. They were transfixed on the mustached man, scribbling away carelessly at anything I could tell them about him. I could have said that he lay with their mothers nightly and the fools would have just continued to unwittingly jot it down." An uncontrollable grunt came from my belly. Our friend Mr. Goodwin had quite the cheeky sense of humor. James though, took insult to the remark and began to intolerantly stir his head at Giles.

"That was not very nice Mr. Goodwin. Those constables are my men," Davis bit, as if he had any real respect *or* authority over the London police staff. Giles motioned with his shoulders.

"Sorry," he said sneeringly, deficient of any chagrin, "didn't mean any harm."

Awkwardness took a stool at the bar next to us. James and Mr. Goodwin had somehow struck a disliking to one another. I tried to cleanse the unease by asking additional questions.

"Mr. Goodwin, a few days ago Detective Sergeant Davis and myself were leaving Miss McCann's flat when we ran into a rather odd fellow studying the interior of your pub from the front glass." Giles ears perked up. "After a brief conversation with the fellow, we found that his name was a Mr...,"

James looked down at his unsheathed notebook, rattling off the name, "Mr. Erni Feld. Does the name ring a bell?"

Mr. Goodwin went silent and his face lost all color. For the first time since meeting the landlord, I saw some emotion wake up in him. In spite of this, I could not gage whether he was nervous that a stranger had been peering into his establishment or if the name, Mr. Erni Feld, aroused some type of dreadful memory. He swallowed a lump in his throat before finally addressing the question.

"Did you say that someone named Mr. Erni Feld was having a look about my pub?"

"Yes," I said simply.

Mr. Goodwin ducked under his bar. I went to my toes in order to have a better look at was he was doing. He leaped back up a few seconds later with a stack of newspapers in his hands and dropped them down by James's drink. After untying the twine that held the papers together and removing the top two publications, he swiveled his finger along the front page of a daily and pointed at a smaller article. The title read…

"Lunatic Escapes Asylum after Faking His Own Death"

Bethlem Asylum staff are baffled as to how a patient, Mr. R.M. Renfield, escaped from their facility last night. Guards reported that during the late evening they found Renfield on the floor of his room, injured and gasping for air. Bethlem guards rushed the patient to an onsite doctor, and although the house physician put forth his best effort, Mr. Renfield's wounds were too severe and he apparently succumbed to his injuries.

However, just minutes after staff returned from putting the final touches on his casualty report, they returned to find Mr. Renfield's body missing. After a major lockdown of the building and full search by asylum personnel, staff discovered that the patient had faked his death and escaped. The lunatic feigned his own demise by ingesting a combination of collected sedatives that helped slow down his heart. After waking from his unconscious state, Mr. Renfield found his way to the employee dressing hall where he stole staff members' personal clothing and keys. Once he was disguised and had full access to every locked door , he slipped through a set of side exits and retreated into the London streets.

Mr. R.M. Renfield is considered deranged and extremely dangerous. He is tall with blackened whiskers, long hair and a half torpid face. It is assumed that he will most likely attempt to flee the city, though some believe that he may try to outwait authorities, holding off until they call off their search. Several witnesses have spotted R.M. Renfield outside of the asylum and claim that he has used the alias, Mr. Erni Feld. If readers have any information about the lunatic, they are asked to contact the Metropolitan Police Department immediately.

I was embarrassed. We'd allowed an escaped maniac to go free. If James and I wanted to redeem ourselves, we'd need to try and find this R.M. Renfield with what little information we had. Beyond the address he'd provided, there wasn't much to go on. I asked James for the notebook with R.M. Renfield's home number, and after looking it over, tried to think of a way to trace the location in a hurry.

"Mr. Goodwin," I called out, "I noticed there was a line wired to the back of the building. Is there by chance a way to send a telegraph from this building?" Mr. Goodwin nodded.

"I have a machine in the back. I'm quite fond of them. It was a pretty penny to have one installed, but I think it's worth it." He nudged his noise upwards towards a door at the rear of the room. "If you know how to use one, you're welcomed to it. Be careful though, my dog Amaethon is somewhere back there in the clutter."

I smiled in appreciation then followed the lane between the bar and patron tables, directing myself to the hind entrance. Pushing inside, I could smell the strong scent of leather oil from the back parlor and noticed several large crates strewn across a messy room. A single candlestick flickered along the frame of a boarded up window. The wax rod barely gave off any light, and as I guided myself through heaps of shadowy casks and stacked bottles, I suddenly heard a shuffling.

A bulging, egg shaped head protruded from the bottom of one of the crates, its skull almost flat from ear to ear. It had unique triangular eyes which were small, dark and deep-set. Its white body was full and round, with robust shoulders and a very muscular tail.

"You must be Amaethon," I said to the dog. The animal patted toward me with a jaunty gait, as if it were the gladiator of the canine race. It sniffed at me briefly, then, unimpressed, turned back around and sprawled out onto its homemade bed inside an empty wood box. After ensuring my safety, I continued my search, hopping from clearing to clearing.

Finally, I spotted the telegraph machine along the south wall. It was a square box frame with gears, pegs and a rotating drum protruding from its top. Though it was far more advanced then the one I'd been trained to use as a sailor, it looked as if it operated similarly. Before long, I was on an open line of communication with headquarters, and after transmitting the WRU code, I found that I was speaking with Falamas.

"Falamas," I typed while resting on top of a stiff wood crate, *"This is Detective Sergeant Nathaniel Brannick. I need you to check an address in the archives for me. It is for a new suspect in our case."*

As I transmitted the address, a sudden pang of guilt struck at me. I remembered that James and Mr. Goodwin were outside waiting in each other's company. I half expected to come out to find the pair strangling each other. Then again, it was worth it. This address might give us our next clue and bring me to my one armed boy. I began to search the room out of boredom. As my eyes corrected themselves to the candlelight, I made out a chalked rendering along the posterior wall. It was a single circle with two vertical lines across the center. I began to wonder why the emblem had been drawn, but before I could dive too deeply, Falamas returned my message. It read…

"You try me too far Detective Sergeant. The address you have provided is the Bethlem Asylum for the Mentally Insane."

"Damn," I hollered. I typed a quick apology then ended the transmission. The frustration sent my veins pleading for opium. When I finally calmed down, I left the backroom to find Davis fixed on a second drink. I approached him and returned the notebook.

"It's time for us to leave."

"Did you find anything?" asked James.

"Nothing good. The address Mr. Renfield gave us is for the Asylum. It is a dead lead." James said nothing. Instead, he polished off his drink and made way to the exit. Mr. Goodwin waved us off mockingly.

"Goodbye Detectives. We'll miss you," he said phlegmatically, causing his customers to laugh in unison. I ignored the bunch, even though their sniggers struck at my pride.

For the remainder of our shift, Davis and I went through the details of the investigation as we walked across London. We spoke about the graveyard and the Ivanescues, but couldn't seem to agree on any one thing. We were at a standstill. I tried my hardest to think rationally, but nothing seemed to add up. We were involved in something beyond my limits, which frightened me. After spending the remainder of our shift turning over previously turned-over stones, the two of us finally called it a night.

"Want me to walk you the rest of the way home old boy," I offered. Davis waved me off.

"No need," he jawed coldly, "here comes the barred wagon." James whistled to a constable who was steering a nearby police carriage on the main road. The driver tugged the reigns, recognizing Davis, and steered towards us.

"Davis, what's gotten into you lately?"

"I could ask the same Nathan. Monsters, banshees and witch hunters! I think the stress of Catherine's disposition has worn you thin."

His words plowed up a fury in me that had been buried for far too long. I swung a wild hay-maker, my leathered glove slapping along James's cheek from where knuckle met fat. A lavender mark emerged from his face. Holding his jaw with one hand, he stared at me, hell bent, debating whether to exchange blows.

"You know what," he blabbered through his fingers. "You *have* lost it. Consider our partnership over. Come tomorrow you go your way and I will go mine until this ridiculous investigation is over. Then I'll be requesting that we're never partnered again." The police horses clanked their hooves until they halted beside us. The constable steering was unaware of what had just taken place.

"Sir," said Constable Callahan to me as James climbed aboard, "might I offer you a hand up."

"No thanks," I said, lifting up my coat collar, "think I'll walk."

CHAPTER 15

I slept for what felt like days, haunted by nightmares of the porter. Finally, a sudden heavy drag of wood at my door woke me up. It was a burly old man pushing at the furniture I'd barricaded the entrance with. He was stocky with a ferocious glare, wearing tan trousers, a matching jacket, and dirty undershirt.

"Good afternoon lad," he said brutishly. His shaved head and crooked teeth made him look like a ferocious crocodile. "My wife says you came in pretty battered up last night. I came to see if you were still breathing."

"I did not know you're wife could speak," I said softly while sitting up, still in excruciating pain.

"Can't, she's a mute. But she communicates in other ways."

He shoved into my room, brusquely ripping the blankets from on top of me before grabbing at my arm. The tender bones under my wound howled in agony, prompting me to curse uncontrollably in my native tongue.

"Now hold still or I won't be able to change your bindings ya'-nutter." The old hooligan unwrapped my bandaged and crooned, appalled at his findings. "Looks like the wife was able to push your bone back in, but the wound is infected. What happened to you? Get done over by some muggers or something?"

"No," I protested, "I ran into an old acquaintance that had some unfinished business with me."

"It serves you right then, an eye for an eye."

He had a grass colored bottle in his hands with an inscription that I couldn't read. The rim was stained a rusty orange. He opened it up and trickled a few droplets onto my wound, igniting a sopping torment that sent my forearm into convulsions.

"Stay still you skirt or you'll muck this all up." The smell of the liquid was sharp and pungent. After letting the liquid dry, he tightened strips of old bed sheet into a tourniquet, allowing the limb to rest in the sling and dangle painlessly over my chest. "Now I don't know what trouble you're in," he said loutishly, "but I don't want you here another night. My wife has a big heart, but not I. The only reason I'm helping is because I saw what you paid."

"Please sir," I said through my clinched teeth, "I beg you by God's mercy- let me stay one more night. I need rest before I carry on with my work. You see, I am..." I paused momentarily, uncertain of what I should disclose to the innkeeper. My thoughts raced back and forth, but ultimately, I decided not to be ashamed by my tasks. "I'm on a charge from God to eradicate the spawns of Satan."

The old man stared at me vacantly, blinking a few times in an uncomfortable silence before finally opening his mouth again to speak.

"That's it, get out!" he hollered. "You damn foreigner, you've lost the plot!"

He hauled me up from the bed by my collar with one arm, and grabbed my belongings with the other, jabbing them into my stomach. Carrying me like luggage, the brute hurled my body out of the room, and into the hallway. I tumbled helplessly, too exhausted to try to fight back. I scampered from the corridor, hopping into my leggings and boots before making it to the clerk's desk in the lobby. There, with tears in her eyes, the old maid who had taken me in waited. She covered her mouth in shame as I hobbled into my last boot, retreating from her husband who followed close behind. He stomped down the stairs and violently pointed at the door.

"I said out! Go back to the funny farm." I bowed my head briefly to the hostess, thanking her for her hospitality before shambling into the streets.

London lay silently in a coat of mist, hiding anything more than a few meters away. My body, still weak from battle, felt weighed down by imaginary chains. I limped at a dead man's pace, ignoring the gawking street folk who must have presumed I was a blundering drunk. *Is this what Jesus felt like during his final hours? Persecuted by the Jews and derided by the Romans.* Finally, after a grueling hike through the foggy avenues, I arrived at the inn that Vasilica and I first visited upon arriving to London.

The small building was family owned, and for less than seven-pence, one could buy themselves a suitable meal. The innkeeper, a portly woman with deep-set lips, a bulbous nose and a pebble sized wart on her chin, chopped at some onions behind the bar. I limped to a stool nearby, and with a fraction of my nine pounds confiscated from the Irishman, purchased some hot stew, bread, and tea. I huddled over the bar for sometime, nourishing my crippled body until I could muster the strength to exchange any dialogue.

"My dear lady," I said between a cough, holding my breath to restrain from choking, "did a rare looking woman with salt colored hair perhaps leave a note or message for me?"

The innkeeper shook her blubbery jowls, letting a string of drool escape her rotted mouth as she opened it to speak.

"Oh, yes. I was wondering when someone would come asking for it. She dropped it off yesterday. I was nearly tempted to open it myself." The fat woman stampeded her way to small drawer, uncovering an envelope stained in wine and broth. She wiped off a few crumbs from the top, and then held it up in the lantern light before wobbling back to me. "Yes, that's the one. Sorry, it's a little colored from a scuffle last night."

I gave the barkeep a few extra coins for her troubles, and then proceeded to remove the note from its envelope, reading it over my bowl of onion stew. It read in Romanian, scribed in my sister's handwriting.

Buna ziua my dearest brother,
I am sorry if my disappearance has frightened you. I am well and in good spirits. Perhaps I should start by first explaining that the mysteries of God are sometimes not for us mortals to comprehend. You see, the night before last, a messenger from the Lord visited me, vowing to help reunite us, and more importantly, guide us to Paraschiva. This angel herded me to your location in Tottenham, but by the time I arrived, it was too late. You'd already fled from your safe house, chased off by a pair of detectives.

I concealed myself amongst the locals and followed the investigators as they made their way with your belongings to London police headquarters. Within my short time of gathering intelligence, I learned that the men believed you guilty of murdering a young woman by the name of Jacqueline McCann. Most upsetting, it seems that people claim seeing you in this woman's home just hours before her death. I knew that this was obviously a plot conspired by one of the nosferatu, but how I would prove it to investigators seemed more difficult. I also knew that if this woman was killed by undead, then it was only a matter of time before the curse reawakened her. With little time to spare, I was forced to act a bit more reckless than usual. I used a trio of local men to help me hunt down one the detectives so that I could persuade him into seeing the truth. While I was able to speak with him, his unwillingness to believe that you were innocent left me no other choice than to invite him to the resurrection of the so called victim.

Miss McCann lay beneath the soils when the detectives arrived at her gravesite. In time, their patience allowed them the privilege of watching her unholy return. While I believe her rebirth helped convince at least one of the detectives of your innocence, it also cost us dearly. Because before I could stop the spawn from carrying out any violence, she poisoned the fat investigator with her venomous fangs. Though I was able to send her to final judgment, it was not without consequence, as the tainted policeman refused to let me help prevent his transformation.

As for the other detective, the angel confided in me that he will play an important role soon. While I want to share with you as to why he will be of value, such details must wait until we meet in person. Know only that with his help, we will

finally put an end to not just Paraschiva, but all of the nosferatu. I will visit him again soon, and it is my desire to arrange for you both to convene. I will return to this inn each evening as we'd planned, near midnight or so. Be here my brother, we are closer now than we have ever been.
Sincerely,
Vasilica

I clutched the letter in my hand, pondering its contents as I let myself thaw out. I was pleased that sister and I would be reunited soon, and even more excited that the end seemed near. Yet for what it was worth, my body was still broken. I sat in agony, fighting back tears produced by my tender back, unsteady legs, and cracked forearm. I had little willpower left in me to remain conscious, and so I tapped at the dirty bar top in order to summon the barkeep.

"Done with your stew then?" she asked, taking the bowl away from under my face. "You hardly touched it."

"My lady," I called out while picking out four shilling from my pocket and placing them on the wood. "Do you perhaps have any vacancy upstairs?" The bar maid gave it some thought while burping a foul stench. She then slid the coins from the table top and between her jiggling breasts.

"Ha, place is empty. It doesn't get busy until night. You can have your pick of any room you want."

"Whichever is closest," I moaned. She handed me a key with a large wood block roped to the bottom then pointed upwards to a set of stairs.

"Take the first one to the right."

"And Miss," I added, balancing myself out of my chair. "If the salt haired woman comes again, let her know I'm merely resting and will be down soon."

I handed over one more coin, unsure of its value, and then shambled towards the steps. It took me minutes to do what should have only taken seconds, but finally I made it up to the second floor. I ignored the mice scurrying across my feet and made it to my door. Turning the key, I found a space no bigger than a privy, with baby blue walls and a dripping moldy ceiling. The smell of moth eggs sickened my stomach, and as I slipped into the cold bed still clothed, a stench of expired sweat permeated from the bedding. As soiled as the room appeared, it took but a few brief moments after laying for my eyes to grow heavy, sending me off into a pain ridden sleep.

I dreamed that I was attending Vasilica's wedding back in our hometown of Sibiu. The small ceremony took place within a garden behind our church. Her groom was adorned in black full plate armor and had a hood that covered his face. He carried a nearly snuffed out candle in one hand and a shield in the other. As I looked upon the visitors, I found a most frightening gathering had come to bear witness. While most of the assembly was foggy and faceless, there was a young soldier in attendance who whispered to a rotten corpse, its absent lips grinning a terrible smile at my sister. Behind the pair, was a woman hidden in a slate gown with matching veil. She was crying, as if at a funeral, though no one seemed to pay attention. I turned to my sister, who winked at me before removing the hood of her new husband. Underneath was a skull that she leaned into and kissed.

Not long after dozing off though, did a rapping come at my inn door. Nearly paralyzed, I gathered what strength remained in me and lurched to my feet. The sunlight from the bedroom window had diminished, and only a weak orange glow from the gas lantern outside my chamber remained. I shuffled to the rotten door and tugged it open. To my delight, there in dim corridor was Vasilica. She wore an English style gown that I had never seen her in before and appeared more radiant than ever.

"My dear brother," she hailed me, using an early form of Romanian I'd never heard her speak before. "Thank God I found you. I was so worried." She held out her arms, and soon we were locked in embrace. Her grip was tight, and as she squeezed me closer to her, I could feel my breath escape from my lungs. My bones throbbed with pain. She must have been feeling better because her strength seemed renewed.

"Easy sister, my arm has been ravaged by one of Paraschiva's minions." Her eyes peered at my sling. She sniffed at it, studying the odor as if recognizing the aroma.

"It's infected."

"You can tell?" I asked curiously. "I smell nothing."

"Worry not, I'll tend to it."

She shut the door behind her. I searched the room for something to use as a fresh bandage, but before I could find anything, Vasilica firmly grabbed at my chin. She forced my gaze upward into her deep, dark pupils. Her temples bent and forehead twisted. "Trust me my brother. I would never steer you wrong. Now, listen to what I tell you." Her words were imposing and uncharacteristic. Yet, as confusing as she was, I listened. "You will go to Scotland Yard and turn yourself in for the murder of Miss McCann. You will tell the police that you and Miss McCann were involved in a love affair that left you broken hearted. It was too much for you to bear and in an uncontrollable rage-you set out to her home where you poisoned her with wolf's bane."

I was baffled as to why my sister would instruct me to turn myself in. I tried to wriggle free from her arms, vexed by her behavior.

"And why would I do that Vasilica?"

She drew back, shrinking in confusion. I couldn't understand why. Her head then tilted sideways, studying me, and then the crucifix hanging around my neck. A glistening sheen came from her mouth. I narrowed my eyes, examining her lips. She took notice and voluntarily opened her jaws. There in a perfect menacing row was a set of teeth that could be forged from no other place than the depths of hell.

"Ah, true faith," she spat degradingly. "Fine, we'll do this the hard way."

Lashing at my collar, she curled her fingers around my neck, lifting me off the ground. *I had been tricked again.* This beast was none other than the great Paraschiva, a wolf in sheep's fleece. My life, now gripped in the midst of her razor sharp talons, was about to end. The Queen squeezed at my throat, crushing my windpipe. Her face transformed from my sister's soft features to a striking fair-haired fiend with sallow flesh, sapphire eyes, and a faultless splendor. I fought to curse her with my last breaths, but began losing consciousness. My vision blurred and my body numbed until it finally all shut down. There, within a meager tavern room in London, I was defeated. The hunter had become the prey.

CHAPTER 16

It was a bloody miserable day. One that makes you wish you could switch places with some wealthy woman's dog, nestled by the fire all day, eating up scraps. Fog darkened my flat's windows, stealing time in its blurred haze. If not for my trusted pocket watch, I would have missed work by half a day. After last night's argument with Davis, I was so troubled that it took several hours with the pipe to nurse me back to par. I'd embarrassed myself with my temper, destroying a good partnership, and even better friendship. Surprisingly, despite the fact that I went overboard with opium, I still managed to find the motivation to get ready for work.

I crawled out of my chair and began to wash up. My chest was heavy and my body worn. Somehow, Ms. Abigail had slipped into my flat during the night, and left me breakfast. It wasn't much more than homemade bread with jam, but it helped me feel better. It pained me to have to go into headquarters, but I'd already missed several weeks when Catherine was ill, and the money I owned was far too excessive. Unless I wanted to end up in debtors' prison, I needed to make every payment from now on.

I buried my stress as deep as possible before retreating into London's streets. The mists outside were surreal, ominous and foreboding, like an earthbound purgatory. I walked the desolate avenues as they threatened to provoke my ever growing state of hopelessness. It took a bit longer to plot my course, but once I arrived, I did my best to avoid going near Davis's office. Falamas worked the counter inside the *Back Hall,* and upon seeing me, stood from his chair in confusion.

"Nathan, what are you doing here? I thought you and Davis were coming in late?"

"What on earth are you talking about?" I asked while signing in my time.

"Last night, Davis came back to the station and said he was going to be working into the late hours of the night. He wanted me to inform Swanson of his tardiness this morning and assured that he was not absent due to lack of obligation." Falamas peeled back a page from our sign in log, pointing at Davis's signature. "See, he didn't sign out until almost four in the morning. He says the case was nearing a close. I assumed that the two of you were onto something?"

I took a moment to ponder why the laziest man in the London Metropolitan Police Force would stay so late for work. I assumed it had to do with my behavior from last night. James was now bound and determined to solve the case by himself. If so, he was going to try his best to make sure that nothing appeared out of the ordinary while at the same time pinning everything on the Ivanescus. Not wanting to lose face in front of Falamas, I decided to play along until I could figure out James's motives.

"Ah, yes. Davis is working the late shifts whereas I'm covering the early ones until we solve this. We are close," I said with false enthusiasm, closing the records log, "*real* close."

Moments later, I found myself at my desk, and after warming up by the furnace, took a few minutes to review the case files. From a practical perspective, which is what Davis would outline in his report, the facts were clear. Police uncovered the body of a Miss Jacqueline McCann one November morning inside her flat. Initially, authorities presumed that the victim had simply passed from consumption, a disease she'd recently been diagnosed with. In spite of this, because of the defensive position that her corpse was found in, and linking evidence of a violent lover named Vasile Ivanescu, a more fastidious inspection was conducted.

Remarkably, as police continued to look into the matters, they inadvertently stumbled across a very much alive Miss Jacqueline McCann, who was found digging herself out from her own grave. Somehow, she had been misdiagnosed and buried alive. The girl was in shock, and as responding officers tried to contain her, the sister of the lead murder suspect interjected. Vasilica Ivanescu butchered the young Miss McCann in front of authorities, eluding them and escaping from the scene of the crime. After responding police left the murder site to report their findings, Vasilica quickly returned and removed any evidence which may have been left behind. When police revisited the gravesite to collect the body, they found only mounds of finely grained ash. The murderer had burned Miss McCann's corpse into dust.

Blimey! How could I be so daft? If Davis reported the false, but ever so practical account, the entire force would think I was mad. All the signs pointed to the Romanians. Yet, my instincts protested. Obviously, I couldn't deny that I've had experiences with the echo that were unexplainable, but they were limited and trifle. What I saw at the cemetery was different. It was bigger. How was I going to convince my superiors that Davis was wrong, when I could hardly believe it myself? Yet, for all the doubt that lingered, it was clear that certain details didn't make sense. For example, what motive would the Ivanescus have to mastermind such an intricate plot, and why would they be foolish enough to linger around London afterwards?

I tried to come to my senses and decided to allow my idle speculations to wane so I could get back to work. There must be something that I'd looked over. Something that would help the entire case makes more sense. Luckily, with Swanson being preoccupied with the body found in the Thames, I had a bit of time to get my facts right. I made arrangements to borrow one of headquarters' carriages so I could revisit the gravesite of Jacqueline. Before I could leave though, the irksome voice of Lord Wilhelm Frederick suddenly came drumming in my head.

"Logic is only as obliging as men allow it to be."

Frustrated, I went into my office closet and pulled out my field equipment bag. Perhaps his scientific methods could be of some use. Plus, I was getting desperate. Maybe I could try to test some of the ash around the grave. After packing it into the carriage, I harnessed a pair of horses from the stable and left for Brompton.

It was early afternoon, and visitors still lingered on the green cemetery grounds. They tainted its fresh features with their drab mourners' cloths like plague sores on the skin. I tied up the horses near the gates and headed towards the burial lot. The earth was still wet and I had to slosh through fields of muddy grass in order to get to Jacqueline's grave. However, what I didn't realize is that there would be someone waiting for me that would be better than any clue.

London's number one murderer on the loose, Vasilica Ivanescu, perched on the headstone, praying in Latin. She looked grief stricken. I waited for her to finish while thinking of some sort of way to rule her out as a swindler. I took inventory of what was in my crime kit. Suddenly, a plot brewed in my head. Though her gentle features, petite body, and *most* importantly, colorless locks drew a picture of someone incapable of committing anything so heinous as murder, I reminded myself of her little hands grasping her blade as she savagely hacked up Miss McCann. Guilty or not, she was a vicious killer, poisonous fruit to be left on its branch.

"Indulgeo mihi Abbas?" I asked aloud in Latin. She turned and smiled.

"And why must *He* forgive?"

"For falsely condemning the innocent," I said while inching closer. I placed my hand on her shoulder, clearing my throat before adding candidly, "Didn't I?" I hoped she wouldn't try to break my wrist or stab me for being so bold. Luckily, all she did was clutch my knuckles, holding my fingers with hers. A silence came over us as we lay in thought, our hands still firmly clasped together. My plan was coming together. "Vasilica, if the authorities get a hold of you or your brother, you'll hang. Let me help."

I pulled my hand away from her shoulder and offered it again palm up so she could use it to stand. She grabbed it and pushed her body forward as to return to her feet. But just before she gained her balance, I pretended to stumble backwards, thrusting her into my arms. As she fell upon me, I plucked a single hair from her head, palming it in my coat pocket. She smelled like sweet flowers and her body was soft and delicate. *My God, I missed having a woman touch me.* I steadied myself so we could both stand, apologizing for my blunder. She took her finger and pressed it along the bruise on my temple.

"It seems you're still weak from your injuries Detective Brannick."

"It appears I am."

"Listen, I know you feel terrible for what has happened," she said as she straightened out her clothes, "but we must focus on what's most important. There are darker forces at hand that need to be dealt with and I will need you to do so." She was standing intimately close to me, like Catherine use to just before we kissed. Guilt-ridden, I drew back until Vasilica was no longer within arms length. I tried not to draw any attention, wandering to the headstone and reading it over.

Jacqueline McCann, it read plainly. Her former employer, who from the looks of things didn't know much about her, had donated the monument.

"Why would anyone want to murder someone who is already dying?" I asked.

"Do you *really* want to know Inspector Brannick? Are you tired of the denial you have put yourself through?" She asked daringly.

"Nathan, you can just call me Nathan now."

"Okay *Nathan*. Do you think you're ready for the truth?"

"Yes," I said with uncertainty, "of course." Vasilica gave a look of doubt. I was undeniably skeptic, but down to my last bullet and out of guesses. If Vasilica had any insight, as inexplicable as it may be, I'd bite. She watched me as I pretended to reevaluate her invitation. I needed to gain her trust. "Yes. I'm sure of it. I most definitely want to know the truth," I said more confidently.

"We'll see."

Vasilica beckoned me to follow her out of the cemetery and soon the two of us were back on Fullham Road. My carriage waited nearby.

"Are these yours?" she asked while looking at the harnessed police horses.

"Yes they are. Care for a ride?" Vasilica wandered to the nearest steed and pet its roan neck.

"Ah, Italian heavy drafts, they're a favorite of mine." The beast huffed its nose as Vasilica went to pet it. She leaned her head on its shoulder, seemingly comforted by the creature. "So, is this a trick to capture me and take me to the authorities?" she asked while looking at the barred windows of the cart.

"Tell you what," I said reasonably, "if you want, you can take the reins. I'd be glad to sit in the cart. The only stipulation is that you'll have to disguise yourself in the constable uniform I have inside. Remember," I reminded her in a dry, yet in jesting tone, "you're a wanted woman."

I pulled out the spare long coat and custodian helmet that one of the boys left in the carriage and handed them to her, attempting to hide my bemused smirk. She stared at the garb like it was a dead kitten, sighing before forcing herself in the cotton blues. Once dressed, I examined her, and after popping her collar to hide her velvet face, took a step back. The disguise would work, as ridiculous as it seemed. Unable to fight my laughter any longer, I let out a wet snort.

"Are you enjoying yourself Nathan?"

"Not a bit."

I loaded into the back and made myself comfortable. I could hear the slap of leather on the horses' rears, then a stern shout that helped kick the entire carriage forward. I peeked out to ensure she was concentrating on the road before finalizing my plan. If what her brother's journal claimed was true, than Vasilica's unusual shade of hair was natural and untreated. Lord Wilhelm Frederick's advanced organic science lessons were finally going to be useful.

I opened the leather kit I'd purchased for Wilhelm's class so many years ago and began taking out the lab tools. I placed Vasilica's white strand into a glass beaker and added a splash of silver nitrate. Remarkably, the dull silver chemical transformed the hair from white to shiny platinum. According to my old notes, this meant that traces of melanin were present, meaning her hair was natural. I continued to follow my journal, trying to find any residue at the bottom of the beaker, but could find nothing. This ruled out hair coloring, as the potent nitrate would wash off the paint, making it curdle like spoiled milk.

At first, my conclusions made me feel as if I'd accomplished something momentous. But as I mulled it all over, I realized that all I'd really done was determined that Vasilica's hair was indeed its natural color. My joy diffused into disappointment. *Call me short-sighted if you must, but science has no place on the field of criminal investigations.* Frustrated, I squeezed the kit between the carriage bars and hurled it out onto the road.

"Keep your methods Lord Frederick," I whispered to myself. "I'll solve this one as I always do."

It was already getting dark due to the short autumn days by the time the carriage stopped. When it did, I found that we were in front of a rundown inn. It was located near the factory house by the built railway ballasts. I could tell from the pedestrians nearby that this was the slums before I even stepped out to discover the street names.

"This is where I find the truth?" I asked hesitantly. Vasilica frowned, handing over the reins to a horse hand that had run over from the stagecoach next door. She overpaid with a shilling, and then grabbed my hand, tugging me towards a door.

"It would be good for you to shut up for once."

We entered the dank inn together, where a rather fat woman I recognized as *Runaway Annie* worked the bar. She was wanted for pick pocketing several drunkards at another tavern close to central London. Annie immediately spotted me and began nervously fidgeting with herself, unsure how to behave.

"Sergeant Brannick, um, how good to see ya'," she greeted with a false cheer, wiping the nervous sweat from her mustached lip as we took a seat at the bar. "Wha'can I get ya'?"

"The money you stole from a thousand men you mutcher," I said spitefully. Annie's eyes grew big. "And it's Detective Sergeant."

"I'm a reformed citizen now Detective Sergeant," Annie replied. "I escaped the social evils of bein' a fallen woman long ago." She kept her gaze low, toying with the barrel levers and glasses to keep her hands occupied. A devilish laugh erupted inside my head. I had the old girl on the ropes. This could prove very entertaining.

"Then a pint for my constable and I."

Annie rushed to a tapped hogshead and began pouring with hellish speed. Vasilica shook her head at me, condemning my actions, though her amused smile told me she was not completely on Annie's side. Vasilica then removed her custodian hat and rested it on the bar as Annie waddled back to us. She clanked the glasses together before licking the froth that flowed down her fingers.

"Drinks are on the house all night for you Detective Sergeant," she bribed, laying the sudsy mugs on the chipped wood beneath. "Oh my," she added as she took in Vasilica's soft face, "how beautiful the constables are now a days. I didn't know that ladies could go into the profession. I might fancy a try myself, aye Sergeant Detective?" I gave Annie a glare that made her tremble. "Anyhow," said Annie as she retreated to the farther side of the bar, "they're complimentary for you as well dear. Enjoy."

"That will be enough Annie," I barked.

"Oh yes, of course." She shuffled a few feet away from us, hiding behind some barrels stacked together, all the while gawking at us timidly like a rat hiding in a wall.

"Wait," Vasilica shouted. "Miss Annie, one more thing. Did perhaps my brother come here and pick up the note I'd left him?" Annie narrowed her eyes, organizing her thoughts. Then, in an act of clarity, she clapped her hands twice.

"Oh, is that you darling? I couldn't hardly recognize ya'. Yes, yes, he did. He's sleeping upstairs in fact." Vasilica propped up eagerly. "Poor boy took a beating from the looks of it. He had his arm in a sling and everything. He bought some stew before getting a room for the night. He said that if you came by, I should let you know he'll be down after a few winks. I'd let him sleep if I were you. He looked terrible."

"Is he alright?" asked Vasilica with concern.

"He's fine. He just seemed to still be depleted from whatever scuffle he got himself into. I really must insist on you letting him sleep a few more hours."

"Fine then," Vasilica said with resolve, "I'll let him rest." I could see that she was trying to hide her delight. I couldn't help but get excited myself, as it appeared that I might finally get some answers. I began to think of questions I would ask, and the order I would ask them in. I just hoped that things would be a bit different then when Vasile and I last met.

"You'll have the truth soon Detective," said Vasilica before sipping a healthy helping of her ale, "very soon." I was tired of feeling confused, and knew that sleeping upstairs were my answers. So I mustered up what patience I had left in me and let time take care of the rest. I gave Vasilica a tolerant smile.

"Well then, what should we do until your brother wakes?"

Vasilica held her mug like a child, both hands firmly covering the walls of the glass. Her head was bobbing to imaginary music, when a casual grin slipped on her face.

"Drink of course."

CHAPTER 17

Afternoon sped into evening, and somehow between our eighth rounds of drinks, a dozen factory workers as well as a traveling Irish band slipped into the pub and filled all of the chairs. The musicians strummed guitars, whistled flutes, and fiddled violins, transforming the inn into something more cheerful. Between the music and clanking of glasses, anything short of a shout was inaudible. Vasilica and I stridently chatted about most anything, including her background. To my surprise, perhaps because of the seven or eight pints she had drunk, Vasilica began telling me about everything since her childhood, and was willing to answer any questions that I had along the way.

According to Vasilica, she and her brother had grown up motherless not far from the Carpathian Mountains, raised solely by their domineering father, Demetri Ivanescu. He climbed his way up the ranks of the Romanian Mountain Force, and was a renowned outdoorsman. One day, while Demetrei was away on duty and the children were with their cousins, his wife mysteriously disappeared from their home. No one could explain what had happened. Once Demetri returned, and learned of her disappearance, he resigned from the armed forces. While his official papers state that it was because of stress, Vasilica claims that it was instead because of what he uncovered in the cliffs, a secret that according to him was the direct reason why their mother vanished.

In what a few of the Sibiu villagers called heroic and most others madness, Demetri exhausted what little wealth he had saved away to put towards his children's military training. It was his hope that someday when his children were strong enough, they'd travel with him to the Carpathians in order to repel what he claimed to have unearthed. For years Vasilica and Vasile prepared with their father, until he felt they were capable enough to hold their own. They followed Demetri blindly along the countryside, hunting down those who were believed to be in league with Satan. That is until Demetri's weak heart stopped on him suddenly. Since then, Vasile and Vasilica had taken it upon themselves to continue what their father started.

As outrageous as it all sounded, much of what Vasilica said corresponded with her brother's diary. She verified dates, people, and places that Vasile had previously jotted down in his journal. She even retold the bizarre account of how her once black hair transformed to its current state of white. The tale was nearly identical to what I had read. While I tried to remain unobtrusive, I also wanted to confirm as many details as possible, listening for any conflicting facts that might prove that her history was all just a well rehearsed story. Unfortunately, I was unable to.

I *was* able however to pickup on a particular individual's name that she tried to avoid. It was her present target, Paraschiva. Vasilica's lips didn't dare to speak the name, though she gave subtle hints that this woman they were after was a monster. It disturbed me to see how unyielding she was in regards to her father's outlandish mendacities, as she otherwise seemed quite charming. She was a bit odd, as most foreigners are, but had a sharp, rapier wit that complimented her peculiar sense of humor. As we continued to trade information, I tried to withhold some of my more personal particulars, especially Catherine. Vasilica somehow saw right through me, and briefly, yet harmlessly commented on my lingering anguish. We talked for hours, and before long, my pocket watch reported that it was nearly nine o'clock. I double checked to make sure I read correctly before announcing it to Vasilica.

"Already nine my dear," I slurred, "Perhaps we should let your brother sleep for the night. I can return in the morning."

I stood up without waiting for an answer, adjusting my bowler as I slipped towards the door. My vision blurred slightly and I could feel numbness in my fingers. Run Away Annie looked relieved to see me go, rushing to remove my pint from the table as I stumbled forward.

"Nonsense," hollered Vasilica as she tugged me by my collar, forcing me backwards and back onto my stool. "Please, give my brother a few hours more?"

Perhaps it was the tone in her voice or the influence of the ales, but somehow, I was lured into a pleasant carelessness that annulled my need to return home. Besides, I still had a job to do, and all that really waited for me back at the flat was loneliness. I'd most likely sit over another one of Ms. Abigail's dinners, and then smoke until I couldn't feel anything any longer.

"Fine," I conceded, "I'll wait a bit longer." Vasilica beamed. "But I'll have to go and pay the stable boy first. You only gave him enough for a few hours."

"Fair enough," she said with her thick accent. "I'll order us another round."

I attempted to step forward but a sudden pull chained my feet to invisible manacles. It seemed that my few pints were finally catching up to me. Carefully, I balanced myself step by step, like an acrobat on a tightrope. Eventually I made it to the nighttime streets. They were cold, but refreshing, especially after being in the heat of the inn. I continued my way to the stables where a young blonde boy serviced the door.

"Young sir," I announced with drunken authority, "I'm here to pay for a few more hours on the police carriage you have here. Let's say midnight." A sudden involuntary spasm of my diaphragm caused me to belch as I handed him a few coins.

"Very well sir," he said with a cockney drawl, "but I'd ask you check those prads. They've been spooked since I took em'."

Nodding, I trundled my way through a separate wood door where all the animals were stored and found myself in a dim, manure ridden barn. The odor was hard to ignore, though the stable was surprising still. I sorted through the collection of horses, mules, and various carriages until I found my two steeds still attached to the stem of the police cart. Petting them with wobbly hands, I burped up a bit more foam before a violent thrash of black caught the corner of my eye.

Spinning it its direction, I could vaguely make out the hazy outline of a feminine figure from the opposite side of the stable. It was the shade I'd seen at my flat. The animals inside began to stir. I slipped one hand into my coat, gripping my revolver. I stretched my neck forward to try and focus on the woman with my foggy vision. The dark shape remained motionless, though I could tell she was watching me. I began to take a step towards it, but just as I did, a small set of fingers suddenly clasped my shoulder.

I jolted to draw my revolver, but the assailant pushed at the barrel with one hand, while releasing my shoulder and blocking a stiff hook I swung with the other.

"Nathan, it's me," said Vasilica while shaking me. Her pallid skin conflicted with the dark blue constable uniform in the barn's lamp light, and I could recognize her flowery scent over the horse shit. I let my guard down briefly before looking over my shoulder to take another glimpse at the dark figure. It had vanished. I returned my gaze to Vasilica, whose breath fumed with ale. I pointed outward towards the hall.

"Whew, am I glad it's you love. Did you happen to catch that *Queen of Darkness* at the end of the hall?" Vasilica gave me a puzzled look. I was clearly pickled.

In spite of this, I tried to put aside my impairments long enough to stumble onto the door of the police carriage. Vasilica followed behind me. I gave her a weary smirk as I tried to straighten my bowler, but instead only managed to tilt it crookedly onto the other side of my head. Vasilica watched with amusement. She had a smile like Catherine, which caused a sudden explosion of naked emotion to wail through me. Where there had once been hurt, now only a need to feel filled up inside me.

"Nathan," she whispered, catching my gaze, "I know you hurt." I cocked my head back and sought to play coy, masking the hidden grief that stirred up. I tried to think of something clever to say.

"I'll be alright love," is all that I could muster.

"Nathan, I am a very honest person."

"You are?" I grinned.

"Yes," she said while getting closer. My face turned sober. "I want to tell you something and you can't be frightened, even if it comes off as very forward."

"Okay," I said nervously.

"I like you. I knew I would when I'd first heard about you, but it's true."

Warmth trickled in my belly. It had been so long since someone was interested in me, and it felt good. I didn't know what she meant about "hearing about me," or how to respond to her directness. I mean, she was beautiful no doubt, with a lovely sense of humor and an intriguing point of view. She also had the sort of back-alley toughness that I liked in a woman. But even if she wasn't a murderer, she was definitely a tigress. I had no idea what to do next.

Vasilica pulled my lower back with both her hands, forcing me downward and curling me within inches of her face. Wordlessly, she reached in with warm breath, and pushing off her toes, laid her moist lips onto mine. *Well, there's my answer.* In all my years, I had never experienced a woman so aggressive. I was slightly taken off guard. But an arousing solace trickled down my spine, allowing for forgiveness. My eyes fluttered as her hands firmly dragged me closer, and before I could stop it, my arms were draped around her.

"*Vasilica, no,*" I wanted to say. "*Stop this, I mustn't,*" I wanted to shout, but none of it came out. I was rendered powerless, and as I leaned harder against her, passion took over. We pressed our lips together for sometime before Vasilica pushed away, her eyes shyly lowered, and her nose pink from rubbing against mine. But by the time she looked back up at me, I was already dropping in with a second kiss. She let out a quiet gasp of surprise, becoming rigid before letting out a low moan. My eyes forced themselves closed as the taste of her skin, the smell of her perfume, and the pleasure of her body stole my senses.

But what started in an instant, and felt like a seraphic forever, suddenly stopped as Vasilica pulled away her head again, this time more assertively. I kept my arms around her and leaned in on her flawless body, relaxing as my eyes became lost in hers. She took her fingers and curled them around my scalp, massaging it with her nails as she smiled. We remained locked for some time, savoring each other's embrace.

Then suddenly it hit me. The arms I was in were not Catherine's. In an illogical conflict with myself, I broke free of Vasilica's grip.

"What are we doing?" I shouted.

"Wait," said Vasilica calmly. "What happened? I thought…"

"Vasilica, this isn't right. I'm supposed to be working, not kissing my lead murder suspect."

"Nathan, wait. You don't understand. This was supposed to happen."

"What in God's name are you talking about?"

"I just know. I can't explain it."

"Well how about you fucking try?" She opened her mouth, and then stopped for a moment, struggling to find her words.

"An angel told me," she finally spat out.

Rolling my eyes in disgust, I gestured my hand dismissively and headed towards the exit. Vasilica chased behind me as I stomped through the hay covered floor, calling out my name. I knew that I was being irrational, but I couldn't help it. I knew Catherine wanted me to move on, and I liked Vasilica a lot, but what if I made her sick? I would never forgive myself. Even if I didn't, how long could I make her happy before I passed, and she was alone and miserable like me? It could never work.

"Nathan, please slow down."

She grabbed me by my wrist, but as I tried to pull away, she twisted my arm until the nerves from my hand to my elbow withered in pain. "Stop!" she ordered. I perched onto my toes, gritting my teeth feverishly, as I waited for her to let go. Releasing my wrist, she hopped between me and the barn door, prodding at my chest with a stiff finger. "Nathan, please, I know that sounds far-fetched."

"Far-fetched? *Far-fetched?* In the realm of possibility, that greatly extends beyond far-fetched. It's fucking ridiculous. This is not a damn game Vasilica. We are talking murder, my career, and lives that are on the line. You have to wake up from this ridiculous dream world of yours. There's no nosferatu, necromancers or missions from God. It's just two crazed foreigners, a dead girl, and a pair of dim-witted detectives involved in a set of bizarre circumstances." Her lips quivered and her saucer eyes watered with betrayal.

"Fine, if that's what you think that this is, then I do not need your help," she said in a callous voice. "But before we part, talk with Vasile. If all that you have seen is not enough, perhaps the words of my brother will knock some sense into you."

"Fine," I roared. "Let's get this over with."

We raced each other out of the barn and into the inn. We flashed by Annie, who was pointing at our fresh ales waiting on top of the bar, and ascended up the stairs to Vasile's door which was already cracked open. Vasilica nudged at the entrance forcefully, revealing a sky colored room with a single candle burning upon a lone dresser. Along the bedside, a pair of cracked wooden spikes surrounded a letter written in Romanian. Behind the paper trailed a small puddle of dried blood that led to wide open window gaping along the far wall.

Vasilica covered her mouth with her hands, letting out a weak squeal before turning towards me and resting her head on my chest. She poured out a stream of tears, mumbling inaudibly while sobbing into my coat. I had seen this a few times before in my career, and not once did it ever prove to be otherwise. Someone had broken in the room, and after a scuffle, fled from the window, dragging the body of their victim behind them. This night had just become a lot longer.

CHAPTER 18

Keys from a soothing organ played throughout the church's grand hall. I remained motionless under the steeple's empty corridor, taking in the rich perfume from the frankincense. Mahogany woods, bright stained glass, and ornate gold statues decorated the cathedral, growing more elaborate the nearer I drew to the altar. Waiting behind Jesus's sacred table waited Saint George in his lion crested armor. I approached fearlessly, unhindered by the blazing halo behind his head. His metallic boot stood a top of a devilish serpent-dragon, who opened his mouth in pain as it bled from the gashes branded by St. George's blade. The saint extended his arm, pointing his sword in my direction. Bowing beneath him, I felt the tap of steel on each of my shoulders, invigorating my body with Christ's power. The lesion on my arm from the porter tingled, as a black mist escaped from its concave surface. I lifted my head just in time to see the great saint inhale a belly full of air that he blew out over me in a flurry of wind, knocking me down onto my backside violently.

I awoke on the cold surface of a brick floor. I could hear muffled sobs assorted with a few mumbles and the clanking of feet. I sat up to find that I was alone in a cell, no larger than thirty paces long, and even less wide. All around me were similar cages, divided by a thin hall. Most of them were empty, except for the cell across from me which held a dirty old man who wept in his stained hands, insensible to the world around him, and a second to my left, which harbored a scruffy thug in red who snored comfortably on a cot.

I peeled myself off the ground, and a sudden rush of blood sent a smoldering pain to my neck from Paraschiva's claws. She had spared me, but for what dark reason, I was unsure. I shivered in bitter misery, dragging myself to the iron bars that made up my cell door. Posted at the end of our thin hall waited a sentry, dressed in police blue with a long coat and funny looking hat. His squinty eyes and cherry shaped nose peeked over a large mustache that smothered his lips. He rested idly on a barrel labeled *Danger*. The cylindrical container stood next to a small caliber cannon that pointed towards the main entrance of the chamber. The guard kept a set of iron keys at his waist next to his club and single shot rifle. It was obvious that no one was getting in or out of here without permission, *but I always loved a challenge.*

This wasn't the first time that I'd been imprisoned. It had happened once before in Grivitsa during the War of Independence. I was just a basic scout then, and was surveying the ramparts when a squad of Ottomans had captured me. They'd violently interrogated me, but were too busy preparing to defend against the incoming invasion about to take place to really try and break me. Instead, they threw me into a mud pit filled with human excrement and dying men, blocking my escape with a fence made of barbed timber. I made that trench my home for several days until the attack finally took place. It was then, while my enemies were distracted, that I finally dug out and escaped in order to rejoin my comrades. If I could survive that horrid pit then this would be nothing.

I cleared my throat and reached out my good arm beyond the gates towards the guard's direction. "Sir," I called out faintly, "if I could have some water." He briefly looked in my direction before returning his gaze to the ceiling. I waved my hand desperately, coughing, moaning, and hoping for mercy, but the policeman continued to ignore me.

"Won't do any use fella," said a colorful voice from my left. It was the rogue in red, now sitting up from his cot. The strange looking gentleman was older, in his early fifties at least, and wore a worn black patch over his right eye. A tall military cap I recognized as a shako covered his long grey bangs. . The hat was quite out-of-date and appeared to be riddled with bullet holes. He looked more like a fallen soldier freshly raised from the grave than a criminal, with his stained red and gold army coat, discolored white pants, and worn-down marching boots clinging to his frame. "Those guards won't do anything for ya.' This sad geezer here has been crying for two days now and they haven't bothered even giving him the courtesy of shouting *shut it!*"

I wiped an unexplainable smear of mud from my forehead. It was still wet. My body must have been dragged. It took me a few seconds to settle, but once I inhaled a few calming breaths, I rejoined the conversation.

"Were you here when they brought me?"

"Aye, I was," he said after spitting, "We both were." I was unsure if this soldier meant him and the old man or perhaps the guard, but I didn't care to ask. "Some fat fool and a few bobbies dragged you in a few hours back. I overheard them saying something about you killin' a young Irish doris. Name they gave was Miss McCann."

Now it all made sense. Paraschiva was cleaning up her tracks, and instead of simply ending me, she fed me to the authorities so that I could either be executed or suffer a hundred years in this caged hell. It was a plan taken straight out of the devil's handbook and I had played right into it. Despite this, I recalled the face of St. George, and knew that somehow this would not be my final verse.

"The name is Vasile," I said while bowing.

"Timothy Dewhirst, but most gabbers just call me the Soldier." Rising from his bed, he approached the pane of bars that separated us. "My friend here is Ravi," he added, nudging his nose towards his empty cell. "Though, I'm betting you probably can't see him." It was true. I had no idea of who he was talking about. Perhaps he kept a small pet of some sort in his cell. "So did ya' have yourself a go of her, or were done wrong?" His English sounded faulty, with jargon I'd never heard, but I assumed that he was referring to the victim.

"If you mean, did I kill that woman, then no. I am part of a large machination my friend. One orchestrated by a great evil." Nodding in approval, the Soldier wiped the snot from his nose onto a finger while coming closer and studying my posture. He slapped his tongue around in his mouth a few times before speaking again.

"I thought not. You stand upright, with pride, like me. You have had military training for sure. We soldiers *will* kill, but only in the line of duty. We don't murder." Intrigued, I limped towards the metal gate between us, putting my hand on the cool metal. He was no ordinary brigand, of that I was sure. Perhaps this Timothy Dewhirst was part of God's plan to free me from this otherwise impenetrable dungeon.

"And why have you been brought here?"

"Use to be a private in the Majesty's army during the Indian Rebellion. As reward for serving, the military took one of my eyes, gave me a gimp leg, and handed me a ticket straight to the poor house. I never lost my honor though did I? I became a rodent exterminator and quite the gambler as well, creating a living out of it for nearly twenty years. Then, just a few days ago while I was in town, some fool had the mind to try to cheat me in cards. I challenged him in an honor bound duel, and was taken away for shooting and killing him. The authorities say it's barbaric, hence why it's been outlawed, but what do they know? I'll most likely be tried and hanged soon."

"Hmm," I groaned, tapping my chin. "I too most likely will be put to death. What a shame." The Soldier bobbed his head along with mine, mimicking me as we lamented, dejected by our circumstances. It wasn't death so much as it was failing to complete what I had set out to accomplish that burdened me. *I couldn't let it end like this.* "Do you believe in God, Soldier?" My words seemed jarring to his ears.

"Oh yes," he answered, crossing himself.

"Then you must believe me when I tell you I am doing his work." The Soldier's single milky eye followed my mouth as he wiped another gob from under his nose and onto his coat. "I will say this bluntly, but honestly. In this world there are nightmares that walk among us, and the Lord has given me the task of driving these wolves away from his flock."

"You mean demons?"

"Yes. They have many faces to them, but they all share the same name."

"Oh, I know," he replied, looking to the unseen person at his side, "Ravi and I have seen our share here in London. Believe you me, they are out there mate, and not just metaphorically. I mean the *real* ones." Timothy was more aware than most. Perhaps he really could help.

"Then you must believe me Soldier when I say that I need to escape from here so I can do God's work- not just to save my own neck." Spearing my open palm between the bars, I reached out to shake his hand. He studied it for a moment. "I need to ask you something very important. Would you promise not to alert the guards if I try to break free from here?" The Soldier tapped his foot like a drum, mulling over my request. I prayed that he would at least consider, and not call for the guard at the end of the hall to alert him.

"Tell you wha', I'll do you one betta'. Ravi and I will help you in your fight. If you truly are a chosen man of God then I've been having a conversation with the redemption I've been praying for. " Timothy grasped my hand and shook it very hard. He nodded, somehow managing to look thoughtful with his vacant stare. Just then a cool breeze flew in from the hall, tickling my skin and causing me to break out into gooseflesh. It reminded me of St. George's icy breath. "I even have a plan on how we'll get out of here."

He glanced over to the guard, who had placed the brim of his hat over his eyes in order to hide the fact that he was dozing off. I couldn't tell if the Soldier was studying the sentry or the barrel beneath him. Timothy then crept closer to me, hunching down as he smiled. He pulled up his black patch, revealing a grotesque cavity where his eye once was. Digging inside the hole with his finger, he removed a single half-match and showcased it. "I warn you though, this won't be easy, and it definitely won't be quiet."

God did have a plan for me. He sent me the Soldier. I looked down, studying the small broken twig of wood pinched between Timothy Dewhirst's fingers. "It never is," I answered.

CHAPTER 19

Though top minds in the English medical field theorize that alcohol can only pass from the blood stream with time, I found that when introduced to extremely intense circumstances, the body has a way of briefly regaining composure. I learned this at sea, when a sailor tried to hang himself from the crow's nest during my watch. Unbeknownst to others, I'd been drunk from an earlier shore leave, but somehow still managed to scale the mast with a cat-like grace, although just minutes before, I could barely stand. Vasilica seemed to be having the very same experience. Not long ago, she was both kanurd from the ales and delirious after discovering that her brother was violently abducted. Now though, she was stone sober, and her ability to mentally recuperate had us racing back on carriage into the city, her at the helm while I dangled from the side, vomiting.

If Vasile had honestly been nabbed, then it was clear that someone else was involved. We deliberated who it might be, and even though Vasilica insisted that it was Paraschiva, we rounded up a practical list of suspects. Now, in desperation, inclination took over. We decided to visit Mr. Goodwin's pub, as well as Ballister's whereabouts. Hopefully, one of them might have Vasile.

We decided to visit my office first so that I could pick up a few spare bullets, a pair of long chained manacles, and anything else that might help us in our pursuit. I decided to return the carriage as the house in question was just around the corner, and the horses return was long overdue. Once we arrived, Vasilica decided to shed the patrolman uniform and return to her dark clothing before disappearing into the streets. I hurriedly parked the carriage then entered the station, my eyes still burning from vomiting. The main hall was busy with patrolmen who were signing in for the nightshift at the clerk's desk. I dodged the lot of them and went straight to my office. After gathering what I needed, I hurried back out, trying to avoid everyone as best I could. However, I could only get halfway to the main exit before one of the constables shouted out my name.

"Detective Sergeant Brannick." I quickened my pace, pretending not to hear. "Detective Sergeant Brannick!" the patrolman squawked louder. I could tell by his soft, dainty voice that it was Constable Jones. He was a young pup fresh out of training who had all makings of a proper kiss-ass. The little runt shook everyone's hand, wished all a good day, and never blabbed any unpleasantries. Parading in my direction, he pulled at my hand and began to shake it. "Detective Sergeant, I just wanted to say congratulations. You did a bang-up good job on the McCann murder. No doubt you'll be looked at for another promotion." I jerked my hand away and bore at my palm as if he'd pissed on.

"What on earth are you talking about Jones?" His face went from proud to squeamish as he nervously tussled with his collar.

"Well, I was told…" he fidgeted with uncertainty, "that Detective Sergeant Davis brought in the murderer this evening. It was said the two of you had been trailing some Romanians for days, uncovering a body snatching outfit they were running." Impulses took over. I latched my hand onto his lapel and dragged him until the two of us were cheek to cheek.

"You better not be playing with me boy," I snarled.

"No, Chief Inspector Swanson told us during briefing! We're holding the suspect until his trial." I pawed my palm over Jones's face then pushed him to the ground, stepping over his sniveling body as I made my way back towards the offices. A few of constables froze, unsure what to do. It appeared that the Chief Inspector and I were due for a little chat. I wasn't leaving here until I'd learned everything.

It was late, but I knew Swanson would be putting in extra hours tonight in order to add the finishing touches to his roster sheet. It was his routine. Swanson was a systematic man with an even more methodical schedule that he followed rather strictly. It made him thorough, but quite predictable. As I knocked on his door, I could hear a sharp pen scribbling on paper from the other side of the pine entryway.

"Come in," he called out tiredly. I proceeded inside, laying anchor at the end of his desk, my arms folded together tightly. He appeared worn, swarmed with sealing wax, telegrams and a stack of papers. "Ah, Detective Sergeant Brannick, I wondered when you'd come in for your much deserved pat on the back."

"What exactly did Davis tell you?" I needled bluntly. *Perhaps this wasn't the best opening.* Appalled, Swanson retaliated with a wicked, icy stare before opening his mouth to speak.

"Detective Sergeant Davis," he answered in a condoning tone, "brought in the Romanian man, Vasile Ivanescu, along with a signed confession affirming that he and his sister murdered Miss McCann. The confession certifies that they were grave robbers, befriending anyone at death's door so they could later lay claim to both their corpse and its wares. They would sell the body to some grisly scientist and keep any goods the family buried them in for themselves. When Miss McCann refused to pass on from her ailment however, the two slew her to speed up the process. Luckily, when they went to claim their prize, both you and Davis were there to stop it. Odd circumstances, but it will all hold up in the courts."

"Rubbish. What of the skirmish with Miss McCann's at the grave site? She was still alive Chief-Inspector!"

"Ah, yes. Davis mentioned you would bring that up. He informed me you had been knocked out cold during the cemetery tussle and kept gabbing about some hallucination involving Miss McCann. He did not have the heart to tell you, but in the report, he stated that while the assailants walloped you, he was able to get the edge and chase them off. Unfortunately, the brother-sister duo returned to the site and burned Miss McCann's corpse while Davis rushed to get you medical attention." Disgust sputtered inside my stomach. I was a loss for words. "Davis said he could not have done it without you." My mouth kept going without checking in with me first.

"But it's a lie," I howled, banging my fist on the desk. Swanson flinched. Thereupon, he took the time to crack his neck before arising imposingly from his chair.

"Now that's enough," he blasted. "I know about you Brannick. Davis informed me of your ridiculous falling out. He told me how he'd confronted you about the opium reeking from your clothes. He's torn up about the whole thing. So much so that the poor old boy even requested a transfer. Now I'll give you one week to clean up before I stop looking the other way. This drug has you acting reckless. Clean up, or it's your job."

An uproar of fury bowled over me. Davis, for whatever reason, had not only gone behind my back, but created some elaborate story to close the case. Now, here I was wasting time trying to argue with the most stubborn man in England. I needed to instead find the underlying cause of all this. I needed to find Vasile. Quickly, my mind began to stir up a compelling story.

"Forgive me Chief-Inspector," I begged reverently, "my wife Catherine has lain heavily on my heart. The drugs have been a way to deal with it, but I'll stop. I swear it." Swanson took a moment to collect himself. His face went soft.

"Well, I'm glad to hear Brannick," he said coolly. "I have high hopes for you. Especially now that parliament just disbanded our shifts on the Thames," he gloated, holding up a freshly opened correspondence. "They finally repaired the Molesey Reservoirs and I could use a man like you to help clean up London. What say we get a few men under you to lead some serious investigations *Detective Inspector* Brannick?" Never did I expect in a hundred years that something so sweet sounding could be so poisonous. I swallowed the lump in my throat, pressed my lips together in a line, and I tried to sound elated.

"Are you having a laugh at me Chief-Inspector?"

"No, orders just came in. Get some rest and we'll talk about it in a few days."

"Right then," I said, bowing my head. "I'm just going to finish up a report, and then I'll get home. Thank you, sir."

I ran out of Swanson's office and to the jailer's area, hoping to find the whereabouts of Vasile. As I rushed through the halls however, an earsplitting rumble suddenly erupted from the back of the building, nearly sending me off my feet. It was a thunderous eruption that sounded eerily familiar, like the twelve pounders on the Black Prince. The source rang from the very direction I was headed in. I sped into a full pace, passing a dozen befuddled constables that were hustling towards the lock-up room.

A cool breeze whooshed past me as I entered the jailor's area. It was a long corridor with barred cells on each side. Looking about, I spotted the guard's cannon that normally pointed towards the entrance now in the middle of the hall. It was mostly just used for show, and Davis and I speculated that the damn thing didn't even work. There it was though, its barrel lodged between the bars of two neighboring cages. Across from the cell, a gaping hole spread across the walls. The breach led outside into the dark streets of London.

"Those bastards," hollered a man locked in a parallel cell, "they didn't take me with them."

"The Fenians are at it again," coughed one of the constables, "Two of the prisoners have escaped." He stared at the opening, his jaw jutted open. "Hurry, get the ranking officer. I was attacked." Constables filled into the room in a panic. I grabbed the sooty policeman who I recognized as Constable O'Malley, and tugged him close to me.

"Who Constable?" I pleaded, "Who escaped?"

Constable O'Malley went flush. I could tell he was trying to hold back. "I'm sorry Detective Sergeant. They snuck up behind me and knocked me out cold. It was the foreign bloke you and Davis had been chasing. He and some gambler called the Soldier got away." *No, it couldn't be Timothy, could it?* Pushing past him, I fought the current of frenzied men to get a closer glance at the opening. A four foot gap centered itself between the two prisoner cells, singed with a blackened outline along the rim. A make-shift rope had been fashioned from cot sheets, lassoed around a splintered cartridge of gun powder that the guards kept near their station. I was astonished. Vasile and a man who sounded eerily familiar were on the run, escaping London's infamously harsh justice system. It seems fate has a way of working itself out.

"Cheeky bastards," I said to myself while staring out the exit.

CHAPTER 20

I slipped past the circus act, slinking out the station and across Northumberland Avenue where Vasilica awaited. I made sure to mix with the small gathering of street folk near the station incase someone was following me. Not far off, I found Vasilica concealed between two buildings. Her cloak's hood was up and its cape hung over one shoulder. As soon as I escaped the light of the street-lamps, and saw that no one was approaching, I ran to her hiding spot.

"Come on, your brother is alive."

"How do you know?"

"Because Davis took him in custody," I answered, dragging her out in the street by one arm while trying to hail a cab.

"Well, where is he then, and what in God's glory was that noise?"

"It was your brother. He just escaped." She smiled devilishly, twisting her arm from my grip, and joining me in my efforts to hail down a carriage. It didn't take long for the two of us to find a coachman willing to drive us. We mounted his pinewood cart shaped like a wheeled coffin. It was twice as unpleasant to sit in as it was to look at.

"Where to?" asked the coachman as we tried to make ourselves comfortable in his crooked cabin. Vasilica waited for my reply.

"Stratford and Allen Street," I said, staring back at my snowy counterpart. "We need to visit the best detective in London."

After an eternity, the two ponies wobbled their way to Davis's block. I paid the coachman, and then waited for him to withdraw from the street before proceeding to James's doorstep. He had lived in London his entire life, housed comfortably in a century old building inherited from his parents. The dwelling, far from any street lamps, shouldered tightly with the other large neighboring houses, projecting a baleful and intimidating black wall. The two of us examined the streets for pedestrians. Once all was clear, we pressed our faces on door's glass.

It took a moment for my eyes to adjust, but slowly, I began to distinguish the contours of James's front room. The shadowy dressers, darkened chairs, and indistinguishable walls that I committed to memory were just as I remembered. James and his family were most likely asleep upstairs. I contemplated returning at dawn, but before I could mention it, Vasilica jabbed a pointed skewer inside the door's lock.

"Whoa, what are you doing? He has kids in there." Vasilica gave me a tired expression.

"We need answers Nathan. I can be silent like a cat. Can you?"

"Fine, we grab James, wake him up, and find out what the hell is going on. Do not involve his family. Do you understand?" Vasilica nodded. I watched as she pushed up at the lock cavity. Her method was cleaner than mine, but far more time consuming. I could hear muffled clicks from the notches inside.

"Now, which room is his?" A delegation of arguments and counterarguments squabbled inside my head. I didn't feel as if this whole idea was going to go as well as I'd hoped. But before I could make any sense of it, my lips answered.

"Last door upstairs." I was shocked at my imprudence. *Had Vasilica bewitched me after all?* She slipped into the house like a specter. Panic stricken, I followed her inside, but couldn't keep up without my feet thudding like bricks. Vasilica softly glided up the curving stairwell. I took the time to gently close the door behind us. By the time I turned back around, she was already at the top step and prowling towards James's room. I mouthed every curse in my head before lifting my foot to follow. But before I could take a step, the sound of heavy wood dragging along the hard floor reverberated from the nearby dining area, causing me to freeze. I calmed myself before trying to peer through the sea of black.

"Hello Nathan," a voice sniveled. "So glad to see you mate."

It was Davis. He dragged and flared-up a match that he used to light a signalman's lantern. The lamp lit up his face and shimmered peculiarly along his eyes. As the bleak glow took my vision, I heeded a set of odd shapes around him. Everything flickered in shadow, and as my sight attuned, I recognized the still silhouettes of Davis's family seated around the dining room table. They were slouched loosely in their seats, hunched and drunken. Sitting at the head with an unbuttoned shirt covered in crusted dribble was James. A bottle of spirits smeared with dried blood rested near his hands which were clenched around the barrel of his favorite rifle. He looked upwards, his hound-dog face shaded by a lurid overcast.

"Did you hear?" he sobbed. "We've been promoted." I browsed the staircase for Vasilica, but she wasn't there. Then foolishly, I decided to move softly towards James. His hands shot up, the barrels of his weapon pointed at my heart. He placed his thumb on the hammer and cocked it back.

"Not another inch," he said calmly, "you'll wake the children."

He steadied the grip of his gun with one hand while picking up the lantern with his other, shining it on his family. It was a nightmarish scene. Each was tied and gagged. Their faces, suspended in terror, were now grey and lifeless. The two boys, both pudgy like their father, appeared dried out and lean. Each tilted back in their chair, nail sized puncture marks in their foreheads and cheeks. Mrs. Davis must have been forced to watch. Salt stains from tears had dried around her eye wrinkles and plum bruises from the bindings on her wrists and mouth showed how she must have struggled.

"By God Davis, what have you done," I lamented, lifting my hands in surrender. Davis peered at his gruesome family sympathetically.

"You were right Nathan. This was no ordinary murder investigation." I could hear him trying to hold back tears as he lay the lantern back down. "The devil came," he mumbled. "She made me do this." I shook my head no, unable to make sense of it all. My mind scattered for resolve while my body screamed for a fix. Keeping my hands where he could see them, I boldly stepped forward, squishing my shoe into something I did not much care to explore.

"Davis, this isn't your fault. Tell me what happened, we can fix this."

"Fix this!" he roared, tears raining from his eyes. "Fix this? No, Nathan there is no fixing this." Stubbornly, I took another inch, letting myself enter the lamp light that encircled him and his family.

"Davis, you were tricked, this isn't your fault, honestly." My blood raced through me like a greyhound. I settled into my natural voice and hoped he'd recognize his old partner. "My brother, he's a priest, he can help. We can send you off to him. He can make you better." He lifted the gun higher. My toes and fingers clutched together, fearing he'd squeeze the trigger. Then appallingly, he turned the barrel on himself, placing the steel along his temple.

"No Nathan there is no fixing this."

"James, jus tell me what happened. I want to stop this. You can help." Davis continued weeping, the gun firmly pressed along his head as he opened his dribble covered mouth trying to speak.

"The devil came," he repeated, slobber falling on his shirt. "He came in the form of a beautiful *woman*." Wiping his eyes with a blood covered hand, he sniffled before continuing. "I didn't know at first. She promised to help solve the case. She told me where Vasile was hiding, even lead me to him. I...I wanted to tell her no," he stuttered, "but I couldn't. It was like someone else steered me. Like...like I was a damn saddled horse. I found Vasile at some inn, and with her help, snatched him from his room. We brought him to the Yard, and after I wrote the reports that she narrated, returned here with her."

My hands began to twitch, linked by empathy for Davis's circumstances. James let out a moan as he stared at his children. He readjusted the rifle, now more securely to his skull.

"No Davis, please. Don't."

"I tried to stop her, but she was hungry. The devil *is always* hungry. She made me butcher my family so she could drink from them." I crept forward, now nearly reaching the table. Davis, unaware, bawled, looking to the ceiling. "Do you think God can forgive me for this?"

"Davis, it doesn't have to end here."

"No, let's end this here," he said with resolve. "It's better this way."

Then, unexpectedly, James whirled the barrel around and aimed it at my face. I tightened up for the shot. "Come with me Nathan. You can see Catherine again partner." His finger went for the trigger, but before he could fire, a glittering knife whirled from the staircase, plunging into his eye. Davis's head kicked back as he fell from his chair. I remained motionless, listening to the gurgle of blood blended with Vasilica's soft boots tapping along the floor. She traipsed down to Davis, checking him for life.

"You were right," she said, pushing the gun from his dead grip, "it wasn't his fault. It was the bite." Both mystified and demoralized, I decided to remain silent. "That bite at the cemetery, it infected him. It is what weakened his will. I tried to warn you." I wanted to fall to the floor, huddle into a ball, and rock back and forth until I fell asleep. This was all wrong. I didn't know what to feel. I needed to get to my pipe. Vasilica, still patting down his body, didn't seem to notice my dismay. "Their bite, it poisons your mind and leaves you pliable for them to manipulate. They've been doing this for centuries." Vasilica unsheathed her blade. "Now don't look," she said coldly. "I need to remove their heads."

I needed resolution to this madness. My mind's eye flashed back and forth from Davis's dopey head nudging inside my office each morning, to the knife now firmly planted in his face. I remembered Catherine's laughter at the Policemen's ball, and then recalled her funeral. As I continued to torture myself, a hushed voice from behind my soul's curtain whispered, calling for me even louder now to go and get to the opium. Vasilica, now aware, came to me and put her small hand on my shoulders.

"Stop Nathan, God needs you now." *His very name insulted me. He'd forgotten about me long ago.* "Nathan, it is the drug, it works against you. It keeps you weak." My torso began to twitch, as a rush of acid shot from my throat to my mouth, spewing vomit along Davis's floor. It was neither the excitement nor the alcohol that caused it. I could tell I was going through some early withdrawal. "Let it out Nathan," Vasilica instructed, giving me a swift kick to the ribs that caused me to fall to the ground. "By God, let it out!" she commanded. Booting me over and over with the soft top of her foot, she compressed the air from my lungs, causing me to spit up more breakfast and beer. My body shivered and my stomach squeezed, but finally, after a couple of minutes, I began to settle, lying face first in my own mess.

Vasilica rubbed the tender muscles in my neck. I began to regain my senses, my ribs now tender where I'd been kicked. I noticed my hands were clasped onto the bible Marcos had given me. My body burned from exertion, and pushing to my feet, Vasilica handed me a silk handkerchief to wipe my shaky chin with. The Romanian designed cloth was completely different from the coughing rags in Miss McCann's flat. I thought it odd that they could be so contrasting. Then suddenly, it all became clear.

"Vasilica," I gargled, "Your brother's journal, it said that this *Paraschiva* took on a sponsor in Munich, what was his profession?"

"We believed him to be a surgeon," she said half wittingly.

"Precisely, what was his name?"

"I can't remember. Vasile would know."

"I can't believe I've been so blinkered this whole time," I thought aloud. "I'll bet you if I were to ask Vasile, he'd confirm that this surgeon's initials are SVG."

"Yes, I can not recall his first name, but I believe his last name was Von Goethe."

"His first name is Sebastian. Your brother wrote it inside his journal. That also means that the handkerchief I found in Miss McCann's flat was *not* Eastern European. It was *Central* European. I'm a bloody fool! The tire marks from a bicycle on Miss McCann's porch, her quarantine, it all makes sense now. The only person who visited her during her last days was her physician, Doctor Timothy Guildford."

"An alias for sure," chimed Vasilica.

"Yes," I cried, wobbling to the door. "The name is codswallop, to hide who this German bastard really is."

"Do you mean he is the child of Paraschiva?" Vasilica asked with consideration.

"Yes, the dodgy prat has been under our noses this entire time."

"Then shall we pay him a visit?"

"Oh yes," I said, lifting Davis's gore covered rifle. "I think a checkup is definitely in order."

CHAPTER 21

I was just a little tyke when I decided to join the British army. My mum was a laborer in the workhouses who died in the spike when I was just eleven. She had told me that my father was some war hero who'd been killed during the first Anglo-Afghan War. I believed her story until the day she was buried. That's when my aunt, who'd reluctantly volunteered to care for me, divulged in the truth. No one knew who my father was. My mum was an *unfortunate* who worked in the rookery, and one day I just showed up, a little bump in her belly.

It didn't matter much to me though. My mind was already set. I was going to be an army man, fighting bravely on the front lines. Life with my aunt wasn't much, as I stayed in the servants' quarters with barely enough rotten wood over my head to keep warm. So, when I was fifteen, I lied about my age and enlisted early in order to get away. I looked older than most boys, so no one seemed to question my enrollment. I think the military was just happy to have another bloke in the ranks, as the empire was well involved in quite a few campaigns at the time.

Military life wasn't half bad. I'd get fed each day, properly clothed, and had a place to sleep at night. I've heard people say that the army was for madmen. How chaps in service would get whipped regularly or march until their feet bled. Truth be told, you only were flogged if you did something you shouldn't have, and the marches were the only way an uneducated man like me was ever going to get to see the world. I visited France, Italy, and parts of India, something I couldn't have done otherwise. Then, in November of 1856, I was deployed for battle, and the real adventure began.

The war started over a city called Herat. British and Indian forces were supporting an ally who'd rebelled against Persia, causing a major uproar. I was just a simple rifleman doing what I was told. I didn't know much about why we were involved, nor did I care. For weeks there were small skirmishes, but no major combat. We trekked through dirt and mud until the soles of our boots were worn. Finally, in February, while we were trying to strategically withdraw from the front, the Persians came at us with a full on attack. We fought like cornered animals, repelling their ambush. Sadly for me, I'd only seen half of the battle, as Persian shrapnel blew right through my face, taking out my eye and cheek. To further exacerbate the situation, while I was sprawled along the field just trying to keep my face from falling off, a cavalry horse crushed my knee, bending it backwards like a chicken leg. I thought I was a dead man for sure, as I was leaking buckets and unable to walk. But then, just before I gave up all hope, *Ravi* came and pulled me out of the muck.

He was in the Indian Infantry, and a hell of a good man. He dragged me from the front lines to safety, where a field surgeon somehow stitched my head shut. I don't remember much, but I do recall Ravi gripping my hand, trying to ease my suffering. The pain was immense, but he never left, talking me through my torture until I pissed myself and blacked out. I woke up a few days later in an infirmary tent, binding over my eye and leg.

My superiors informed me that I'd be honorably discharged, and would be home as soon as I healed. I couldn't walk or see properly any longer, so I was considered unfit for duty. While the news was devastating, I took solace in the fact that I'd done my part to help repel the Persians. As for Ravi, I asked a few of the men at camp if they could find him, as I wanted to thank him in person. The man saved my life after all, and I was greatly indebted to him. Sadly, as I continued to investigate, I'd come to find out that a reunion wasn't possible. Ravi Mahajan had been killed in the battle of Mohammerah just weeks after my injury. *Or so I thought.*

I came back to London coopered. My body was ruined and my spirits were crushed. I had practically nothing to fall back, as I'd wasted it all on trinkets and toffers during my tour. Lonely, poor, and repulsive, I took to drinking, gambling, and painting. Day by day I wasted away without goals or ambitions. Then, late one particular evening, after a night of spreading the broads, I went to sleep on a rickety boat that I owned only to be awoken by a most curious incident.

While in the midst of forty winks, someone, somehow, had slipped into my chamber and was now at the foot of my bed. At first I thought it was a snoozer who'd mistaken me as a proper mark, but as I looked closer, I discovered that a burglar would be lovely compared to what I'd found. Hovering above my bed post was a decayed young man in military dress, his face sunken and crumbling. He had no lips, and beamed a ghastly smile worthy only of the grave. His eyes were a deep-set olive and his neck aslant and broken. From out of his belly oozed his putrid innards, swinging like the rope of a hangman's noose.

Alarmed, I leapt at the ghoul with everything I could conjure, but plummeted right through him. That's when I noticed the rank on his shoulder, and knew that it was Ravi. He'd come back to check on me, and make sure that I deserved the life that he had saved. Throughout the night we had the strangest conversation, but ultimately, it ended with an even odder promise. Ravi was caught in his own hellish limbo. He had no friends or relatives, much as myself, and didn't know what to do in the afterlife. He pledged to help me fix myself, as he felt I'd been dealt a bad hand. In return, I agreed to be his companion until he could move on from his purgatory. It was a soldier's deal, which is one of the most honest, and it has been abided by ever since.

Vasile and I had just escaped Scotland Yard's salt boxes, and were looking for someplace to hold up. We hadn't much time to talk about what we'd do after the get away and were desperate for a hiding place. We were covered in brick dust from the explosion, and warranted a quick clean up before we committed to any further activities. We were too far away from my boat, but I knew of a flophouse nearby where people wouldn't ask any questions, and decided to make our way to it. Ravi acted as a scout, keeping an eye out for any miltonians.

Now I chose this inn because the owner, Patrick Cooper, owed me a favor for assisting him with some ruffians a few months back. Once we arrived, I chatted with him briefly, and before long, was in a storage room with Vasile wiping ourselves down. Vasile's arm looked pretty serious, and as I aided him with his bandages, I couldn't help but take in the horrid smell coming off it. It was infected alright, but we didn't have much time to bleed it. Vasile must have seen the concern on my face, because he quickly covered up his arm, as if half embarrassed.

"Don't worry about it," he said while grinding his teeth in pain. "Saint George has cleansed it. I can take care of the rest later."

"So then fella'," I asked, "What's the plan?"

"I have an address that I need to look into," he said while pulling a piece of paper from his pocket. He held the parchment up in my direction, grunting, as if to say I should take it. I grabbed the crumpled note even though I couldn't read. Ravi looked over my shoulder, and after examining the writing for a moment, translated it to me. No one seemed to be able to hear Ravi, or see him for that matter. Occasionally someone would describe feeling a chill when he came into a room, but even that was rare. I don't know why I saw him, but guessed that it has something to do with me almost dying myself.

"I have an idea of where this is," I said while folding up the paper. "What should we be expecting though when we get there?"

"Death incarnate my friend. This is the child of Paraschiva we are pursuing, whose blood flows with the strength of Vlad Tepes himself."

"So…is that bad?"

Vasile snorted.

"Yes, it's bad my friend." He dangled his injured arm back into its sling causing his half smile to turn a shade wolfish. "Unlike lesser nosferatu, those closest decedents of the Prince of Wallachia have many cursed talents, including immeasurable strength, bestial instincts, and vast array of hellish powers. I don't know exactly what to expect, but I do know it will be very dangerous."

"You're a cheerful one holy man," I said while taking a rag to my red coat. "So is there any good news?"

Vasile took a long pause. His eyes gleamed, flickers of anger and amusement sharing space in them. "Yes, I think there is."

"Think?"

"Paraschiva's child from Munich has only been damned for a very short amount of time. He will not be well versed in all of the capabilities at his disposal. Think of an infant. With time, they can walk, speak, and reason. But first, they must familiarize themselves with their latent potential. It doesn't just come naturally."

"So, is that the only good news?"

"Well," he added with a sore grin, "I'm hoping the element of surprise might do something for us."

Vasile and I continued to clean up until we were presentable. The holy man was a gift. I'd been praying for someone, or something, to redeem this hollow existence I'd been living for far too long. So when Vasile was thrown into the holding cell next to me, I jumped at the chance to help him. I'd overheard the constables talking about him when they first dragged him in. They said he was just some flummut foreigner, wanted for murder. I could tell they were wrong. The cross around his neck, his militant posture, and bold candor, it told me he was a pure, devoted soul. Or perhaps I'm just losing my mind. I mean I do have a specter for a best friend.

"So then mate," I said once we were polished and ready, "onward to battle?"

"First we need weapons."

"Oh, I think I can help with that." Before I was arrested for dueling, which was entirely the other fool's fault, I'd arranged to stay at Patrick's drum for the night. Although my room was cleaned out, he'd collected my belongings and put them aside. After reacquiring them, I presented the equipment to Vasile in hopes they'd be enough. Besides my clothes, I had a saber, flintlock pistol, basher, knife, and irons. *I'm a bit of a weapons enthusiast.*

Vasile took inventory of the arsenal, picking up a Bavarian cavalry saber that I'd won in a card game, and tested it in the air with a few solid swings. The weapon seemed to lift his spirits. He slid it in his waist sash then puffed out his chest proudly. I could tell from his fluid technique, that even with his bad arm, he'd be a formidable opponent. He wasn't tall or overly brawny, but fearsome nonetheless. His eyes were constantly dissecting his surroundings, and even at Patrick's inn, he turned corners with a calculated approach. He had faint scars across the brunt of his knuckles and breakneck reflexes that only a highly experienced man attains.

"This is good," he said as he pocketed the knife, "but we'll need fire."

"I'll ask Patrick if he has anything potent enough to set ablaze." *He did.* We made a few improvised fire hurlers by filling up some bottles with a mixture of potato alcohol and lamp oil. I fit the top of the containers with cloth wicks soaked in our flammable concoction, holding the fabric in place with bottle stoppers. It wasn't the most reliable design, but they'd do the trick.

At last, with our clothing unsoiled and arsenal plentiful, we trudged to Vasile's address. We took the back roads to avoid the crushers who were searching for us. They don't seem to take nicely to prisoners escaping from their headquarters. Ravi continued to act as our crow, keeping an eye out for anything suspicious. Finally, we arrived at the building, which wasn't too far from one of my favorite gin palaces. We crept to the entrance located in the back of an old clock repair shop.

The door was ajar and I could tell from the damp footprints along the threshold that a pair of people had come in fairly recently. Vasile and I drew our weapons, ready to rush inside. Just before we did though, Ravi called to me and pointed behind us. I followed his indicated direction with my one good eye and spotted a dark figure clinging to the wall of the gloomy passageway. It was a bloke to be sure, wearing a wool frock coat with a cravat underneath, black trousers and leather boots. He had an ornate walking stick that he clutched tightly and a squat white dog at his feet. I couldn't make out many features besides his full set of sandy hair.

Vasile picked up on my uneasiness and quickly spun around. He withdrew one of the bottles we'd assembled and readied to throw it. The blonde man sprung from the dark, arms reaching for the sky in surrender.

"Easy now gentlemen," he murmured in a low voice. "I'm not here for trouble. I was just looking into a matter."

"What matter?" I growled lowly. Vasile remained stock-still.

"A lady of mine was murdered and I was trying to find out by whom. It brought me here."

"What are you?" I said accusingly, "some sort of Haymarket Hector?"

"Not exactly. I'm a community leader. This girl was under my care."

"What's your name?" I challenged.

"Community Leader."

"Don't test my patience," I said crossly, "What's your name?"

"Piss off!" he jeered with contempt. I lifted my basher, ready to meet him in mêlée. Vasile stepped in front of me, his eyes still fixed on the stranger.

"He's a druid," he said.

"A wha'?" I questioned. The flaxen chap's expression seemed to wash with disbelief.

"They're ancient priests who lived in this area hundreds of years ago," Vasile continued. "Look by his feet." I did, and spotted a circle drawn in chalk that I hadn't previously noticed. It had three twisted lines that all came together at the center. On top of the outline lay an actual wreath with two small twigs resting on top. Both he and his dog stood inside.

"What the hell is that?"

"A ward against evil," the community leader announced, "Though I wouldn't expect you to understand."

"Try me."

"Listen, I don't have time for this," he whispered in a low but sharp tone. "I can tell by the likes of you that you're not what I'm chasing. However, I did notice that the pair of you are fully armed and walking into the exact place where the Will-O'-Wisp brought me."

"The what?" I said while lowering my sword. Both Vasile and the community leader looked warn from my questions.

"Nevermind," he replied. "What's important is that there is something unnatural inside that building. Are you or are you not going inside to dispose of it?"

"Nosferatu," Vasile said stridently, his accent clearly audible. "And yes, we are here to do away with the demon. However, if you're so concerned, please, come and join us."

"Yeah," I added, "I know what my companion is getting at. How do we know that we can trust you?" Ravi floated near the man, ignoring his growling dog. He stopped at the border of the sketched ring and glowered at it. I'd never seen the specter so bothered. He looped around the community leader several times, waving his dry dead hands near the border. Afterwards, he flew back to my side and whispered something frightening.

"Real magic."

"You can't trust me," said the community leader, "but then again, I don't care. If you want to run me through, then go ahead. Perhaps I'll be reborn someplace a little less miserable next time around. Otherwise, I suggest that you stop fucking about and stop whatever is in there."

"Or else what?" I protested.

Gunfire resonated from inside the building. It was faint, but distinct. Seconds later, a loud crash, as if something large had fallen over, hammered under our feet. Something serious was going on in the building.

"Or else *that*," the blonde man said mockingly. "A pair of fools had gone into the building just before you arrived. If you would let me speak, I could have told you about them. There was the policeman with the witches' mark whom I'd met before and a white-haired lass in a cloak."

"Vasilica," shouted Vasile.

"It sounds like they woke the dogs," said the blonde man. "Now, are you going to go help them or not?"

Vasile changed directions and bound for the door. I jumped to follow him, taking one last glimpse at the community leader. He gave me an icy stare, and then dug in his pocket, pulling out a square package wrapped in newspaper and tied with yarn.

"Give that to the one who speaks with the dead," he ordered, fog billowing behind him.

"Who?"

"You'll know when it's time."

He nodded before walking towards the roadside and into the misty street, his dog tapping after him. I couldn't tell what to make of him, but I knew I was scared. He seemed to know more than he was telling. Plus, anyone who can frighten Ravi is worthy of mention.

Regardless, I raced into the building with a mysterious man who claimed to communicate with God in hopes of stopping an insidious fiend. From what it looked like, we were undermanned, out powered, and had lost the element of surprise. All we had at our disposal were but a few blades, bashers, and flammable bottles. They had the very forces of hell. *Now I know I am losing my mind.*

CHAPTER 22

London never goes completely quiet, no matter what the time. There's always a vagrant begging or lushington stumbling to the next pub. Yet, for as many people may have been lurking, an unmolested silence seemed to follow us as we strode across town. I was working on subduing my emotions during the walk, burying the mental images of Davis and his murdered family. It was important to keep a clear head when you're trying to problem solve. I'd utilized the suffocating method to keep from becoming sentimental during some of my more paramount cases. But try as I might, James, now spread across his floor in two halves, kept appearing in my thoughts. *Someone was going to regret this.*

I tried to recall my visit to Doctor Guildford, dredging up what I could about his office. The lobby, a make shift room for his assistant, had only one doorway leading directly to the hall that trailed into his lab. It was just the assistant and Guildford. *Was he some psychotic murderer or one of these night demons the Ivanescus spoke of?* I wasn't sure, but some of James's last words haunted me. *The devil came.*

"Vasilica, this may sound rather silly," I said as we hurried down the wet and hazy streets, "but when I questioned Dr. Guildford, it was morning. I thought your brother's journal stated that these creatures had to sleep at daybreak?"

"Yes," she said flatly, cognizant of where my question was leading. "It's a capability some of the stronger subjects possess. It takes a great amount of focus on their part, but if your Dr. Guildford *is* in fact the child of Paraschiva, then his potent blood would allow him to stay conscious long enough for your visit."

"Well that explains the dark cellar, but wouldn't that also mean he knew we were coming?" Vasilica eyed me wildly.

"Yes," she frowned.

We reached the office doors of Doctor Guildford, also known as Sebastian Von Goethe, and anxiously prepared for our assault. I tallied the ammunition that I'd taken from Davis. There were two loaded shells in his firearm and four extra that I found on his table. Shielding my back along the wall near the entrance, I waited for Vasilica to have a go at the lock with her infiltration tools. She moved like a seamstress, swift and steady. I stared at her petite hands, and this time, instead of remembering them with a blade, I harked back to when they were pressed along my naked chest.

A few clanks later, the door pressed inward, and together, we filled inside. The front office, cool and still, lingered in silence, as if the very walls were holding their breath. I took out a box of matches from my coat pocket and flicked a stick on the strike pad, letting out light that sketched the room in charcoal and pumpkin orange. I could make out a few shapes, including the clerk's desk and hanging bicycle. Vasilica moved forward, her curved steel in hand as she scurried along the east wall. Slowly, my match began to fade, and as I pinched inside the box for another, I could hear hurried footsteps coming towards us from the hall that led to Guildford's lab. I quickly flicked my wrist with the match and sparked another flame. To my dismay, the light immediately gave way to the frightening shape of Dr. Guildford's assistant closely in front of me, chopping axe suspended over her head.

Her face was no longer striking, but twisted maniacally like a rabid swine. Her blonde hair, now bushy and frazzled, hung over glittering rows of serrated teeth.

"You won't hurt him. I love him!" she squealed, leaping into the office.

Vasilica skipped backwards and lifted her blade in a guarded position while I tried to take aim with the rifle. However, just before I could fire, my match died out, leaving me sightless. I scattered about for another one, and as I did, the fearsome sounds of clashing metal rang beside me. Sparks flashed like lightning and I could feel a whoosh of air kiss my face from the whirling skirmish next to me. As I lit a third flame, I found both Vasilica and the assistant sprawled out on the ground. The blonde fiend, still silently screaming in death, had taken Vasilica's sword halfway through her neck. Vasilica meanwhile, held her shin, which hosted a broad gaping wound. Rushing at her side, I ripped off my coat and wrapped it around the gash. The cut, half the size of finger, squirted ruby onto the base of her boot. I tried to remain calm, tying a sleeve around the wound to isolate blood flow.

"It's not too bad," she sniveled through clamped teeth. "Just the edge nicked me."

"How did you do that," I asked.

"Do what?"

"Fight like that? I couldn't see a thing."

"Most of Satan's spawns stalk their prey in the night. Our father taught us how to master the art of blind-fighting. It looks as if I'm a bit rusty."

"You are amazing," I applauded. Vasilica gave a half smile. "Can you walk?" She nodded her head *yes*, grabbing at my shoulders to pull herself up. Hobbling forward, she took a minute to regain her wits before bounding over the body blocking the hall. I followed after, staring at the dead girl's milky eyes. "What was she?"

"How should I know?" she said while lopping off the girl's head. I tried not to recoil.

"Some witch hunter you are." Vasilica gave me a bemused expression before cracking a sly smile.

"It's a big world. No one can know everything. Now come, we can take care of her corpse later."

I pushed past Vasilica to take point, handing over my matches. The old wine cellar was littered with cob webs, and edging forward, I could smell the familiar stink of embalming fluid. With the rifle as my guide, we closed the distance to Dr. Guildford's lab. I heard cloth ripping behind me, and as I glanced back, I found Vasilica in the midst of constructing a torch out of a wooden stake, coat cloth, and flask she'd procured from her belt. Soon, she had assembled a crude torch, and the two of us continued with a new flush of fire. We gingerly tiptoed nearer, fretfully crossing the hall. Finally, the passage reached its end. Lingering next to the dome-shaped mouth that lead inside Guildford's lab, we paused momentarily, giving each other one last look. Vasilica sheathed her blade and peeled out a dagger from her belt.

"Ready?" I whispered.

"Ready," she repeated while lifting the dagger to be hurled.

We leapt into the surgeon's chamber and were stunned to find Dr. Guildford in his white surgeon's coat with his back to us, tranquilly carving into a cadaver. The corpse was male, his face covered by a caubeen hat. Vivaldi lightly played over a gramophone next to him.

"Good evening," he greeted courteously, his attention still focused on the body.

"Palms up, Dr. Guildford," I commanded, "or should I call you Sebastian Von Goethe?" The doctor put his scalpel down on the bloated stomach of his subject, turning slowly while displaying both his hands. However, instead of lifting them above his head, he began to clap, slowly and sardonically.

"Ah, the golden child has finally come," he said with a heavy German accent I hadn't previously heard from his tongue. "I'm rather disappointed it took so long. Didn't I leave you enough bread crumbs Detective Brannick? What *does* she see in you?"

"Come again?" I spat irritably.

"I thought you would take a more logical approach to it all," he said while taking the needle off of his record, "but you went ahead and avoided the path of least resistance. What a pity. For a rational man, you went about this rather violently."

"Don't listen to him Nathan," Vasilica whispered.

"Ah, the witch hunter," said Guildford in disgust, nearly ready to spit at her. "Don't worry my darling. She has plans for you too."

"Shut it," I ordered, stabbing my rifle in the air. "I want answers Guildford, what's going on?"

"*Nein, Sie haben keine Antworten*," he scalded in German while taking off his surgeon gloves to expose a pair of long, burned finger. His claws, curled and ugly, clicked against one another. "No my friend, I'm afraid you're mistaken. It's time that *I* get answers!" He took a commanding stride forward which was grounds for Vasilica and me to lift our weapons and take aim. The doctor halted. Then, in a moment I could have never predicted, he began scratching at his raven hair, shedding the false mane from his crown. Underneath, a bald scalp plagued by blisters and scorch marks swelled across his skin. His gums receded, fashioning a gnarled set of vicious olive teeth. Both of his mismatched eyes, now luminescent stared at us from their sunken frames. He resembled more of a beast than a man.

"Why, why you?" he roared, pointing a razor finger at me. I slowly crept backwards, planning our retreat. "I served her loyally. I gave her anything she wanted." The doctor lurched forward, pushing away the body he had been working on. Panic stricken, I squinted out of one eye, targeting my sights along his forehead. Drips of cold sweat poured down my spine as his sickening face scowled at me. "You really don't understand do you?" he snapped. "I brought you here you fool. Everything to this point has happened because of me."

I shot a look to Vasilica, who was seconds from throwing her dagger at Guildford's chest. "No doctor, I didn't know that," I said while returning my aim to him, "Care to elaborate?" Guildford's shiny, charred scalp spew a trickle of sickly red glop from its burns. I tried not to gag.

"The boy with one arm, my minion Sam, he said you would hear from me. He told you I would lead you down this trail, didn't he?"

My mind flashed back to the night I found the one-armed boy in my flat, his morbid smile beaming as he delivered Guildford's message. *Miss McCann's death, Davis's family, had it all been a plot orchestrated around me? Why in God's name would anyone want to center a scheme of this magnitude around a drug addicted cynical fool like me?* I jerked back to life and tried to focus. Even if what he was saying was true, he was trying to break me down. In any case, I had my own agenda. If I could buy time, perhaps Vasilica could position herself behind him. It was time to pick a fight.

"Yes good doctor," I said lightly, "I can already fathom why someone would pick me over you. Look at yourself, crying like a little school boy because you can't have your way. It's pathetic." Guildford clenched his fists while Vasilica began slinking to his flank."And I can only presume that the woman in which you speak of is none other than the great Paraschiva. Am I correct?" The doctor lifted the corner of his lip, displaying a single putrid fang. "Well then, I suppose the only reason you'd led me here in the first place is because you have absolutely no idea where she is, do you? This explains your little minion hopping about my flat. Moreover, if you don't know where *she* is, that means she clearly wants nothing to do with you. You're like an old whore, all used up." Guildford began to shake. Vasilica, now nearly behind him, readied her weapon. "What I find most amusing is that you figured *I'd* be able to help track her down. I'm good Guildford, but I'm not that good. As if, the bride of Vlad Tepes would reveal herself to the likes of me? You really are daft old boy."

"No," he sizzled, "I knew you wouldn't know." His marble shaped eyes blazed brightly. "But I hoped if I tried to kill you, she'd come to help!" Within a flash, the doctor squatted to all fours and scrambled towards me. He crawled savagely, using his lanky fingers to help him move. A thunderclap from my firearm shredded the flesh around his neck. Unyielding, he batted the gun from my hands and grabbed my throat. Vasilica leapt at the monster, stabbing the knife at the doctor's head. With his free hand, Guildford clawed at her arm, catching it before the blade made contact. He stood upright and hurled her across the room. Vasilica collided with the wall, sliding unconscious onto the floor.

"Come now my master," he called out, grinding his claws in my neck, "reveal yourself and save your little pet."

A disturbing silence went over the room, pierced only by my choking gasps. Turning his nose in my direction, Guildford studied my panicked features. My toes and fingers began to go numb. I peered back at him, catching a glimpse of the man that lay behind this foul visage. He had one sharp brown eye, a cleft chin, and a pair of dimples. He was perhaps handsome in life, but now, a network of ebony veins weaved around his flesh, making a tree branch pattern that pulsed faintly under his pallid skin. I dangled like a hanged man, suspended in pain for at least a minute, slowly losing consciousness. Finally, with his fingers still firmly around my neck, he shrugged his shoulders, and in a farewell voice blubbered, "Have it your way my Queen."

Tightening his grip, Guildford squeezed the life from me. I began to fade away. The pain washed from my body as my vision tunneled. I took one last gulp of air before all went black.

Then, after a moment, my sight returned. I was in a luxurious white parlor, adorned in gold and silver. Candelabras lit the room, flickering off of a long and lean woman with deadly curves, sitting in a nearby chair. Her pale skin looked soft and smooth, the very image of feminine perfection. She had gold curls of silk that hung down to her bare shoulders, and blood red lips. Her face was angular and exquisite with breathtakingly blue eyes. She wore a flowing crimson gown and a black ribbon around her neck with a hanging ruby.

"It's your final night," she said in a deep sensual voice.

A feeble looking man in a tailcoat that I recognized as Von Goethe trembled nervously in an opposite facing chair. He was healthier looking, with flush cheeks and a straight posture.

"Will it hurt my lady?" he asked with his accent. The woman gave a mirthful, yet frightening laugh.

"Of course," she said through a smile, "but it is necessary. The body dies before it can be reborn. But in three days, once the process is complete, you will never worry about pain again." Sebastian seemed pleased by her answer and hurriedly stood up. He pulled up a sleeve and showed her his wrist.

"Then do it my lady. Together, we will find your necromancer. Once we have him, we can take him back to your home, and use him against your foolish master."

The woman backhanded Sebastian with unnatural speed, and then, grabbing his hair, pulled him towards her. Suddenly, her remarkable features turned nightmarish. Her eyes transformed into fine white beads within black sockets, like stars in the night sky. She had prolonged pointed teeth that drew down to her chin, and a serpent's tongue.

"You do not speak of him like that," she snarled. Sebastian gave a baffled look.

"But…but, you said it yourself that you want him dead." The woman pulled harder on his scalp, drawing him backwards.

"Perhaps once you've seen death," she said maliciously, "then you'll understand."

She pierced her long fangs into Sebastian's neck. An odd popping sound came from his collar, as if bones deep inside had snapped. Sebastian flailed his arms and opened his mouth as if to scream, but only a gasp came out. A suckling noise came from where the woman's lips met Sebastian's flesh, red running between. His eyes fluttered and his skin paled before finally, he went limp.

"My lady," he gasped, "If the process fails and I do not return, remember me…remember me…remember me."

CHAPTER 23

"**R**emember *me*?" shouted a guttural voice. A storm of battle sounds besieged my tender senses. There was no longer any pressure from cold dead hands lassoed around my neck. Though my vision blurred, I could make out a few figures scattered across the chamber. I wiped my teary eyes, and was delighted to see Vasile, and for some odd reason, Timothy "the Soldier" Dewhirst, whirling weapons at Dr. Guildford. The monster hissed timidly as Vasile continued to taunt him. "I said, do you remember me?" he hollered. I peeked at Vasilica, who was still motionless on the ground. I braced myself upward to my feet and hurried to the scuffle, unsheathing my revolver and pointing it at the grotesque terror.

"Ah Detective, that won't do any good," said Vasile while thrusting his sword at the doctor. Grabbing my sleeve, the Soldier slapped an old bottle of spirits in my hands.

"Fancy seeing you here Nathan," Timothy said with a thick grimy voice. "See if this does the trick." A tethered sheet of cloth hung from the lips of the bottle. The sting from the liquor's odor told me that it was a relatively high proof, and very combustible. This was no drink. This was a method of execution. I reached for my matches, but nearly forgotten that I'd given them to Vasilica. Before I could speak, Timothy struck his own match and lit my wick. "This beats painting on the boat, don't it old boy?"

Meanwhile, Vasile continued to do battle, fighting with only one good arm. His other was bandaged and in a sling, though it did not impede his efforts. Vasile moved like a dancer, dodging Sebastian's razor sharp fingernails with quick footwork, while thrusting his blade at the beast. Von Goethe clawed wildly at Vasile, snarling and slobbering.

"Go ahead friend," Vasile said to me in his sloppy English, "do what needs to be done."

Vasile gave a broad swing of his sabre while leaping backwards, providing me a brief opportunity to hurl the bottle without harming him. Unfortunately, before I could, Von Goethe's lightning reflexes allowed the beast to grab the sharp end of Vasile's blade, pulling the witch hunter back into striking distance. Black blood sprayed from the nosferatu's palm as the weapon's edge cut into his flesh, but the monster did not falter. Even after a pair of Sebastian's fingers dropped to the ground, he continued, tearing the handle from Vasile's hand and disarming him. He then lifted the sabre over his head, ready to strike Vasile down, but before he could, a loud shot roared behind me. Von Goethe's hand exploded into several pieces, dropping the sword.

I turned to see what had happened, and found Timothy pointing an outdated flintlock pistol. He gave a triumphant smile as smoke rose from the weapon's barrel. Sebastian held onto his blood stump, more angry than hurt. He locked eyes with the Soldier and let out a guttural growl. Panicked, Timothy lifted up the pistol and heaved it at Von Goethe. The firearm harmlessly bounced off of the monster's chest. Timothy watched as the pistol fell to the ground, shrugged, and then lifted the club in his other hand and charged.

The fray was far too chaotic for me to safely hurl the lit bottle. I watched as the flame continued to climb up the strip of cloth, and wondered when the glass container might burst in my hand. While I kept an eye on the burning fabric, Vasile and Timothy continued to fight off Sebastian. Vasile had rearmed himself with his sword, and tried to cleave at the beast's head, while the Soldier swatted at

Sebastian's reaching claws. But the nosferatu was unnaturally quick, and avoided their every blow.

Then inexplicably, the monster leapt high into the air, gliding to the ceiling. He latched onto a beam like an insect, hanging upside-down. The distance was too much to toss the bottle, so I lifted my revolver and aimed. Seeing me, he hissed, let go of the ceiling, and fell downward, crashing onto the Soldier. Timothy gave a harsh gasp and went prone. Sebastian, who lay next to him, took his remaining hand and grabbed at Vasile's nearby heel, jerking it. The force caused the Romanian to drop hard on his backside.

The heat from the glass burned at my hand. If not for the leather of my glove, I'd have abandoned the bottle long ago. Sebastian shot me look, then after glancing at the firebomb, crawled towards my direction with nightmarish speed. His stride was overwhelming, and before I could fling the bottle, he was within arm's length. But suddenly, just before the monster could pounce on top of me, he jerked backwards. Somehow, Vasile had clutched onto Sebastian's surgeon jacket, and though the material from his coattail tore in a long strip for several feet, the witch hunter managed to hold on.

I stretched my arm back, preparing to throw the bottle. Guildford's dilated eyes begged me not to, but it wouldn't save him. I kept reminding myself of all the hell he'd put me through. Crashing the glass upon him, the monster let out a piercing shriek as he tried to get to his feet. Vasile, struggling to hold him down by his blazing coat, looked to the Soldier. "Help me you fool."

Clumsily, Timothy stood up and collected Vasile's sabre. He shuffled to Sebastian and jabbed the blade into the scorching flame. Black smoke curled onto the ceiling. Sebastian continued to thrash, but the Soldier fought hard to pin him down. The nosferatu tossed and wailed as the flames devoured him. Gradually, his screams stopped, as life slowly sizzled out of him, and his arms and legs wilted down onto the ground.

All went quiet for a moment. The three of us exchanged glances while catching our breath. Then unexpectedly, a bizarre chorus of harrowing shrieks poured out from under the burning body, causing Timothy to abandon the sword and dive backwards. To my horror, numerous demonic hands sprouted upward from the floor, tearing away at the burned remains of Guildford. The arms were constructed out of flame and ambers. They ripped chunks of singed flesh from him until he was nothing more than a burnt husk. Only then did they lower back down into the earth and disappear.

Hell is real.

"Get to my sister," Vasile barked, waking me out of my stupor. I hobbled over to her and put my ear along her mouth, listening for breathing. Her panting fluttered in and out, but it was steady.

"She's alive," I called out.

I lifted her into a sitting position and waited for Vasile. He limped to us and went to a knee, digging in his sister's belt pouch. After a short while of searching, he removed a tiny bottle. He waved the blue glass under Vasilica's nostrils. I could smell the stench of ammonia. Eyes wide, Vasilica started to life with a gasp and coughed uncontrollably. Vasile and I nodded to one another in relief before focusing back on Vasilica.

"Brother," Vasilica moaned, "you know I hate Sal Volatile." The two hugged briefly. "How did you know where to find me?" Vasile stroked a strand of his sister's chalky hair behind her ear with his fingers.

"A brother knows all," he said smiling while using his good arm to bring Vasilica to her feet. "Besides, it was not you I was looking for as much as it was the nosferatu. Now that the demon has been vanquished, we can strike at his creator."

Nosferatu, demons, creators, it all overwhelmed me. I tried to open my mind to this new uncharted territory, but it was difficult. The Ivanescus had been familiar with it all since they were children. I, on the other hand, was clueless. I felt cheated.

An acrid stench steamed from Sebastian's charred body. Vasile, Vasilica, the Solider and I, were a questionable ensemble for sure, coming from very obvious different walks of life. Somehow though, we had managed to come together and stop Sebastian. After gathering our thoughts, and treating our injuries, the four of us deliberated over the entire episode. We each gave our personal accounts and described our involvement over the last few days.

I'd come to find out that Vasile was under the distinct assumption that Paraschiva somehow had learned to mask herself with false faces. It was a discipline that he'd never come across before, but it explained why she'd been able to elude him for so long. He'd witnessed it first hand at the inn, when Paraschiva disguised herself as his sister in order to capture him and turn him over to Davis. Luckily, it was only by chance that Timothy had been dragged into Scotland Yard a bit earlier for illegal dueling. The two not only befriended one another, but devised a way to free themselves from their confines. Nonetheless, if Paraschiva was behind the kidnapping of Vasile, and worked closely with Davis, then it meant that she'd been keeping a close eye on us.

After a bit more speculation, we collectively agreed that it would be in our best interest to continue sharing our thoughts elsewhere. Shots had been fired, a rare occurrence in London that, if heard, draws attention quickly. Firstly though, we'd need to clean up any evidence linking us to tonight. Vasile and Timothy decided to straighten up any signs of scuffle, while Vasilica went through Sebastian's possessions, leaving false clues that made it appear as if the physician had left town. I, on the other hand, had the distinct privilege of burning Sebastian and his assistant's bodies in the subbasement where we'd discovered a furnace.

I dragged the corpses one by one to the dank sublevel. Not only did I avoid leaving evidence for responding constables, but I refrained from directly touching the assistant, using sheets and a gurney to my advantage. The echo didn't always work, but it didn't stop me from being cautious. I was already too weary, and didn't have it in me to see how the poor assistant had been corrupted. After hauling the pair into the boiler, I lit the stove and watched from the cracks of the furnace door to ensure the cadavers burned.

But something was amiss. As I continued to watch the blaze, the hairs on my neck stood up. I'd somehow become aware of a presence in the room. Then, from the corners of my eyes, a shadow wavered in the distance. I turned to investigate, only to find a most bloodcurdling scene. It was the woman of shadow, her hair and gown wavering in the darkness as if floating in water. Her body drifted tranquilly and a vague smile crept along her hazy face. It occurred to me that this was the first time we'd met without me being under the influence of opium or ale. It made it all more frightening.

"You're not my wife are you?" I asked. The figure shook her head. "Are you Paraschiva then?" My hand began to slip towards my revolver, though I knew it would have no effect.

"Nathan," the ghostly voice hummed, echoing lightly throughout the room. "I'm not here to hurt you. I'm here to warn you."

"Warn me?" I scoffed. "Oh, that's funny, counting that you've been trying to kill me this entire time."

"No, Nathan," the voice said softly, "I've been trying to keep you alive. I need you."

"For what?"

"You have the gift," she said admirably, "An ability that most other people can only dream of. You *know* of what I speak." *I did.* The echo was an oddity that I'd hoped to someday be able to explain, but the last couple of days made me think of it in a new light. *Was I this necromancer after all?* The room went quiet for a moment. I could hear the group upstairs pacing about, clueless as to what lay under their feet. "They will try to use you, and if you can't help them…they'll most likely kill you."

"What are you talking about?"

"The stories of the Ivanescus' father are true," she said coolly while drifting closer to me. "He'd found our home so many years ago in the mountains, and attempted to destroy us. He failed, but not before slaying one of us brides. For his cruelty, my master took his wife, and made her his own. She is now my beloved sister. But the Ivanescus hope that the necromancer can help reverse what we've done. Make no mistake, they know that you're the necromancer, and in their narrow-mindedness, they will deem you as evil, much as they do with our kind.

"But you *are* evil."

"Are we? Or is it just that one bloodthirsty fool, Sebastian, left a bad taste in your mouth?" Her cloudy head looked towards the furnace. "We have century's worth of knowledge. We understand that only the most trustworthy should have the strength that we possess. Such is why I allowed you all to slay Von Goethe. He was undeserving."

My mind began to race. What Paraschiva said about the Ivanescues did match what I'd read in Vasile's journal, and spoke about with Vasilica. Their father, Demetri, *did* claim to have found something in the mountains that led to his wife's disappearance. It's why he trained his children to be killers. If it were true, then Vasile and Vasilica were not only hiding things from me, but they might be trying to use me as well. I was familiar enough with the two to know that they couldn't think that the *echo* was inherently good. But would they be willing to kill me? Before I could say another word, the shadow spoke again.

"Ask them. Hear the truth firsthand. They are not bringers of holy justice. They are merely vengeful fanatics." *She's trying to manipulate me.*

"To hell with you! They might be keeping secrets, but it pales in comparison to your schemes."

"Nathan," she sighed, "I've been holding back from you because men can't possibly fathom the existence of immortals in a simple conversation. I needed to give you time to see for yourself that your reality isn't what it seems. I apologize if things have become messy along the way. But, I stand before you now, ready to help you recognize your true power. Let me change you. Turn you into one of us. Not only will it cure your consumption, but it will help you finally fulfill your destiny as a great necromancer."

"Ribbons and bows," I spat. Her head tilted with uncertainty. "Ribbons-and-bows," I repeated, annunciating more slowly. "You're trying to fancy up what you really want from me. I know that you want me to kill Vlad Tepes. I read it in Vasile's journal."

"Nathan, whatever you've read is only an inkling of the truth. Vasile can not possibly comprehend what immortals are blessed to understand. My grudge with my master is more sisterly than malevolent. I don't need you for that. I want you as a companion, someone to love." My mind coursed with uncertainty. "You are too unique to let go. Please, let me help you?"

Paraschiva was offering me a new chance at life, and I was half tempted to take it. The consumption would only get worse. My body would eventually falter, and I'd be forced to quit the force. I'd be poor and bedridden, living out my last days alone and miserable. Maybe being one of them didn't necessarily mean that you had to be evil. Maybe, just as Paraschiva had said, the dramatics of the investigation only made it appear that way. I mean, I have the echo, and although I'm no saint, I definitely wasn't a monster. Perhaps their offering worked the same way.

"If your words are true, then you'll give me time to work this out by myself. I'm going to see what the Ivanescus have to say about your claims. If you're right, then we can talk." Paraschiva glided back to the wall.

"I'm glad to hear you're willing to consider it," she said with a composed voice, "And although I would wait for you until the end of time, let it be known that the witch hunters won't be as patient. If you turn your back on them, they may kill you. Be careful my child."

I nodded to her. As I did, the shadow began to melt away, dissolving back into the blackness of the walls and ceiling. Once she was gone, I removed my revolver from its holster and held it at my side. I could hear the group upstairs dragging furniture. I began walking up the steps of the subbasement, unsure of what I'd do next.

I'd always known something was amiss with the witch hunters and now it might make sense. If Paraschiva was being straight with me, then it wasn't coincidence, nor was there signs from angels that brought us together. All the Ivanescus really wanted to do was use me. They wanted to see if there was more to my echo. I'd hoped that they could explain themselves, but it wouldn't be easy, especially if what Paraschiva said was true.

Then again, I'd seen what the nosferatu were capable of. Could they be trusted? Was Paraschiva manipulating me *or* did her centuries of unlife give rise to some sort of elevated perspective. Maybe if I saw things from her viewpoint, where death and life coexisted as one, I might consider Sebastian's actions, my illness, and the entirety of the case, all very trivial. Perhaps she really did just want to help me because she thought that I was her necromancer. There'd be only one way to find out. I'd need to speak with the Ivanescus.

I closed my eyes briefly and gathered the strength.

"Quite the predicament," I said to myself.

CHAPTER 24

"T**his night has run afoul," said Vasile as I made it up the stairs. "There is no more that sister and I can do at the moment. Perhaps it's time we escort you home Detective."

I raised my revolver at him.

The group was taken aback. Timothy speedily drew his flintlock pistol, but was unsure who to aim at, while Vasilica shouted my name in alarm. But all Vasile did was raise his good hand in surrender, locking eyes with me in a daring and unafraid manner. He stood up carefully from a shelf he'd been leaning on, a composed look on face.

"Detective," he said calmly, "Think about this. You are being foolish."

"Tell me about your mother?" I demanded. "Tell me why you've been lying to me?"

"Nathan," Vasilica said heatedly, "Stop this at once."

"No," Vasile interrupted, "Let him speak."

"I know what has happened to her," I said condemningly. "I know she's Paraschiva's sister."

"She is not!" Vasilica roared. Vasile gestured his hand at his sister, calming her down.

"Nathan," he said in a composed tone, "Who has told you such things?"

"It doesn't matter," I barked. "Answer the question."

A long pause suffocated the room.

"It is true. Our mother was taken by the dark prince when we were just children. As time went on, we learned that she had not been killed, but changed. We vowed to destroy the monsters that cursed her soul to the depths of hell, and have been trying to vanquish them ever since."

"And what about this necromancer? Are you going to try and use them to save your mother?"

"Necromancers are inherently evil. We would never work with one evil to deal with another. However, it is our hope that this death speaker is not a necromancer, but instead, a guardian of the dead. If so, they would be of divine nature, and could perhaps cure our mother."

"And if they were a necromancer?"

"Then," Vasile delayed for a moment, "We would slay them."

"And how long have you known that I might be the necromancer?" Vasilica gasped, as if startled, while Timothy gave a bemused expression, his pistol still readied.

"This," Vasile said through an exhausted breath, "Is something that I've only recently put together. It was the one-armed boy, Sam, who recently helped me figure it out. Vasilica had no idea."

"So then," I said boldly, "Are you going to try and kill me?"

"Of course not," Vasilica broke in, "Nathan, I've told you the truth. The messenger told me you going to help us."

"Sister," said Vasile while keeping his eyes on me, "Let's not be impulsive." Vasile bowed his head to me. "I hope that it doesn't come to that. If what my sister says is true, and a messenger from heaven said you would help, then surely you must be a guardian of the dead."

"But if I wasn't?" I challenged. Vasile remained mute, his eyes looking down in shame. *He'll kill me if he has to.* A blend of fury and fear surged through me. I'd done everything I could to save him, and here he was, admitting that he'd slit my throat if I gave him the opportunity. I shook my head angrily. "That's what I thought."

I slowly began sidestepping my way towards the hallway which led to the exit, my revolver fixed on Vasile. He remained still. Vasilica raised her hand towards me beseechingly, following me as I crossed the lab. I glanced at Timothy, who cocked his head to me.

"Timothy, I've known you for sometime," I said anxiously, "These people are mad. You'd be wise to come with me." Timothy turned back to Vasile and Vasilica who were watching from afar. He then returned his gaze to me, focusing on my pointed weapon.

"Would I, old boy?" he spat rhetorically.

"Detective," Vasile called out, "Before you do anything irrational, think about the source of your new found information? Think about who said it, and what they've put a good man like you through."

"You don't know anything about me Vasile," I said as I made it to the mouth of the hallway. "And on that note, do not follow me. If I see any of you *ever* again, I'll shoot you."

I didn't wait for their reactions, instead retreating into the hall. Hurriedly, I made it through the corridor and out of the building. The streets were foggy, nearly completely drowning out the light of the gas lamps. I didn't hear or see any constables fussing about, and knew that no one had taken notice of the commotion we'd made. My chest hurt from the cold air, causing a bout of bloody coughs to surface.

My conscience was burdened and my heart was heavy. I didn't know who I could trust any longer. I'd spent this entire case trying to convince myself that the Ivanescus were innocent, only to find that they'd likely kill me if I'd let them. In the process, I not only abetted them in evading Scotland Yard, but I broke several dozen laws myself. *What have I become?* I needed to go someplace where I could think it all over. I needed to get somewhere safe. I needed to go home.

By the time I made it to my flat, it was nearly dawn. My body was weak, and all I wanted to do was chase the dragon. Hades, who usually harassed me by ramming his forehead into my leg, was nowhere to be found. I threw my bowler on the table, nearly hitting an assortment of breads that Ms. Abigail had left for me. Hurriedly, I went for my pipe hidden in my drawer. I stared at it for a moment, curious if it was wise for me to smoke and let my guard down. Then, before I could explain why, my arm drew back and threw the apparatus at the wall. It cracked in two and fell to the ground.

I still felt anxious and uneasy, and decided to double check the house. I moved to draw the curtains, examining the small park across the street. The dark sky had been shaded with a streak of pink from the rising sun, casting a ghostly shine over the grass and trees. I continued to stare, when suddenly, something daunting caught my eye. Sitting on a park bench near an old oak tree were the Ivanescus and Timothy. Their eyes were fixed on me, watching as I speedily closed the curtains. *Those bastards, they were watching me.*

I took a frightened step back, withdrawing from the window. As I did, something small and polished caught under my shoe, causing me to lose my footing. After regaining my balance, I examined what I'd slipped on, and found that it was a single metallic cufflink. I picked up the buttoned clasp, pinching it between my fingers. It was painted black, with gold lettering on top that spelled *M.B.* Curious, I continued to study the floor. Smeared across the wood were small white lines that I'd looked over previously. They were light, barely noticeable, and trailed towards my front door.

I removed my revolver and followed the tracks out of my flat. The marks were even more faded in the hall, lightly tracing down the stairwell every few feet. It was very early, so I treaded softly, as most of my neighbors were still asleep. As I continued to track the white stains, I found that, to my horror, they'd snaked down the second floor corridor, stopping at Ms. Abigail's door. *No one better have hurt that poor old woman.* Instinctively, I hurried to the entrance and rammed at the door with my shoulder, breaking her shabby door lock.

Cold air and the smell of rot were the first things to meet me. There was no light coming from Ms. Abigail's home, and I had to use the glow from the hallway lamps to see inside. I slowly crept in, my pointed revolver leading the way. All of the windows were draped with thick curtains and the furniture was flipped over or torn apart. I carefully made it towards the kitchen, where the intense odor strengthened. It took my eyes a moment to adjust, but gradually I made out some items resting on the counter. There were putrid legs of meat, moldy clumps of dough, and a single butcher knife stabbed into the wood. As I inched further, my foot unexpectedly kicked into something large and heavy. It was a body.

The figure was facedown, slumped next to the stove. I could tell from their outline that they were too large to be Ms. Abigail. As I lowered to a knee to examine them, I found that they were wearing a set of coattails and white performer's gloves. I seized the corpse by their jacket, turning them over until they were face up. Marcos's face was fixed in a painful cringe. It was still caked in stage makeup, though there were large blotches where he had been dragged. His broken jaw drooped into a gaping frown just above his neck, which seemed to have been torn open by a wild animal. Near his shoulder was an envelope with a broken seal. I pried the parchment from under him and opened it.

Dear Amico,

I have compiled some basic information for you as promised. Below is a summary of two major practices that focus on authority over the dead. As you will see, though these traditions have very similar channels, their philosophies are extreme opposites.

The first tradition is necromancy. It is a form of dark magic that allows the living to speak with, and control, the dead. It has roots in both Babylon and Egypt, and is said to be employable by only the darkest of souls. The church sees invoking and manipulating the dead as a violation of nature, and therefore a sin against God. Most practitioners were wiped out during the late fourteen-hundreds under Ferdinand II of Aragon, and according to legend, there are very few who remain.

The second form is called Divinum Mortuus, roughly translated as Divine Death. It is said to be a holy gift from the mysterious angel Samael, given to those who he sees fit in helping him protect the sanctity of life and death from Satan. It is written that those who possess Divinum Mortuus can use the memories, knowledge, and senses of the dead in order to help with their grim duties. It is said that extremely capable practitioners can hollow grounds, ward off evil, and even repel undead in order to protect the dead from disgrace.

While I am not acquainted with your case, perhaps your suspect believes that the victim used necromancy to cheat death? Or maybe your person of interest thinks that he is an agent of Samael, and must protect the purity of life and death? Either way, you should know that what you deal in is far more disturbing than any simple murder. The history of both of these practices is stained in blood and littered with corpses. Still, I hope this may be of some use.
God bless,
Marcos

I crumpled the letter in my hand, trying not to cry. This was entirely my fault. Marcos had been murdered, and I wanted to know by whom. There was only one way to learn how. I removed my glove, opened my palm wide, took a deep breath. Then, after drowning my thought, I placed my hand on his forehead. My vision began to fade.

Marcos was whistling a tune as he knocked on my flat's door. The drive from his knuckles pushed the door slightly opened. Marcos shrugged and ambled in. He called my name several times, but to no avail. After a moment of waiting, he removed an envelope from his coat pocket. Suddenly, a shriveled hand violently grabbed at his wrist.

"What have we here," said a rickety woman's voice.

Marcos turned to his assailant, only to find Ms. Abigail staring at him coldly.

"Ciao," Marcos said merrily.

Ms. Abigail's head contorted from round with a wrinkled face and grey hair, to a sharp and striking woman with gold locks, ruby lips, and eyes like sapphires. Her mouth opened, and a pair of dagger-like teeth glistened. Though parts of her were fiendish, the rest of her was so beautiful that it almost excused her wretched features.

"I'm afraid he won't be reading that letter," she hissed before savagely ripping into Marcos's neck.

My vision returned, and I could see someone in the doorway blocking the hallway light. I looked over my shoulder and saw Ms. Abigail lingering at the entrance. Her stance was stiff and her features were shaded.

"So now you know?" she said in a macabre tone that didn't match Ms. Abigail's usual falsetto. Suddenly, the door slammed behind her and all went black.

CHAPTER 25

"Nathan," Ms. Abigail called out through the darkness, "Come, and let me help you." I crawled blindly along the kitchen floor, trying to remember where the windows were.

"Oh shut it," I said cruelly, concealing the anguish inside me. "Don't play games with me, not anymore. You're foul, every part of you." I crept on hands and knees from the kitchen towards the sitting area, trying to feel for the drapes. "You're not Ms. Abigail. So drop the act *Paraschiva*."

"Well done," she said in a deep sensual voice. "I'd expect nothing less from you."

I continued grasping at the air, hoping to find the drapes. Finally, the soft touch of cloth fell into my hands. I tugged hard, pulling the curtains outward. The tangerine glow from dawn poured into the flat, brightening the apartment. Ms. Abigail's face transitioned from a look of terror to disgust. Then suddenly, her skin shifted from pale rose to a wintry shade of blue. Her simple clothes changed into a crimson gown with rubies encrusted in the embroidery, and a scarlet ribbon with a red jewel tied tightly around her neck. Her locks of flaxen hair curled beautifully around her lean and ravishing face, and a pair of fiery eyes bore into my soul. This was Paraschiva's true form and it was easy to see why so many people had become obsessed with her.

"Know this Nathan," she said in a composed voice, unaffected by the light. "I'm not what they say I am. This ruse, this great plot you think I'm part of, is merely a misinterpretation of motive."

"Oh, bullshit," I hollered.

"No, it's the truth. My master's ritual had found you and I'd come here to London on his behalf to claim you. When I found you, you were a mess, drifting lifelessly as a shell of the man you once were. I witnessed all of your amazing potential going to waste. You were brilliant, tenacious, entertaining, but the pain you carried was holding you back. So I continued to watch from afar. I should have known though that the great necromancer, the one who I would invite into our kingdom, *The Eternal Kingdom*," would figure me out."

Her words had an inexplicable way of tugging at me. She spoke comfortably and relaxed, as if she'd known me for decades.

"I knew you were frail, both mentally and physically, so I chose to look after you. Ms. Abigail had caught your wife's consumption, and was secretly withering away. She tried to keep it from you, but once she passed, I traded places with her. I planned on gradually introducing you to my world, as I knew it would take some time to understand. I wanted you to fully comprehend all of my intentions, and was nearing that time when I'd come forth, but then, the outsiders began to meddle."

"The Ivanescus?"

"Yes, but not just them. My retainer as well. The child I made out of need in Munich. He grew blood drunk with his new found power and was out of control. I tried to guide him, but he just wouldn't take. Since it did not suite me, I abandon him and left him to his own devices. If he wished to live like a rabid animal then I knew it would catch up with him. He would soon find out how quickly power can turn upon itself, and it did."

"And what about Miss McCann?"

"She was an unfortunate bystander. Before I abandoned Von Goethe, I made the mistake of mentioning that I'd found the necromancer, and was fascinated with you. He grew jealous. After I abandon him, he tried to get me out from hiding by going after you. He'd already begun experimenting with progeny of his own and decided to use his latest creation to toy with you."

"You mean the one armed boy?"

"Yes, but the young man was only his first, and he was created by accident, tainted by Sebastian's bite. It's what we immortals call *thin-bloods*. The only true way to pass down all of your gifts involves a thorny ritual that takes many nights, a ritual that Von Goethe could barely understand. He began courting Miss McCann, trying to experiment and change her into one of us. She had come to him in desperation because of her sickness, and was vulnerable. He promised her a cure and attempted to replicate the rites I'd bestowed upon him. Then he used his abilities to deceive your Chief Inspector into giving you her case. He wanted it all to come together so he could prove that you were worthless while he was invaluable. I wanted to come out from hiding to stop him, but I knew the Ivanescus were trailing me. So, I interceded by changing my visage to match Vasile's and visited Miss McCann on the night before her transformation. I purposely drew a spectacle from the patrons at the pub below, allowing them to watch as I heatedly warned Miss McCann that her beloved Dr. Guildford was nothing more than a murderer. The performance helped slow down the Ivanescues by drawing attention to both them *and* my child. I knew it was only a matter of time before one killed the other."

"And Ms. Abigail, where is she now?" Paraschiva frowned.

"I let her rest in the Thames. It seemed fitting, as the river is the life blood of your city. She is shared and drank by many. I thought you would like that. She was a wonderful woman." *The body in the river.* The one that Swanson had been in a panic about. It was Ms. Abigail.

"And Davis?" Paraschiva went quiet.

"I'm sorry about that Nathan. I was merely trying to keep you all on Von Goethe's trail. I guided James Davis to where he needed to be, but unfortunately, I could not control myself. You kept that bible in your pocket, and I could no longer feed off you as you slept. You even left me with a nasty reminder of what would happen if I tried." She pointed to the burn on the uppermost part of her breast. "James Davis was already slipping from the wound that he'd received from Miss McCann and began losing his grip on reality. In my absence, he tortured his family in a state of madness. When I discovered what he had done, I had to finish them off. Feasting on them both filled my appetite and mercifully ended them."

"You are lying! He told me you made him watch." Anger took over. I stomped towards Paraschiva, unsure of what I'd do next, but before I could make it close enough, she dissolved into shadow. With the doorway now exposed, I hurried out of the flat and ran up to the stairs to my own rental. Hurriedly, I slammed the door behind me, locking and latching it. I turned around, half tempted to rush to the window and call for the Ivanescus. But when I turned around, lo and behold, there was Paraschiva on the far side of the room.

"Please, Nathan it takes a great amount of exertion to use my abilities in the daytime. Don't make me chase you around."

"Do you want to know what I think?" I asked while pointing an accusing finger at her. "I think that you're trapped. You have to fulfill your master's wishes and find the necromancer as he ordered. Only you had plans to turn me on Vlad Tepes. But your plans were halted when both the Ivanescus started trailing you and your minion went batty. So you tried to turn them all on one another, which left only a larger blood trail. Meanwhile, you've been patiently waiting for me to get closer and closer to death so you can offer me a new chance at life. That's what I think!"

"Believe what you want Nathan. I am telling the truth." I stared at her grudgingly, clueless as what to do next. Half of me argued to *finish her* and the other half felt that leaving with her might be what I was meant for all along.

"So now what then?" I asked bluntly. She perked up, adjusting her posture.

"I have narrowed it down to three different possibilities," she said sensibly. "First, you could refuse to join me, and in a violent temper, try to destroy me. That ends with you dead, and me very sad."

"Second?"

"The second possibility is that you can refuse my invite and request that I alter what memories you have. I can make it seem like this entire episode is something you dreamed up due to stress after Catherine's death. I would leave you to your opium until your eventual demise."

"And the third possibility?"

"The third possibility," she said in a hopeful tone, "is that you take my offer. Let me lead you out of here. We can return to my kingdom where I can introduce you to your new family. Oh Nathan, it is paradise. There are uncountable servants, resources ever plentiful, and no more worries for ever after. We're the blessed children of the revered stars and sacred night. We want for nothing."

I appraised her every word, boiling it all down between two real choices. Die in misery or go and live forever in paradise. My will bent closer to her desires. It seemed like leaving might be the right choice. Maybe living forever would give me a different perspective on everything that's happened to me thus far.

Then suddenly, I thought of everyone who'd died during this damnable case. Miss McCann, James, Sebastian, Sam, the assistant, Marcos, Ms. Abigail, they were all gone. Their deaths were a terrible tragedy. I hoped they were at least at peace. On the contrary, the paradise Paraschiva promised would not last forever. It would not take more than a few decades before the bronze tarnished, castles crumbled, and my mind unfolded. Her offer, though enthralling, was a sentence, not salvation. I would spend the rest of eternity begging for a death I could no longer administer. Suddenly, I realized that the woman I was talking to wasn't some tragic angel, misunderstood and fallen from grace. She was a monster.

No," I said defiantly. "I'll not join you in your eternal agony. Drown in your curse." Paraschiva, seemingly deflated, sulked very briefly before looking me straight in the eyes. She shook her head in disgust.

"What a shame," she moaned. Then, all at once, her eyes turned beady and began to glow white. Large, dragon-like fangs grew from her lips. A meshwork of purple veins pulsated through her skin and a pair of long claws grew from her fingers. "Goodbye then Nathan."

Without warning and inexplicably, the nosferatu dipped her hands into the wood floor as if it were water. A long shadowy hand protruded from the ground and grabbed at the table closest to me, lifting it into the air, and ramming it into my arm. The impact pitched my revolver from my hand. I fell to one knee, the air stolen from my lungs. Horrorstruck, I tried to get back to my feet, but a second black talon caused the chair behind me to kick under my legs, dropping me into its cushioned seat. The dark limb drove the chair towards the wall, wrecking it into the surface. Blood oozed from my nose as I smashed to the ground, and I could feel one of my teeth loosen.

My instincts chased around the floor, probing for my firearm. I could hear Paraschiva's light steps walk beside me. She slapped at my ankle, her sharp fingernails tearing at my skin as she tightened her grip. My legs lifted from the ground with ease. *Death was near.* However, as my hands scratched desperately at the floor, I spotted a hand sized shard from the opium pipe just a few inches away. The pipe had split from when I'd hurled it and it was now sharply pointed like a dagger. I stretched out my arm as Paraschiva continued to lift me, clutching the wooden stem and hiding it behind my back.

Paraschiva dangled me upside down, raising me higher until we were face-to-face. She smiled with her salient icicle-like teeth, taunting me with them as she readied to rip me apart.

"Such a waste," she muttered before opening her gaping mouth to devour me.

Then, strangely, impulse took over. I gazed into Paraschiva's eyes and with everything in me, willed her to stop. The nosferatu halted. A baffled expression leaked across her face, though her grip on my leg loosened. With no time to spare, I lifted my arm and rapidly jabbed the edge of the pipe into her chest. The makeshift weapon went through her skin and bone with ease, causing a spurt of crimson to spray from the yawning hole. She wailed in pain while dropping me on my neck, taking the sight from my eyes. I crawled backwards, a flash of purple, blue and red exploding like fireworks inside my eyelids. I could smell a putrid, malodorous stew from my nostrils and the crackling of fire from my ears. I scampered into the corner, still blind. I heard Paraschiva's cries as they whittled down to whimpers. Hot sparks spit on my cheeks, and as I guarded my face, a final hiss of heat screeched through the room. Then all went still.

Shortly after, as my vision resurfaced, a humid air filled inside the flat. Though my eyes were still blurry, I could see a mound of smoldering ash and claret ambers where the bride once stood. It was over. The beast was dead. Though my body was racked with pain, I stood up and took in my surroundings. All that remained was ripped wallpaper, broken furniture and the gloomy emptiness from the apartment. I had lost everything.

I couldn't logically explain why Paraschiva had stopped, except for the fact that I'd emotionally demanded it. If that were the case, then make no mistake, I was the necromancer, evil to the core. I needed to be stopped before I could hurt anyone else, before I caused anyone else to die. Quietly, I looked through the rubble, searching for some sort of desire to carry on. Only the revolver remained, its plating shining near the corner of the room. *I know what must be done.*

I retrieved the firearm, raising it to my mouth. I prodded the barrel between my lips, savoring its metallic flavor. A quiet peace came over me, and as I drew the hammer, I knew this life had ended. Farewell misfortune, so long tragedy, goodbye London. Every breath was now a choice, every second, an option. I closed my eyes and slowly squeezed at the trigger. This was the end of Detective Sergeant Nathaniel Brannick.

CHAPTER 26

The sky was vast, and streets, a hint less ominous. I took in the cool air from the front doors of my apartment building, listening to the clanking of horse hooves, chattering people, and far off trains whistling sweetly in the distance. It all came together like some sort of symphony. The atmosphere outside was peaceful, and as light flakes of autumn snow fell from the heavens, a great mirth warmed my stomach. The day felt more welcoming than usual, perhaps because I was no longer afraid.

I peered across St. Mary's road and spotted three familiar figures staring back. They waited patiently near the park and seemed relieved to see me. Vasile clutched two briefcases while the Soldier hauled an old rucksack and bedroll. Vasilica, meanwhile, was posed in front of the pair with nothing more than a smile I'd never seen her with before. The trio must have looked out of place in the middle of London, but for me, it was quite the sight.

I buttoned my coat, then after dodging a procession of carriages riding on the street, assembled with the group along the outskirts of the park. Vasile looked concerned, darting his eyes between myself and my flat's smoky window. I gave him a nod that said *everything is okay*. The Soldier and Vasilica were a little more sanguine, with smiles smeared across their faces. I hoped it was because they understood that I'd chosen to start anew, leaving that bastard Detective Sergeant Brannick to die within the confines of the flat.

"We have a train to catch Mr. Brannick," declared Vasile with enthusiasm. He held up a handful of tickets. "We could use a master of *Divinum Mortuus*. Won't you join us?" I huddled close to the small gathering and tried to get a closer look at the papers inside Vasile's hand. Vasilica, who had tears in her eyes, broke the tranquility and leapt into my arms, hugging me fervently. The Soldier gave a crooked smile before picking a ticket from Vasile's fingers, and handing it to me.

"Here we go Nathan. That one is especially for you."

I collected the pass from his grasp, inspecting the charter. It read, *Rail Route 107 from London to Transylvania. Transfers at Cologne, Vienna, and Budapest.* A strange, unfamiliar tingle tickled at the back of my throat. It was a laugh.

"Remarkable," I snorted.

The group, who'd stood here across the street for God knows how long, had never given up on me. I had accused them of murder, persecuted them, condemned them to death, and still they did not falter. Even in my darkest hour, they stead strong and endured. It took all of this grief and conflict in the world around me to realize that the utmost return a man earns for his struggles is not what he gets for it, but what he becomes by it. There would be a time to mourn for all those who suffered because of Paraschiva. For now though, hope had a way of overshadowing the past, if not for just for a day. I had been reborn a new man, created out of choice. Vasile placed his hand on my shoulder and smiled.

"My friend, we have been waiting for you for a long time." I smirked and adjusted my bowler before picking up one of Vasile's suitcases.

"So have I."

Brannick's Journal, Entry 1
Life, no one can predict its course. Sometimes it's snuffed out like a candle, extinguished before its time. More often it burns for far too long, squandered, but never put to good use. Only the

biggest fools try to explain it and most arrogant strive to conquer it. It is an eternal mystery.

Now that I've become acquainted with the devil's work, I have decided to join the Ivanescus in their campaign. For nearly twenty years, they have fought on their own, protecting unknowing souls from the grasps of what most people believe to be fairytales. It was time to lend a hand. We make our way to Sibiu, stopping briefly in Le Harve so that Father Babineaux can try to cure me with the Rite of Expulsion. Afterwards, we will go to the Ivanescus' home to build a foundation that can finally stop the great evil that lives in the Transylvanian Mountains.

Vasilica tells me that there are others like me, masters of Divinum Mortuus, who protect the barrier between the living and the dead. She tells me that through time, we may be able to find another like myself, who can help me develop into the guardian I'm meant to be. Until then, I plan on doing everything I can to hone my own power. Not only do I wish to grow stronger so that I can help the Ivanescus' mother, but I want to finally put an end to her maker. If Vlad Tepes is in fact stronger than Paraschiva, then I'll need to have everything at my disposal to stop him.

I don't quite know why I was chosen. Yet, I speak with certainty when I say that what I'm embarking on is only fitting. Because this entire episode has shown me that no matter what the circumstances, somehow, we must always use our gifts to try and preserve what is virtuous. So long as we sin, let us also restrain. So long as the devil influences, let God also guide. And so long as there are nightmares that prey on the weak-let there always be those, like me, who try and put a stop to them. My name is Nathaniel Brannick, witch hunter.

EPILOGUE

A cacophony of thundering hooves pounded across the Carpathian Mountains. Four coal-black steeds galloped at a grueling pace, towing a withered stagecoach. A driver with a long beard and great charcoal hat lashed at their backs, directing the horses through a rutted passage smothered in snow. Two lanterns clank on each side of the driver's box, lighting up the narrow roadway ahead. Gradually, the beasts clambered to the top of the peak, shaving rocks from the cliff's edge hemmed sharply along the path.

Suddenly, a faint blue flame glimmered in the distance. It was dim, barely illuminating the ice around it. The wall of fire blocked the lane between the carriage and a set of wrought iron gates. As the stagecoach grew nearer, the horses began to neigh and snort. The driver hollered at the stallions, convincing them to move more hastily with his whip. Finally, the animals reached the blue pyre, crossing the threshold. A sputter of light burst outward until the steeds protruded from the other side. They were unharmed, and began slowing their stride until they reached the fringes of the massive gates.

The fence lay abandoned, wilted and rusted by time. All stood still except for the wafting snow and plumes of steam escaping from the horses' nostrils. Then all at once, the roll-up curtain from the stagecoach drew up and a dark figure nervously looked outward. The wagon door swung open and a pair of feet, one donned in a black boot and the other a dress shoe, stepped onto the ice. He was a tall man nearly the size of the carriage, with a shined top hat, buttoned long coat and undersized pair of trousers. His face slouched as if parts were nerveless, covered only by a wispy mustache. In his hand was a small animal cage with a single, plump calico cat inside. The feline gave a look of discomfort from the frigid air, and after sniffing at it a bit, curled into a ball.

The towering man, with cat at his side, began to high step along the ankle high snow with his broomstick legs. His good eye, bulging and yellow, studied the flame behind him.

"Remarkable," he said in a glassy voice, revealing a stained set of incisors. He spun around, seemingly fixed on speaking to the driver, but to his confusion, the coachman had vanished. A dumbfounded grin trickled down the tall man's face. He encircled the carriage, searching for footprints, but found that there were none. Laughing, half-astonished, half-fearful, he took a moment to let his thoughts settle before lifting the cage to speak to his pet.

"We are finally here Enoch. Our deliverance is at hand."

He directed himself to the gates and peered past them. There, behind the fence was an imposing courtyard with wintry garden and single stone cottage roofed with thatch. Behind the old hut was a massive granite wall with a set of stairs on its back that ascended upwards to a decaying slate castle. The ancient stronghold, most likely a majestic sight in its day, poised along the cliffs forebodingly. Its windows neither shed any light nor presented any life from within. The tall man continued to gape, leaning on the gate's bars.

Then suddenly, the iron entrance thrust opened, creeping inward towards the courtyard. Screams of metal resonated through the cliffs as the gates stretched. The visitor hopped backwards in fright, his arms protectively hugging at the cat's cage. He watched as the slow moving fence continued to extend until finally its rigid wings were fully spread.

"Lovely," he exclaimed, "simply lovely."

He lifted his leg up to nearly chest level, then apprehensively placed it across the fence's threshold and froze, as if waiting for something miraculous to happen. Nothing did. He shrugged then continued crunching along the snow, making his way to the ascending wall. The barrier's flight of steps was made of flat, carved stone. They rose to the castle base, scaling by the hundreds. The visitor clambered up the first stair, kicking the slush off his feet as he went.

All at once, a choir of wretched wolves howled across the mountainside. Though the song was bloodcurdling, the traveler did not recoil. Instead, he casually continued up the stairway, stopping nearly every few feet to catch his breath. After a grueling hike, he finally made his way to the base of the castle, only to find that there was no entrance. Instead, a crescent shaped path with even more chiseled stairs waited, curling towards the back of the castle. He dropped his shoulders, mumbling at his feet as he labored up the trail.

Finally, he reached the back of the castle. There in the moonlight lingered a single door, stained in red and splintered. A bronze devil head with a tarnished knocking ring braced in its mouth glared at him. He used the knocker to rap on the scarlet wood, staring at the ornamental face as it frowned at him. The traveler could hear no activity inside, and after a moment of waiting, he lifted the ring to knock again. As he did, the door swung open, and the silhouette of a young maiden greeted him.

She was short and lean with a rigid stance. She wore a black funeral gown with a veil that draped over her face and carried an ebony handkerchief in her hand that she squeezed onto tightly. As the visitor looked her over, he could see a set of soulless eyes piercing from her shroud with a haunting white glow. A pearly milk substance dripped from under them, and as the visitor continued to watch her weep, he could smell rotted meat breathing from her clothing. He cleared his throat and stuck his chest out proudly, giving himself a moment to collect himself.

"I am here to see the Master," he declared.

The hostess looked at him blankly, then with the door still ajar, turned backwards and walked inside. She seemed to glide like a sailboat in calm waters, sinking deeper into the unlit confines. The tall man hurried into the castle, closing the door behind him. He rushed towards the pair of pearly embers floating before him, trying to catch up. The building was cold like a tomb and he could barely make out the outlines of furniture and walls around him. His only guide was the two twinkling eyes. He could hear his cat growling and hissing inside its cage. There was movement all around him, of that he was sure, and though he could not see or hear anyone else, he felt their presence.

He followed for quite sometime, until at length, the set of jouncing eyes stopped and waited for him to draw near. He did so, and as he approached the hostess, he could feel her putrid bitter hand touch his, placing a wood handle between his fingers. Then, without the flick of a match or spark from kindling, the tip of a torch ignited. A long oak shaft burned brightly within his grip. The visitor adjusted his eyes to the light before recoiling in horror as the features of his guide were now plainly in view.

She had a shrunken face swathed in flakey paper like skin which wrinkled deeply along her chin and cheek bones. Her fiery eyes were buried within black sockets that wavered over a pitch nose. The top of her lip only partially enveloped a pair of buck teeth that were sharpened savagely at the ends. A netting of mauve veins weaved throughout both her chest and neck and a rattling sound came from deep in her throat.

She coiled a finger, beckoning the visitor to follow as she floated up the steps. He studied her tracks, watching for shuffling, but the long dress covered her feet. Together, they made it up a narrow, cave-like stairwell, shrouded in puce rock. It opened up to a long hallway with dozens of windows strewn across its walls. He could see the delicate waver of the blue flame from outside. The fire seemed to be very far away now, nearly concealed in the murky night.

The pair continued to walk across the corridor until finally they reached the end where a single door awaited. It was heavily reinforced with strips of iron bolted to the timber. It sat between two royal tapestries dyed in deep black, embroidered with an ivory loop at the center. Within the circle, the depiction of a dragon, wings spread viciously, sprawled across it. The beast appeared to be nearly strangled by its tail and pinned down by an odd double breasted cross which protruded from its back. The tall man gawped at the drapery while his guide removed a set of iron keys and unlocked the gold lock fastening the door.

A warm brush of heat landed on the tall man's face as the entry opened. He could see a cackling amber fire greedily devouring the wood it danced on within a cobblestone fireplace. The rich aroma of burning oak captivated his nostrils, coaxing the tall man to enter. The hostess gestured for him to enter, and as he did, he took in his surroundings. White granite covered the entirety of the massive, windowless bedroom. A birch canopy bed, with matching furnishing, clung along the walls. Over the bed, a bear skinned blanket concealed the cushions, the beast's head staring furiously at its guest. A single set of silvery armor positioned near the cobble fireplace, shimmering in the firelight. It bore a shield and tunic with the same dragon insignia that had been sewn into the tapestries. The visitor rested his cat on the floor and familiarized himself with the sleeping chamber.

"*Renfield,*" echoed a hundred hushed voices.

The tall man leapt up, panic stricken. He tried to calm himself, holding his hand above his heart, before politely removing his hat. He stroked his bale of long hair and after gauging its untidiness, spit on his palm and combed it through his locks. He then straightened his wrinkled coat collar before using a finger to polish his front teeth. After deeming himself presentable, the traveler leaned an arm onto a nearby chair and casually posed.

"Yes," he replied. The room settled. Renfield looked up at the ceiling as if expecting an answer. Everything lay still until finally, a second set of whispers filled the room.

"*Renfield, you have failed me,*" said the harmony of voices in an overwrought tone. Renfield held up his hands in submission. He took a few frightened steps backwards, probing the room for anything substantial. He waved his finger in the air, as if scolding the heavens.

"No," His lips quivered. "No, I did what you said! I kept an eye on her. I did what I could. If I were stronger perhaps, then maybe I could have intervened. But I am just a simple mortal." He began to rub at his hands nervously.

"Master, you promised me. You told me you would give me new life. You said you would deliver my salvation. Please Master, stay true to your word."

The atmosphere swelled, and all at once, a spectral apparition appeared at the center of the room. It was a sooty and gossamer, like coal smoke. In the blink of an eye, it flung itself at Renfield, lifting him into the air and crashing him along the wall. Renfield squirmed and wriggled, gasping as the intangible force engulfed him. Shrieks and shouts from several corners of the chamber called out collectively.

"Do not go about reminding me of my promises Renfield. Your inaction has caused my bride's death."

Renfield, terror stricken, shook his head. He scratched at his neck, throatily trying to speak through his crushed vocal chords. "No, I-I beg your forgiveness. I am a weakling, trapped by my mortal coils." He tugged at his collar, croaking for breath. "However, I have information that can....help us exact revenge upon those who murdered your precious Paraschiva." He gulped for another mouthful of air. "I know where the killers are traveling. They have the necromancer." The ghostly figure released its grip, dropping Renfield to the ground. Sprawled along the cold floor, he wheezed and panted, coughing up a thick spit that dribbled down his chin. He watched as the misty shape fluttered before him, whirling and transforming itself into a solid form.

The figure was a man with a sharp face and deep set eyes. His flesh, pallid and taut, clung around a sharp aquiline nose that hooked over a pristine sable mustache. His fine chin and cheekbones gleamed in the firelight, and his thin, menacing eyebrows furrowed savagely. He had a silky black mane that mostly hid under a feathered scarlet cap, except along the sides, where it dangled loosely onto his shoulders. He wore an extravagant red robe sewn with white furs along the collar, which clasped around his clavicle with a gold starred broach. He decorated himself in jewelry from his slender fingers to his ashen neckline. He protected his forearms with an ornate set of metallic bracers, etched with ferocious drakes. His eyes flashed like lightning as he studied Renfield, sickened by his slobbery spectacle.

"You will tell me everything you know," said the domineering man in a deep Eastern European brogue as he stood over Renfield. "Then, I will determine if you are worthy of," he halted briefly, considering his thoughts, "salvation."

Renfield scurried to his knees, crossing his hands as if praying. He drew open his jaw and began to stutter out a few unrecognizable whimpers before sputtering a slaver of words that made up a sentence.

"Oh yes," he said beseechingly while massaging his knuckles, "I will tell my master everything he needs to know." Renfield looked to the ground sheepishly as he recalled his crooked memories. Snot trickled from his nose as he bit on his lower lip. Gradually, his thoughts came back to him and the light trace of a maniacal half smile smeared under his ratty whiskers. "Shall I start with the one called...Nathaniel Brannick?"

Arthur: Shadow of a God
By Richard Denham

King Arthur has fascinated the Western world for over a thousand years and yet we still know nothing more about him now than we did then. Layer upon layer of heroics and exploits has been piled upon him to the point where history, legend and myth have become hopelessly entangled.

In recent years, there has been a sort of scholarly consensus that 'the once and future king' was clearly some sort of Romano-British warlord, heroically stemming the tide of wave after wave of Saxon invaders after the end of Roman rule. But surprisingly, and no matter how much we enjoy this narrative, there is actually next-to-nothing solid to support this theory except the wishful thinking of understandably bitter contemporaries. The sources and scholarship used to support the 'real Arthur' are as much tentative guesswork and pushing 'evidence' to the extreme to fit in with this version as anything involving magic swords, wizards and dragons. Even Archaeology remains silent. Arthur is, and always has been, the square peg that refuses to fit neatly into the historians round hole.

Arthur: Shadow of a God gives a fascinating overview of Britain's lost hero and casts a light over an often-overlooked and somewhat inconvenient truth; Arthur was almost certainly not a man at all, but a god. He is linked inextricably to the world of Celtic folklore and Druidic traditions. Whereas tyrants like Nero and Caligula were men who fancied themselves gods; is it not possible that Arthur was a god we have turned into a man? Perhaps then there is a truth here. Arthur, 'The King under the Mountain'; sleeping until his return will never return, after all, because he doesn't need to. Arthur the god never left in the first place and remains as popular today as he ever was. His legend echoes in stories, films and games that are every bit as imaginative and fanciful as that which the minds of talented bards such as Taliesin and Aneirin came up with when the mists of the 'dark ages' still swirled over Britain – and perhaps that is a good thing after all, most at home in the imaginations of children and adults alike – being the Arthur his believers want him to be.

**Broken
(Book I of The Breach Chronicles)
By Ivy Logan**

BROKEN BUT NOT LOST

The dark shadow cast by an ancient prophecy shatters an innocent family, but all that is broken is not lost and will rise again.

Half-blood sorceress, Talia, had a unique childhood. It might have been bereft of dolls but not of love. Instructed in combat skills and trained to escape detection, she was schooled to face an unknown menace. Yet, when her family's worst nightmare comes to pass, Talia finds her protected life spinning out of control. Everything she believes in, and everyone she loves, is cruelly snatched away. Talia is forced to flee the attentions of a mad king and denied her supernatural legacy.

She chooses the path of retribution, devoid of love and friendship, but learns that sometimes love is received even if not sought.
'Broken' is a tale about Talia's coming of age, reuniting with her family and seeking vengeance. Most of all it chronicles Talia's rise from the ashes and her journey into finding herself again.

Read Talia's epic saga of love, sacrifice, friendship, and discovering the hero within set against a background of time travel and supernatural forces.

A Storm of Magic
By Ashley Laino

Being brought back from the dead is an impressive trick, even for magician Darien Burron. Now he must try and use his sleight of hand to swindle modern-day witch, Mirah, to sign her power away, or end up a tormented demon in the afterlife.

Meanwhile, sixteen-year-old Mirah is starting to lose control of her powers. After an incident at her aunt's Witchery store, Mirah is sent to a secret coven to learn to control her abilities. While away, Mirah meets up with a soft-spoken clairvoyant, a brazen storm witch, and the creator of dark magic itself. The young woman must learn to trust in herself before she loses herself entirely to the darkness that hunts her.

Weirder War Two
By Richard Denham & Michael Jecks

The Second World War was the bloodiest of all wars. Mass armies of men trudged, flew or rode from battlefields as far away as North Africa to central Europe, from India to Burma, from the Philippines to the borders of Japan. It saw the first aircraft carrier sea battle, and the indiscriminate use of terror against civilian populations in ways not seen since the Thirty Years War. Nuclear and incendiary bombs erased entire cities. V weapons brought new horror from the skies: the V1 with their hideous grumbling engines, the V2 with sudden, unexpected death. People were systematically starved: in Britain food had to be rationed because of the stranglehold of U-Boats, while in Holland the German blockage of food and fuel saw 30,000 die of starvation in the winter of 1944/5. It was a catastrophe for millions.

At a time of such enormous crisis, scientists sought ever more inventive weapons, or devices to help halt the war. Civilians were involved as never before, with women taking up new trades, proving themselves as capable as their male predecessors whether in the factories or the fields.

The stories in this book are of courage, of ingenuity, of hilarity in some cases, or of great sadness, but they are all thought-provoking - and rather weird. So whether you are interested in the last Polish cavalry charge, the Blackout Ripper, Dada, or Ghandi's attempt to stop the bloodshed, welcome to the Weirder War Two!

Click Bait
By Gillian Philip

A funny joke's a funny joke. Eddie Doolan doesn't think twice about adapting it to fit a tragic local news story and posting it on social media.

It's less of a joke when his drunken post goes viral. It stops being funny altogether when Eddie ends up jobless, friendless and ostracised by the whole town of Langburn. This isn't how he wanted to achieve fame.

Eddie knows he's blown his relationship with rich girl Lily Cumnock. It's Lily's possessive and controlling father Brodie who fires him from his job - and makes sure he won't find another decent one in Langburn. And Eddie doesn't even have Flo to fall back on - his old nan died some six months ago, and Eddie is still recovering from the death of the woman who raised him and who loved him unconditionally.

Under siege from the press, and facing charges not just for the joke but for a history of abusive behaviour on the internet, Eddie grows increasingly paranoid and desperate. The only people still speaking to him are Crow, a neglected kid who relies on Eddie for food and company, and Sid, the local gamekeeper's granddaughter. It's Sid who offers Eddie a refuge and an understanding ear. But she also offers him an illegal shotgun - and as Eddie's life spirals downwards, and his efforts at redemption are thwarted at every turn, the gun starts to look like the answer to all his problems.

Burning Bridges
By Chris Bedell

They've always said that three's a crowd...

24-year-old Sasha didn't anticipate her identical twin Riley killing herself upon their reconciliation after years of estrangement. But Sasha senses an opportunity and assumes Riley's identity so she can escape her old life.

Playing Riley isn't without complications, though. Riley's had a strained relationship with her wife and stepson so Sasha must do whatever she can to make her newfound family love and accept her. If Sasha's arrangement ends, then she'll have nothing protecting her from her past. However, when one of Sasha's former clients tracks her down, Sasha must choose between her new life and the only person who cared about her.

But things are about to become even more complicated, as a third sister, Katrina, enters the scene...

**Citizen Survivor's Handbook
By Richard Denham & Steve Hart**

The prepper's guide with a difference. Includes a foreword by TV star and best-selling author Cody Lundin.

During the 1940's Britain suffered a national catastrophe that would become known as 'The Great Tribulation' by its survivors. The remnant of His Majesty's Government formed a department known as The Ministry of Survivors, the mandate of this office being to help, guide and inform the public through the anarchy around them. During the early years they produced and issued a handbook known as 'The Citizen Survivor's Guidebook'.

However, as the situation became more desperate, the guidance within this book quickly became redundant. The Ministry deemed that the only remaining course of action was to produce a second edition; informing people to evacuate the chaos of the towns and cities and flee to the countryside, focusing on wilderness survival and how to be self-sufficient on the move.This is a surviving copy of that handbook.

www.blkdogpublishing.com

www.ingramcontent.com/pod-product-compliance
Lightning Source LLC
Chambersburg PA
CBHW012013050726
47590CB00009B/3167